*Wedding Treasure*

The eighth Mark Treasure adventure is a classic country house whodunnit with all the ingredients that have earned the author his wide and appreciative audience – tartly drawn, often outrageous characters, a richly contrived plot, a baffling *modus operandi*, the whole presented with style and wit.

Mark and Molly Treasure are invited to the wedding of Fleur Jarvas, step-daughter of a business friend. As the banker and his actress wife drive to Herefordshire for the event, they speculate on why the arrangements have been made with almost indecent haste. When they arrive at Much Marton they hear their conjectures being echoed by other guests. The disposal of Fleur's capital is getting the most attention, particularly as her true father, known to be opposed to the wedding, is living off the income. When he arrives un-announced there's open discord – and violence at the church rehearsal.

As the wedding eve rituals gather pace, so does the tension, and when the next day dawns it is not to bells and confetti but to two unexplained deaths, a pointed disappearance – and a testing case for Treasure.

We are delighted to welcome David Williams to our list with a very satisfying mystery.

# David Williams

# WEDDING TREASURE

Never mind the
prose — look
at the dedication!

With love

*David Williams*

March 21st. 1985

**M**
MACMILLAN

*First published 1985 by*
MACMILLAN LONDON LIMITED
*London and Basingstoke*
*Associated companies in Auckland, Dallas, Delhi, Dublin, Hong Kong,*
*Johannesburg, Lagos, Manzini, Melbourne, Nairobi, New York,*
*Singapore, Tokyo, Washington and Zaria*

*Typeset in Great Britain by*
BOOKWORM TYPESETTING
*Manchester*

*Printed and bound in Great Britain by*
ANCHOR BRENDON LIMITED
*Tiptree, Essex*

British Library Cataloguing in Publication Data
Williams, David, *1926-*
    Wedding treasure.
    I. Title
    823′.914 [F]      PR6073.142583

    ISBN 0-333-38715-5

*This one for*
*Mike and Mary Loxton*

# CHAPTER ONE

'Of course, we're only assuming Fleur is pregnant,' said Molly Treasure, keeping her eyes on the road.

'Because having a baby's not a good reason for getting married? Not any more?' Her husband, Mark, pouted over the questions.

'Pressing rather than good.'

'Pressing certainly. Whether good or bad, debatable,' the merchant banker responded pedantically. 'We could be wrong about Fleur. You think she's a virgin unsullied?'

'Not that, I'm afraid.' Molly frowned. 'I do wish this dreary man in front would go away, in his tired little hatchback. He obviously wants to turn off. For Wales or somewhere.'

'That'd mean turning left. Too much river down there to make it possible.' Now he made a puffing noise with his lips. 'Unless his hatchback's amphibious.' He paused again. 'He's turning right. To Gloucester. On the other hand, he may just feel safer in the middle of the road.'

'Well it's very inconsiderate when it's so narrow. And he's so slow.'

'Mmm. Expect we'll lose him before Monmouth. It was your idea to take the scenic route. Like me to drive again?'

Molly Treasure shook her head and reduced the speed of the Rolls-Royce a little. She drove the big car in the way she rode her ancient bicycle around Chelsea – chin up, back straight, arms well stretched, both hands firmly devoted to steering, and, in the case of the car, set like a racing driver's at ten to two.

The actress's patrician profile, which her husband caught with his glance of approval, was a very well-known one throughout the English-speaking world. Her expression was characteristic – natural off stage and frequently applied on stage – showing a too conscious but determined effort in tolerance. It also emphasised her resolve not to allow minor irritants to spoil a largely dutiful if still promisingly agreeable country weekend.

The river was the Wye – famous for salmon and for reaches of breathtaking beauty. On the right was a high, wooded bank.

'They should widen this road,' said Molly, in summary judgment.

'Probably not allowed. Historical conservation. That bank is a bit of Offa's Dyke. Eighth-century earthwork. Erected by the English. . .'

'To keep out the revolting Welsh.'

'The English being quite as repulsive,' responded Treasure with acerbity: he was partly Welsh.

It being mid-October, the cascading early autumn foliage on the bank was beginning to look its picturesque best. Glimpses of unbroken blue sky struck through the trees that overhung the road. Sunlight shimmered against the surface of the rippling, fast-flowing water. Altogether it was a day where nature was beating art on every turn.

The Treasures' ultimate destination was the Orchard Hotel in the village of Much Marton, some miles south-west of the city of Hereford. Coming from London, they had left the M4 motorway at Chepstow, where it thrusts west into Wales. The A466 road they were on heads north, but not always with determination since it follows the vagaries of the river, first on its west bank, then on its east. They had just crossed the water after the village of Llandogo and touched the outskirts of Lower Meend on the other bank – the language contrast impressing that they were coursing the natural boundary in ancient border country; Offa's Dyke, always to the east, notwithstanding.

As Treasure implied, they might have moved faster over a less pretty route, but there was no hurry. The wedding they were attending was not until the following day. The demands of their separate careers had kept them largely apart for more than a month: he had been travelling in West Africa and the USA: she had been appearing in a short repertory season at the Haymarket Theatre, and filming in the daytime. In all, they considered they deserved a relaxed weekend together.

It was now early on Friday afternoon. They planned to arrive at Much Marton for tea, after stopping to see an ancient church in Monmouth. That evening they were to dine with Jack Figgle and Amanda, his second wife, at Marton Manor. Amanda was the bride's mother.

The Treasures were not sleeping at the manor. They had accepted the room Jack Figgle had tactfully offered as an alternative at the small but many starred hotel close by.

The manor was middle Georgian and architecturally a delight – the furnishings special, and the plumbing surprisingly adequate. The food was usually excellent, because it was just as usually sent in from the Orchard, which Jack and Amanda Figgle considered their local 'take-away'. At ordinary times the visitors would have settled for the manor despite the competing attractions of the hotel – a late Victorian country house converted with taste ten years before and equipped with, amongst other benefits, a cook of international fame, an indoor swimming pool and a well-maintained nine-hole golf course.

But this was no ordinary time.

'I think we were right to take the hotel,' said Molly.

'Good. I thought you were having doubts this morning.'

She smiled. 'Well, it might have been fun to be at the. . .the vortex of the wedding, as it were.'

'Romantic delusion. It'd be hell. Place'll be crammed with aged relatives and impecunious hangers-on. After all, it's not that large. Not as manor houses go. And there are bound to be crises.'

'Why?'

Treasure shrugged. 'Because there always are at weddings. Besides, they don't keep enough staff to cope with a full house. Amanda's charmingly casual at the best of times. Comes of being brought up in San Francisco.'

'Nonsense,' countered Molly who didn't subscribe to the concept that California was entirely populated by drop-outs, cranks and zealots.

'Well, I'll bet breakfast won't materialise till mid-morning tomorrow, if at all.'

'That's quite possible.'

'Much better to be remotely in touch.'

'You can hardly be that since you're making the most important speech at the reception.'

'*A* speech at the reception,' Treasure responded modestly, looking down at the notes he had been making since Molly had taken over the driving.

'The longest one, then, judging by the time you've taken preparing it.'

'Unlikely, I'd say.' He stretched his neck slowly. 'I'm aiming at four minutes, not allowing for polite laughter. Anyway, a minute of riveting oration. . .'

'Rates an hour of fastidious preparation. I know,' Molly interrupted. 'I was joking. Can't wait to hear what you're going to say.'

'Neither can I.'

'Of course, the Orchard's going to be full too. They've only twelve rooms.'

'But all with private bathrooms.'

'*That* being the deciding factor.'

'Well, I couldn't see you queuing for a bathroom at the manor on the wedding morn.'

'We'd probably have got the main guest suite.'

'Couldn't be certain, and one could hardly have asked.'

'And can't you just hear Amanda at the last minute begging if we'd terribly mind letting the bridesmaids use our shower?' She caught the look of mild speculation on her husband's face. 'Or the best man perhaps?'

'Quite.' The speculation had changed to a disapproving frown. There was silence for a few moments. 'I still find this rush to the altar inexplicable,' said Treasure. 'If Fleur's not having a baby, the fact her future husband's got a job in Hong

Kong doesn't really justify anything.'

'A wedding at such short notice, you mean?'

'That certainly. The sacrifice of the money looms larger though. It's so unnecessary.'

'If Fleur marries before she's twenty-one she doesn't inherit from her grandfather's trust? Not until she's thirty? That's if one or both parents disapprove the match?

'And her father, Kitson Jarvas, disapproves strongly. She also loses the income from the capital she's been getting.'

'But it's Jarvas family money?'

'What's left of it. They were merchant tycoons in previous generations. Shippers and traders in the East Indies. Don't amount to anything now except complicated trust funds. Well, not complicated really, just a bit eccentric.'

'Fleur's nineteen?'

'Nearly twenty.'

'And she's been getting income from the trust up to now?'

'Limited income. Ten thousand a year since she was seven. Intended broadly to cover her education.'

'Well, one assumes she's managed to muddle through on that. Remember she's had a wealthy step-father since Amanda remarried.'

'Jack isn't that wealthy, not any more. Even so, I know he hasn't allowed Fleur's income to be used in the eleven years of the marriage. Had it invested for her. Paid for her upbringing himself.'

'So she has a nest-egg in any case?'

'Could be something approaching a quarter of a million, I suppose. Depends how the money's been invested. Probably a good deal more than Jack himself could lay his hands on right now. The recession hit him hard. Did I tell you he's looking for buyers for the company? Pretty modest asking price.' He paused. 'Must admit, I'd rather lost track of his affairs until this sudden engagement cropped up.'

'But you've lunched with the lovely Amanda?' There was a touch of archness in the enquiry.

'That was about Fleur's financial situation. At Jack's

11

request.'

Treasure liked Figgle, who was a more or less lapsed corporate customer of Grenwood, Phipps – the merchant bank where Treasure, still in his early forties, was Chief Executive. Figgle, a widower before he married Amanda, was owner of a family automotive component business in the West Midlands. Ten years before there had been the prospect of the firm being floated as a public company. It was why Figgle had become involved with the bank. The hopes of a floatation had died following a general recession. Figgle and Treasure continued to see each other socially from time to time, when the older man came to London. Often he brought his attractive wife with him. This was how Molly Treasure had come to know the Figgles.

The friendship between the two couples was not an especially close one. The Treasures had stayed at Much Marton only twice before, once at the manor, and once at the hotel. Both visits had been brief, and some years earlier. In the previous spring, Fleur had spent a night with the banker and his wife at their house in Cheyne Walk, Chelsea, when she had been in London for a party. It had been at her mother's request.

In the circumstances, Treasure had found it a little surprising that he had been invited to propose the toast to the bride and groom – traditionally a job reserved for a very old and close friend of the family. He shook his head as he went on: 'If the girl had waited a year to get married she could have been independent of everyone. She'd have come into the thick end of a million pounds on her twenty-first birthday.'

'Why not her eighteenth?'

'Because people came of age later when the trust was set up.'

'She'll still get the money eventually?'

'In ten years, yes.'

'And meantime that ten thousand a year dries up?'

'Because of an especially spiteful clause in the trust deed. Kit Jarvas and his lawful wife get it. Except he doesn't have a wife at the moment.'

'But he still gets the money?'

'Yes. And knowing a bit about Mr Jarvas's way of life, my guess is it'll be his main source of income for the next decade.'

'But that's obviously why he's opposed the marriage.'

'Possible, but not proven. One of the reasons why Jack asked me to see Amanda. For advice. Our legal people looked over the trust deeds. The conditions are clear and specific. Grandfather Jarvas obviously didn't hold with early marriages.'

'And Fleur absolutely refuses to wait? Or give any reason except that her beloved's off to Hong Kong at short notice? Sorry, I've forgotten his name again.'

'Jonas Grimandi. Father originally Italian. Naturalised British. Jack says very bright – the boy, I mean. Got some kind of business school degree in the States. Computer whizz kid.'

'And he's well off?'

'Only reasonably, I gather. Still very young. Twenty-six, I think. But Jack says hand-picked by his company for the Hong Kong job.'

'And Fleur's afraid she'll lose him? If he's allowed to go off on his own?'

'Amanda says not.'

'And he doesn't have to be married? To get the job?'

'Apparently not.'

'So there's nothing to stop them waiting the year? If she's that desperate she could go out and live with him meantime. I mean, that's almost the norm today in any case.' Molly sniffed before adding firmly, 'No, I still think there's a baby on the way. And full marks to them for wanting to keep it.'

'And being old fashioned enough to want it born in wedlock,' Treasure interrupted. There was a touch of speculation in the tone.

'That too, of course. But it's curious she won't admit it to Jack and Amanda. Strange child. Highly strung and quite impetuous, I'd say. I hardly know her, of course. That time she stayed with us, we chatted for a bit. Woman talk. I don't believe she finds Amanda altogether sympathetic.' And

13

neither, as it happened, did Molly.

'Plain daughter and glamorous mother. Source of mutual resentment?

'Fleur's not that plain.' Molly nearly volunteered that only men found Amanda that glamorous. Instead she added, 'Amanda was bothered about the boy who was taking Fleur to that party. . . .'

'Which is why she made Fleur spend the night with us.'

'Yes. You know they have a town flat of their own? Amanda insisted they'd lent it to someone. I think it was a ruse to get Fleur chaperoned. Anyway, Fleur found her mother's concern absurd. Said the boy couldn't lure her out of a burning building, let alone get her into bed. I remember her turn of phrase very clearly.'

'It wasn't this chap she's marrying?'

'No. A young Guards' officer. I must say I found him rather dashing and nice when he came to collect her. You were out.' Molly sighed. 'But then, I may be getting to the stage when all young Guards' officers look dashing.' Molly was thirty-eight, a strikingly handsome woman and wearing well.

'That's quite untrue,' her husband replied without elaboration and rather too absently. He was preoccupied with another thought. 'What you mean about Fleur. . .'

'Is she's a pretty liberated young woman. And uninhibited. But I wouldn't expect her to be stupid or careless,' Molly snorted. 'Which is more than can be said for this driver in front.'

It was the same car they were tailing – except Molly had purposely dropped the Rolls back some distance. There had been a good deal of traffic coming towards them but nothing behind. While it would have been dangerous to try passing the small car, the driver was delaying no one save themselves. Now he had slowed perceptibly and was travelling even closer to the centre of the road than before.

'Give him a blast on the horn,' said Treasure impatiently.

Molly did as she was told – with immediate and disturbing consequences. The offending vehicle accelerated abruptly, first swerving dangerously on to the other side of the road which fortunately was empty. It then swung around, still at speed, through nearly a hundred and eighty degrees, wobbling perilously on two wheels. For a moment, it seemed to the horrified onlookers that it was about to be driven straight into the river. And then it was.

'*Mamma mia*, it's a disaster. I'm falling asleep, you understand? It's why I'm in the water. Like you say, in the soup. Uh?' Only the front of the steeply sloping car was submerged. The head sticking through the window was male, bald, and elderly. The accent and idiom were a mix of Italian and American. 'You think I'll be sinking some more?' The speaker leaned further out of the window the easier to view the river line. This was running a few inches below the top of the front wheel, but was only just lapping the forward lower corner of the door.

'You're all right while the brakes hold. You're on gravel at the back. Sand, not mud at the front. Are you still dry inside?' asked Treasure. He and his wife were standing close by on the bank, Molly wearing a look of the deepest concern because she felt responsible for what had happened.

The head disappeared into the interior of the car, then re-emerged. The expression was confident. 'No water. Only noises. Like in the bath. This river. It's tidal?'

'Not here, no.'

'Maybe that's good. It can't go out to free me. But it can't come in and drown me. My name is Grimandi. Silvano Giorgio Grimandi. For the headstone. Catholic rites. In case I don't make it.' The fleshy, cherubic countenance broke into a wan smile. 'You think I should open the door?'

'Not that one. It'd be better if you can climb out through the back.'

'So.' Mr Grimandi's head went in again while he considered the suggestion and worked out the logistics.

'Better still if he stays there and we winch him out. Half a minute.' The owner of the voice that came from behind the Treasures was a youngish man in grey overalls. The small

15

open truck he had been driving was stopped behind the Rolls. Its door carried the legend 'R. Jones. Garden Machinery. Sales & Maintenance'; behind the driver's cabin was a power-driven winch.

Treasure and Molly held back the traffic while the marooned car, complete with driver, was pulled out of the water and up the bank. They then helped to push it into a safe position on the narrow verge. Throughout the operation Mr Grimandi evinced a keen if somewhat detached interest in the proceedings. His expression as he was being propelled backwards was one of deep wonderment. When it was eventually appropriate for him to alight he did so with hesitation, first testing the ground outside suspiciously with one foot.

'Shall I see if I can start it, then?' asked Mr Jones.

'*Si*. Please. You are very kind. You are all very kind.' The speaker made an embracing movement with both arms. Mr Jones went back to the car. 'There'll be trouble with the police?' the old man whispered to Treasure.

He was as short and rotund as he had seemed when seated. His age, Treasure guessed, was in the mid-seventies. But he looked fit, and his movements now were agile. He had the darkest blue eyes Molly ever remembered seeing – and they radiated good humour. The one curious thing about Mr Grimandi was that he was wearing two suits – two jackets and two pairs of trousers in contrasting colours.

'I don't think the police will bother you. But I see it's a hired car,' said Treasure, noting a sticker on the windscreen. It wasn't one of the well-known rental companies. 'Bit old and battered. . .'

'Like the hirer.' Mr Grimandi gave an impish grin. 'I pick up near the airport. This morning. Very early. Small company, you understand? Not so concerned with the age. Not mine. Not the car's.' He searched for something in a jacket pocket, then discovered it wasn't the right jacket. He looked sheepishly from Treasure to Molly. 'When I come off the plane, I can't be certain I get to rent a car. So I travel light.

16

One suitcase. Is why I wear two suits. Also. . .' he looked about him, as if for eavesdroppers, 'also extra drawers. Three pairs.' He nodded earnestly to confirm the prudence of such measures.

'Very sensible,' offered Molly, affecting a warm approval her husband was sure she didn't feel for practices so bizarre. 'Tell me,' she continued brightly, 'are you perhaps related to Mr Jonas Grimandi?'

'Sure. Sure.' The little man looked both surprised and delighted. He smote his barrel chest like an over enthusiastic penitent. 'I am great-uncle. Head of the Family Grimandi.' Now his palm opened as his arm flourished heavenwards in a wholly operatic gesture.

'On the way to Much Marton for the wedding? Just like us. What a lovely coincidence. Isn't it, Mark?' Molly didn't wait for her husband's response. She had taken a liking to Mr Grimandi who could certainly no longer be identified with the dreary, dangerous road hog of half an hour before. 'And you've come all the way from. . .?'

'From Brooklyn. New York City. Is a nice section. I was born in Palermo, Sicily, Signora . . . Signora . . . er. . . ?'

'Treasure. Our name is Treasure,' put in the banker. 'No wonder you fell asleep. Long drive on top of a night flight,' he went on, not wishing to be outdone in the display of unctious bonhomie towards a fellow wedding guest.

'And you're here at such short notice too,' Molly added amiably, the more so since Mr Grimandi had formally kissed her hand. 'Expect you wished the wedding had been later. Next year, perhaps?'

For the first time Mr Grimandi's expression turned to a frown. He drew himself to his full height with an *Il Duce* type lift of the chin. 'Next year? No, Signora Treasure. The wedding is tomorrow.'

'Wouldn't count on this as the going-away car,' came the voice of R. Jones emanating from deep inside the engine and in an accent emanating from deeper still in the Welsh hills. 'Soaked right through, d'you see? Have to be dried out proper,

I'm afraid. Tow it in now, up to my place. If you like. If the gentleman will sit in to steer.' He brought himself into full view, throwing a doubtful glance in Mr Grimandi's direction. 'It's not far. That'd be best. I can bring it up to you tonight or in the morning. Much Marton isn't it? I heard you say.'

'That's right,' Molly confirmed. 'And that's the perfect answer. Mark, you'll steer, won't you, darling? To save Mr Grimandi after his frightful experience.' She avoided her husband's gaze, but smiled benignly at her aged protégé. 'Then he can come on with us, and er . . . and tell us why the wedding has to be tomorrow,' she ended brightly, and with disarming candour.

# CHAPTER TWO

'Will you and Daddy mind terribly letting the bridesmaids use your bathroom? Around eleven-thirty in the morning? They're sweet girls.' Amanda Figgle, a muddle of papers in her hand, looked across at her mother, Mrs Harriet Cartland Ware, grandmother of the bride. There was doubt in her voice. She was well aware that sweetness of disposition had no clear bearing on an entitlement to extra bathroom privileges. If Molly Treasure had been present in the drawing room of Marton Manor, which she wasn't, she'd have found it hard not to laugh.

The manor, made of dressed stone and in the Grecian style, was rebuilt in 1798 to a design by Joseph Bromfield of Shrewsbury. The house had two storeys plus an attic. There were five sets of apertures on the side elevations, seven on the northern façade from which protruded a grand Ionic portico and porte-cochère spanning three openings, its four slender columns rising through both main storeys to support a flat entablature. On the southern elevation the matching four columns were not free-standing but built into the semi-circle of a central bow. This last feature provided three windows on both floors, extending and lighting the important rooms behind – the one at ground level being the drawing room.

The two women were seated opposite each other on unyielding, authentic Chippendale settees set at right angles to the heavy and ornate marble fireplace. An antique mahogany table lay between them. There was no fire, though Mrs Ware had some minutes before been on the point of suggesting there should be. Not wanting to create work for anyone – but sure

19

there had been a dangerous drop in the temperature – she had fetched a red woollen cardigan from her room instead, and slipped it across the shoulders of her tailored, white linen dress. She had left her home in San Francisco only two days earlier.

The table held a tray with coffee cups. Lunch, taken in the dining room, was just over.

The room was well proportioned, nearly twice as wide as it was deep, furnished in the main with good eighteenth or early nineteenth century pieces. The pictures were notable – a Sickert, a Mary Cassatt, a Seago, a Bonnard watercolour, several oils by lesser members of the Camden Town Group, a Dufy and a dozen paintings by contemporary artists, including two Alexandra Cotterell interiors.

The three double casement, venetian windows in the bow and the two flanking windows let on to the long terrace. Today the centre bow window, immediately opposite the fireplace, provided more than simple egress.

An awning in red and white striped canvas, with scalloped pelmets on both sides, stretched from the window to a colourful marquee on the upper lawn. The big tent was also striped, and hung on the inside with billowing pink nylon swagging. Baskets of pink and white hydrangeas dangled from wires above head height. The tent support poles were artfully festooned with the pink drapery, their bases set around with boxed evergreen bushes.

In contrast, thirty or so bare and stained, small collapsible tables were arranged roughly around three sides of the tented area, flanking a circular portable dance floor, and facing a long and also unadorned trestle table at the far side. There were fragile gilt-painted chairs upturned on all the tables and looking, in some way, to have been lewdly exposed.

The tent and equipment suppliers had finished their work. The caterers would not begin theirs until early the following morning. Meantime the uncompleted scene for the wedding reception on the morrow was visible from southern aspects of the house. Side sections of the tent facing the house had been reefed up to allow free passage of air to keep the plants from stifling. As well as exhibiting a scene of somewhat alloyed elegance, this also served to funnel a sharp draught into the drawing room through the window which, because of something to do with the awning, could not be properly closed.

'I'm sure we shan't mind about the bathroom, dear.' Mrs Ware was sixty-three – twenty-four years older than her daughter. She cared a good deal about her comforts normally, but she was determined to help out where she could over the wedding.

Mrs Ware had been a noted beauty in her day. Studious application, a little cosmetic surgery and – as she was given to insisting – a great deal of positive thinking had served to preserve her good looks. Even so, she tended to comport herself as though she were encased in an invisible band-box.

'They'll need a half-hour each. They're sharing the only bathroom on the top floor with all the others.' Amanda was affecting to care more than she did. It was one of a dozen things on her list. 'It'll be murder up there by mid-morning.'

Amanda was still very much a beauty. Slim, and taller than her mother, she had an especially clear complexion and naturally fair hair which she wore in loose waves to shoulder length. Her movements were languid like the tone of her husky voice. She was wearing an undyed, heavy-knit, wool sweater with a loose roll-neck, and a greenish Welsh tweed skirt over light brogues. The sleeves of the sweater were pushed back, displaying slender, bronzed forearms.

'I guess we'll be through upstairs by eleven-thirty.' Mrs Ware now sounded less positive. One hand moved in a reflex way to touch the back of her coiffure – a kind of over-sized blonde meringue. 'Do you think so, Byron?' she called with pointed uncertainty to her husband. He was sitting in a Hepplewhite wing chair across the room reading the London edition of *The Herald Tribune*. It was one of the few chairs in the house he found genuinely comfortable – even with a recumbent Old English Sheepdog lying across his left foot.

'Anything you say, my dear.' Only the bare question had

registered. It had been answered along with a smile. The instruction in the tone had missed. The dog – called Palmerston – had raised his head at the exchange, in case human movement was presaged: it wasn't, so the head thudded back again on to Byron Ware's shoe.

Ware was a short, genial man with crinkled, grey hair and a military moustache. He had not long retired as senior partner in a stockbroking business. In dress, general appearance and attitude he was an American who, accent apart, could easily have passed for English – as easily as his wife, who had retained her British nationality after her marriage, was always assumed to be American.

'This seating plan's a disaster. And a mistake. We should have had a stand-up buffet,' said Amanda, unfolding a large sheet of paper and directing a disconsolate glance at the canvas cavern outside. 'I mean, you'd think people could at least have answered the invitations by now. As for people who've accepted then cancelled. . .'

'It was pretty short notice,' said her father, over the top of his paper and his half-glasses. 'I suppose folk are having to re-arrange things to get here. The ones that live a long way away.'

'You and mother came six thousand miles to get here yesterday.'

'We're a little different, dear,' put in Mrs Ware. 'You always get last-minute cancellations, of course. I remember at your wedding – your first wedding – I had the same problem.' She sniffed confidently. 'A properly served luncheon is a whole lot nicer than a buffet though. And there just has to be a seating plan. I mean otherwise people get to sit with people who bore them. I don't know why it happens, but it always does. You have to arrange for it not to.'

'But with over a hundred and fifty coming, how am I to know who bores who? Anyway, I don't even know the Grimandi friends. Not that they seem to have many.' The eyebrows arched briefly. 'Well, I suppose I'll have to leave the final plan till the morning. The place cards are done, at least.'

She folded up the seating plan and applied herself to a different piece of paper. 'And I do think Fleur could be more helpful. Be around more. Like this morning. I mean, why can't Jonas meet his own relations, by himself.' She sighed. 'It's Fleur who got us into this whirl. Of course, I'll never understand why she couldn't have waited.'

'She did want to settle for just a registry office wedding,' her father offered gently. 'Something quiet with no fuss.'

'A hole in the corner affair she'd regret later – and blame on me. Honestly, we went over that so many times. Jack and I would have hated it, anyway. And besides, it would only have confirmed what people are guessing.'

'Fleur seemed happy enough this morning.'

'Yes, Daddy, and why shouldn't Fleur be. . .'

'Why shouldn't I be what?' The tall young woman who had just entered had nothing of her mother's colouring, and only a hint of her physical attraction. Fleur was dark where Amanda was fair: there were the same involving eyes, the same long bone structure in the face, but the skin was pale and pinched. Fleur's figure was less svelte than plain underdeveloped, her movements nervously sharp, the under-set of her expression uncomfortably morose. She had on an old shirt and a shapeless black sweater pulled down over equally ancient blue jeans. In summary, her appearance was more careless than casual.

'God, it's hot,' the girl exclaimed. She pulled the sweater off over her head, then pushed her hands twice through her short black hair before dropping into the empty place beside her grandmother.

'Don't catch cold, dear.' Mrs Ware nodded. 'Your mother thinks everything's working out for the best. Over the wedding. We all do. In the circumstances. We missed you both at lunch. Pity you had to drive into Hereford. We've hardly seen you since we got here. What a pretty pink blouse that is.'

'You mean it's better than this, Grandma?' Fleur grinned, pushing the rolled up sweater behind her on the seat. 'Actually it's one of Jonas's shirts. Very Jermyn Street. So we're all happy about the wedding? In the circumstances.'

There was silence for a moment. 'Provided you are, of course.' It was Byron Ware who spoke, quite slowly.

'And provided I don't want to call it off? For the sake of that dreary money? I mean, if I did, would you cancel the whole charade? Still? Topple the tent? Send back the presies? Astonish the Vicar?' She glanced round at each of her three listeners. 'Even if I was preggers? In the club? Like everybody thinks?'

'You know, I've never cared for either expression,' said Ware, but affably enough.

'Sorry, Grandfather.' She looked straight across into his eyes.

'What I meant was, it's my understanding your parents, that is, your mother and Jack,' he corrected himself, 'are dedicated as much to fulfilling your desires as they are to guarding your best interests.'

'You mean they indulge me? That I'm a spoilt brat?' Sharply, she thrust her legs out in front of her, letting them form a V-shape. She lay her neck back on the hard top of the settee.

'I didn't say that, and I don't even believe it. I do believe they'd let you call it off. Even if you were . . . preggers.' He grimaced. 'If that's what you wanted. They're very good people.'

'I know. I don't deserve them.' Fleur jumped up, skipped around the table and kissed Amanda on the cheek. Then, as though she regretted the impulsive show of affection, she moved away quickly from her mother. With hands in pockets, she took three long strides towards the centre window, stopping there and staring at the tented enclosure. Palmerston, the dog, watching her movements, had lumbered to his feet, stretched, then come purposefully to sit beside her, appearing to study the same scene, and glancing up at her from time to time.

'The trouble is, Jack isn't my father. . .'

'No, dear, Kit Jarvas is your father.' It was the girl's grandmother who had interjected. 'And even though he doesn't approve your marrying Jonas – right now, that is – it really is a lot of money to throw away over a . . .'

'Principle, Grandma? Mummy would say a lie, wouldn't you, Mummy?' Now the girl swung around fixing her mother with a sardonic stare. Palmerston got up, turned about, then sat down again. He started panting, letting his tongue hang out.

'I'm not sure what you mean, Fleur.' Amanda looked up, a pencil poised in her right hand. 'But then that's not unusual. As you said this morning, we don't communicate any more.'

'You said Jonas has nothing to do with. . .with my father's attitude. That my father just wants the money. . .'

'The income for ten years.' This was Ware. 'That could be true. I could be prejudiced, of course. Kit and I never did hit it off.'

'He could also have your interests at heart you know, dear? Really believing you'd be better to wait that year,' said Mrs Ware.

'You buy that, Mummy?'

'Well, since Jack and I don't know exactly what your father said to you after Jonas saw him . . .'

'I told you.'

'Did you? Not enough to explain why you just couldn't wait to marry.'

'It wasn't like that.' The girl switched her gaze to her grandmother. 'Honestly, it wasn't till Jonas talked with Silvano Grimandi. . .'

'That's Jonas's American uncle, dear? Great-uncle. Not his father? I'm sorry, I'm not good on foreign . . . on Italian names.'

'Well that's who he is, yes, Grandma. He's the one Jonas lived with when he was studying in New York. Jonas says he's the wisest man he knows. You'll meet him. He's coming to the wedding. Or supposed to be. They saw each other when Jonas was in the States about the Hong Kong job.'

'And wise old Great-Uncle Silvano advised you to go ahead and get married despite your father's objection,' said Ware without emotion. 'Is that what Jonas's parents think too?'

'They don't come into it, Grandfather.' She noticed the glance that passed between him and her mother. 'It's not that Jonas doesn't respect them and all that . . .'

'It's just he respects his great-uncle more.'

'He's closer to Silvano.'

'I'm beginning to understand. And how about your respect for your mother and Jack.'

'I love them very much. They know that. It's just different in this case. We've really made our own decision.' She folded her arms across her body and began walking towards the door. Palmerston followed, sitting when she stopped. 'As for my father's motives, you can ask him yourselves. We just picked him up at Hereford station. By mistake. We went to meet old Mr Grimandi. He wasn't there. My father was. He's staying at the Orchard. Jonas is arranging a room. He's coming to the wedding. Well, don't look so shocked, Mummy. You did invite him.'

'But you didn't tell us. We never expected . . .' Amanda began, clearly dumbfounded.

'Here's his acceptance.' Amanda pulled an envelope from her back pocket.

'Don't you think you should ring Jack, Amanda?' suggested Ware, breaking the awkward pause.


'Voluntary liquidation's your best bet, Jack. Better than having your creditors liquidate you. You'll have over a year to sell up. We calculate you can meet the liabilities with a bit over. Not much, but a bit.'

'And you definitely don't think I should hang on? That there could still be a buyer for us? As a going concern? Up to now, the fact we're for sale's only been put out very circumspectly.'

'Look, there are companies available all over the West Midlands. Perfectly good manufacturing businesses like yours. . .'

'And this is your formal . . . instruction? As our accountant, Peter?'

'If you like. And advice as a friend,' replied Peter Brown. He and Jack Figgle were finishing lunch at the Plough & Harrow Hotel in Birmingham.

Figgle was host. The way things were, he ruminated, it would soon amount to a defiant gesture to come to places as grand as this one. 'I needed another two years. I'm sure I could have turned the corner by then.'

'Two years with the bank pretty close to calling in a million-pound overdraft. You need another million fast to tool up, and then start building stock on those new contracts. You have mountains of unsaleable finished products. . .'

'Not strictly unsaleable. They're standards, most of them. They'll sell out over the years. Either as original equipment or replacements. Here or overseas.'

Brown shook is head. Figgle made metal-to-plastic high-impact mouldings for motor cars: bits for a wide range of models. When the British car industry had slumped, he had gone on producing to be ready for the recovery he was sure would come: the recovery had taken too long. His export trade had suffered even more.

When demand started to pick up Figgle was over-stocked with product – a lot of it obsolete: models had changed. There were new sub-contracts available from the car manufacturers, but the cost of financing slow-moving existing stock as well as producing new had proved too much for the under-capitalised company.

'If only the car makers would underwrite us.' Figgle re-lit his cigar.

'Well, they won't, and this is the least likely time in the history of the industry for them to start.' Brown's accounting firm were auditors to a number of car-component makers in the area. Figgle was the least up-to-date of them, also the most uncompetitive. 'If they could afford to guarantee you financially, they might as well own you and take the profit along with the risk.'

Figgle frowned. He looked a good deal older than his sixty-three years. He was a heavily built man – an ex-athlete, as well as a war hero – an infantry officer who won a DSO at the Normandy landings. He had inherited the family business from a father and grandfather who had been on first-name terms with William Morris, Herbert Austin and the Rootes brothers.

The company had had its ups and downs. Jack Figgle had never consolidated enough on the ups: he knew that now. There came the point where he could only look back reproachfully at himself for procrastinating too long on whether to go for a public floatation – also the times when he had turned down some very attractive take-over bids.

He supposed he had never been professional enough: too content with the way things were: too jealous of his independence when it came to going public or becoming a paid manager for some conglomerate.

To his credit he had always protected the welfare of his employees: earned their loyalty – or thought he had. It had been a strike a few years back that had led to the cancellation of the company's biggest ever contract, due to the impossibility of maintaining delivery schedules. The experience had changed his paternalistic attitude quite a bit: not enough probably. He had remained the sole shareholder though – gone on believing he could still please himself about the future.

He had married Amanda not long after the death of his first wife. Later, when he was fifty-seven, he had made up his mind to sell out and retire in five years. That had been six years back – during the last of the company 'ups'. It was why he'd bought the manor house at Marton. It was nearly fifty miles from the factory – much too far to make daily commuting sensible on a long-term basis, even with a chauffeur.

Life with Amanda had proved expensive from the start, and had become more so. Furnishing the manor had cost a fortune. She had insisted on doing the thing properly, in a style that matched the provenance of the place. Jack had approved at the time, even when it became apparent she paid too much for things, especially pictures – buying at galleries instead of auctions. The cost of maintaining the place had never been a problem – until lately: neither had adding to his modest collection of antique weapons, educating an eight-year-old son, marrying off a step-daughter in style, and, damn it, taking friends to lunch in first-class restaurants. The prospect of bankruptcy concentrated the mind no end.

'You mentioned Mark Treasure was coming to the wedding. I should have thought. . .'

'That he could over-rule the decision of the team he sent up in June? That he could have Grenwood, Phipps back us, ignoring the facts?' Figgle interrupted. 'It's not on, I'm afraid. I told you, his people are trying quietly to find us a buyer.'

'He might have provided some loan capital. Enough to. . .'

'The report was pretty damning. Well, you know it was. You got a copy.' Figgle poured them both more coffee. 'The recommendation was to sell or merge the company. I accepted it. Haven't bothered Mark since. Not professionally. Gets embarrassing. His chaps said we're too small. We didn't expand, diversify when we should have done. Management out of date. In all senses.'

'That wasn't in the report.'

'Not in so many words. Clear enough it was meant though.' Figgle paused. 'Mark's a good fellow. Good friend. But why should he put a million plus at risk in an outfit with a track record as bad as ours? He knows the local bank would probably want Grenwood, Phipps to guarantee our existing overdraft with them for a start. It's the cost of borrowing that's killing off companies like mine. It's not as though we're brand new. Young. Innovative. We're the absolute opposite.'

'There's plenty of risk capital on offer for developments in high technology, of course,' said Brown, forgetting to deny the last proposition. Absently he pinched the top of his nose. He was putting on weight again: the flesh on his nose was always the sign.'

Peter Brown was a self-satisfied, middle-aged accountant in a flourishing practice, thankful he was in a profession, and one in which the incidence of failure and deprivation was almost nil, even in times of slump. He was sorry for Jack Figgle, but deep down he had little natural respect for people who inherited businesses and let them fade away. Brown had come by his qualifications the hard way: he doubted Jack Figgle had ever made much effort at self-improvement – or ever had to.

'You suggesting we should switch to making bits for computers?' asked Figgle. 'Bit late, I'd have thought.' He ruminated for a moment. 'Strange, though. The chap my step-daughter's marrying had a similar idea. Fleur went along with it too. She was supposed to come into a good deal of money next year. She offered to put it into the firm – naturally in return for shares. Ordinary shares at a nominal price, and loan capital at very low interest. Very decent of her, I thought.'

'I see. Computer components? You could do it?'

'In tandem with the old business. Jonas Grimandi, that's the fiancé, he's in the business. Could have put us on to some useful contracts. Long-term stuff, too. So he said. Could have worked, I suppose. Very little tooling involved.'

'So? What's stopping you?'

Figgle explained briefly. 'There was nothing definite, you understand?' he ended. 'It was just talk. Fleur has no idea how much it could have meant to the business. How much of a mess I'm in. I wouldn't want her to know, either.'

'And Kit Jarvas is really against the marriage?' Brown enquired thoughtfully. 'Or is he feathering his own nest? I only know him by reputation. Who doesn't? Incidentally, haven't heard of him in years.' If Brown had less sympathy for Figgle than he was affecting, he had none at all for Jarvas. Like many others, he recalled the man as a socialite of nearly three decades before – debutante's delight, occasional escort to royalty, trend-setter, favourite of the gossip columnists, a drone who had frittered away a fortune, wrecked a number of marriages, including two of his own, been in trouble with the law, and actually served a jail sentence for fraud, before crashing into obscurity.

Figgle grunted. 'You know, I've always been grateful to

30

Jarvas. In a curious way. I mean, if he hadn't left Amanda she couldn't have divorced him and married me.'

'I think that's extending charity too far, old boy. And you haven't answered my question.'

'I can't see anything wrong with young Grimandi. With Jarvas it could be a case of genuine dislike. I mean, can you credit Jarvas has to grub so low. . . ?'

'Yes. And with respect, you're much too naïve in such matters, Jack. My guess is the swine's on his uppers. Thinks you and her future husband quite capable of looking after his daughter. He's going for the ten thousand a year. Nothing to do with his opinion of the bridegroom.'

'You may be right. Everything's happened in such a hurry. . .' Figgle stopped and looked up at the head waiter who had just come over to the table. 'Yes, Cornellio?'

'Sorry to interrupt, Mr Figgle. Mrs Figgle is on the phone. You're welcome to take it in here at my desk, sir. If you wish.'

# CHAPTER THREE

'Room all right, Mr Jarvas? We do our very best, even at no notice.' The words 'right', 'Jarvas', 'best' and 'notice' echoed through the oak-panelled hall of the Orchard Hotel. Tim Shannon was given sharply to amplifying the key word – usually the last – in every phrase he uttered, marking each such emphasis with a lightning, semi-circular, upward movement of the head. The ensuing lift of the chin and wiggling of the cheeks put people in mind of a stalking cockerel with short legs.

Stocky, broad-chested Shannon, aged forty-two, and proud owner of the Orchard, was keen by inclination and fit through application. As an experienced colonial administrative officer – retired early through lack of colonies – he owned a string of other, equally predictable and generally commendable attributes.

There was no one behind the small reception counter at the bottom of the stair-well. Between two and four in the afternoon at the Orchard, if you needed attention you picked up the telephone on the counter: there was a notice to say so – quite a small one.

Informality was the aim at the hotel. Guests were encouraged to feel they were staying in a well-appointed country house without any obligation to entertain the host – Tim Shannon assured everyone jovially. Requirements between lunch and tea were usually met, but they tended to be few when guests learned the staff numbers were too.

The building was red-brick Gothic, three storeys with a

basement, and L-shaped. It had high pointed gables, monstrously tall chimneys, and an incongruous central turret. The short arm of the L protruded on the north side and encompassed the entrance in its crook – with a high pointed porch, all stained glass and coloured tiles.

Most of the rooms on the ground floor were still employed for their original purposes: only the dining room was now an extra sitting room. The upper floors were given over to bedrooms. In the basement was the cellar bar, restaurant and kitchens – all latter-day conversions. The connecting old kitchen building – an extended basement on falling ground to the west – now housed the swimming pool and exercise area.

'Room's topping. Absolutely fine,' said Jarvas. He had been obeying the printed directive about the telephone when Shannon had approached him from behind. He was thin and fair, about six foot three, concave, fiftyish – a disquieting, energised, humanised leaning tower. After swinging round to face Shannon, his limbs continued moving as if he was responding to a staccato and irregular rhythm. 'I was wondering. . .'

'About car parking?' Anticipating the needs of guests was second nature to Tim Shannon: in his zeal he often defined the wrong ones.

'Actually golf.' The hands came together in a prayerful way, elbows outward. 'Didn't bring a car, d'you see? Thought of hiring one. Not worth it.'

'Quite. Stupid of me.' It was the 'stupid' that this time got the biting emphasis. He had been in the drive when Jarvas had arrived in Fleur's car.

It was just as well Fleur and Jonas had been with the chap, otherwise there'd have been no room. Not on your life. Not for Kitson Jarvas – at least not until Shannon had checked with someone at the manor. The Jarvas attitude to the wedding was pretty common knowledge. Had it changed? It was obvious Jarvas hadn't been expected. Shannon had guessed that squeezing him in at the Orchard had been less embarrassing than putting him up at the manor.

Now the hotelier came to regard him closely, Fleur's father looked more dissipated than even legend had it. His features suggested earlier good looks – debonair and aristocratic – but he was fast fading at the edges. The mid-weight tweed suit was in the same condition. The impressive Old School tie was no doubt merited – though the Old School probably wished it weren't.

'Golf? Follow me. Did you bring clubs?'

'Actually, no.'

They had traversed the short corridor behind the stairs. Shannon, a fast mover, was holding open a heavy, half-glazed door that led out, under an open porch, to a terrace even wider than the one at the manor.

'Plenty of clubs you can hire. Much Marton village there. Due south.' Shannon pointed directly away from the building, over a pleasing and undulating landscape. 'You can see the church. West end of the village. Mostly fourteenth century.' The hand moved ten degrees to the right. The church tower and rooftops nearby lay beyond a stretch of falling ground in the middle distance. 'Church half a mile from where we're standing. That's as the crow flies. That path you can see beyond the lawn, it leads straight down along the line of trees. Runs between the vicarage and the churchyard at the end. The manor's beyond the church. Can't see it from here. Down a drive on the other side of the road, the one you took when you came off the Hereford road. You may have noticed it divided soon after? Left for the hotel. Right for the village.'

'I see. Absolutely splendid. And the first tee?' Jarvas took a cigarette from its packet, but didn't offer one to his companion.

'I'm sorry. One gets in the habit of doing the whole commercial. So. Driving range on our far right. In front of the car park. Changing rooms over there too. For day visitors. Swimming pool closer, at the end of the terrace. Residents only, except by arrangement. First tee directly in front of us, down there. Course laid out to the left, as you can see. Nine holes only. Good par thirty-four. Normal ninth green at present out of action. Attacked by fairies. Rings.' The head jerked hard on the last utterance.

'I'm sorry?'

'There's a proper name for them, but they look like fairy rings. Circles of toadstools. Bloody nuisance. Come and see.' Shannon led off sharply across the lawn. 'There's a cure though, and we're winning.' They stopped at the first tee. The offending green began thirty or so yards further on, and was roped off. It was covered in a white powder.

'Looks very sick,' Jarvas sympathised.

'But getting better. It'll take six months. For the time being I've made the ninth fairway run straight on, over the path, instead of doing a dog-leg back up here. You can't see it now, but there's a gap in the tree line down there.' He pointed to a spot some two hundred yards distant and a little to the right. 'Made a temporary green beyond. In a hollow below the practice range. Keeps people out of the area we're curing. Interesting variation for players who know the course.'

'Look forward to playing it. Take you up on borrowing clubs.' Jarvas had turned the proffered hiring into borrowing. 'Travelling light, d'you see? Having to carry wedding clobber, of course.'

'Just ask at the desk. Probably fix you up with a game too, if you want. Nobody about at the moment. Lull before the storm.'

'Wedding guests?'

'Arriving from about now. Place is full tonight and tomorrow. Your room was available through a booking error.' Tim turned about. 'Better be getting back, if you'll excuse me. We're doing the wedding catering tomorrow, plus dinner for about twenty at the manor tonight. My wife will be looking for reinforcements. D'you know whether you'll be dining here tonight, Mr Jarvas?'

'Almost certainly at the manor,' the other answered with only the smallest hesitation. 'By the way, my bill should go on the manor account. Fleur mentioned it, I expect.'

The hotelier nodded uncertainly. She hadn't mentioned it to him, and the fact would need checking. Jarvas had made the statement with the assurance of a practised sponger.

'Could I have a word, Mr Shannon, sir?' The speaker was a tallish, heavily-built man, square-jawed, muscular and very dark. He looked to be in his late forties. His face was weather-beaten and he was wearing a cap and labourer's clothes. The accent owed more to Kent or Sussex than the Welsh borders. He had emerged from the line of trees. 'Thought I heard your voice,' he went on. 'I'll put that peat and phosphate dressing on the temporary green this evening. If that's OK with you?'

'Good idea,' Shannon nodded vigorously.

'There's showers forecast. It'll work in fast enough. Turf'll need more feeding if we have to go on using it next year. It's . . .' The man stopped speaking when Jarvas turned around to face him. His changed look was one of surprise – and not a pleasant surprise.

'This is Dick Clay,' offered Shannon who seemed not to have noticed the reaction. 'He's our chief green-keeper and unofficial pro. I'm his assistant.' He guffawed energetically. 'Dick's also head gardener. This is Mr Jarvas, Dick. But hold on. Of course, you two know each other.'

Neither of the men introduced had made any verbal acknowledgement of the event, nor of the following correction. Both had nodded briefly, while they eyed each other with distinct suspicion.

'Any more problems, Dick?' Shannon subscribed over-heartily, after suffering some seconds of an uneasy silence.

'It was only about dosing this green here, sir. Been no rain for three days. Give it a miss today, I thought.' Clay indicated the roped area, but his gaze came slowly back to Jarvas.

'You're the boss, Dick.' Shannon also glanced at Jarvas. 'We're using a special organic cure. It's new. Put it on every day provided there's moisture in the soil. Gets toxic if it doesn't soak in. Bad for dogs and children.'

'Can't use a hose, I suppose. To much chlorine in the tap water.' This was Jarvas.

'You've just confirmed one of Dick's most fervent beliefs,'

36

answered Shannon. He turned to the green-keeper. 'Seems Mr Jarvas also thinks you can kill with kindness, Dick.'

'Reckon he does that all right,' said Clay with considered sourness.

'Mummy's in a panic. Jack's belting back from Birmingham where he was lunching. The grandparents are stunned. Wait till the news gets to the village.'

'And that shouldn't be long. Tim Shannon took it in his stride, I must say.' Jonas Grimandi stepped away from the window of Fleur's room. She was holding up two dresses for his opinion. He pointed to each in turn. 'Like. Don't like.'

'Too bad. They're both going on the honeymoon.' She dropped them on the bed.

'Good. So there's one I can tear from your lovely, young body with relentless passion, and no loss to anyone.' He walked across and put his arms around her.

The young man had a style and elegance about him of the type which an uncharitable observer might easily have described as suave. He was dark haired and olive skinned. In build he was slight, with slim hips. He was taller than average – certainly taller than the average Italian. His accent was cultured Glaswegian with no trace of his North Mediterranean antecedents: he admitted to speaking Italian only inexpertly, and also with Hibernian inflections. His country clothes were very new, very expensive, and very correct – only he looked as if he was modelling not wearing them.

'Thought I was being married not pillaged.' She kissed him, and took some time over it. The belligerence and taut nerves displayed earlier had disappeared. 'I wish it was the day after tomorrow,' she said when their lips parted.

'Because being married will end your bourgeois sense of guilt?' He watched her expression change, and wished he had said something else.

'Nothing of the kind.' She stiffened, then moved away from him abruptly. 'I just want to be married. All right, I need the feeling of permanence. The commitment. But I still wish it was

37

all over. The formal bit. I wish we'd just got that special civil licence . . .'

'And disappointed all the relatives?'

'To hell with the relatives. Half of them are phoney anyway.'

'Jack Figgle may not be related, but if what your father says is true, he's behaved pretty well towards you. I'll bet he's not that anxious to blow another five thousand on champagne and the rest of the trimmings. Not if he's already on the breadline.'

'You think Jack will go along with what my father's cooked up? Oh God, it's all so obscene.' She had gone back to her packing.

'Since it gets Jack out of a hole, I'd say he'll play along. It's not as though Mr Jarvas intends to take an active interest in the business.'

'We can probably be thankful for that.' She frowned. 'Except I can't help being sorry for him. In an odd way. Despite everything. He is my father, I suppose.' She paused. 'He's so pathetic with his posing. Pretending he's been protecting my interests from the start.'

'Well, his formal consent, his giving you away, it cuts out any legal come-back. For ever.' He watched her expression carefully.

'Suppose you're right.' But she made a long face. 'And he'll keep his word?'

'At the price. The deal he's worked out gives him a guaranteed salary from Figgle & Sons for the next ten years.'

'How much?'

'That's for negotiation,' he answered, purposely dissembling because he knew the figure. 'He also wants a pension after that. Whatever's agreed, it'll probably be a lot better than purloining your income from the trust. More secure too. And more tax efficient.'

'You mean if something went wrong through the trustees? How could it?'

'It was he who said it could. You'll have to ask him.' He had parried the question successfully.

38

'I don't care. The money's not important to us. Only for Jack and my mother.'

'Your father won't be doing badly. Except, like he said, he's not going for a flashy deal. Not the best he could get. Not if he pressed. It's mature though. Suppose he's fed up with flashy deals. He as good as said so in the car.'

'That he's looking for security? His timing's tight. He wants Jack to sign that contract before the wedding.'

'Of course. But it's not complicated. It took me five minutes to understand. If Jack's in as tight a corner as your father says, and if you're still ready to invest in the company. . .'

'If *we* are still ready, you mean. It's your idea. Our money.'

'OK, if we're still ready. After the wedding you'll – sorry – we'll have around a million to put in the company. Hands you the controlling interest.'

'So Jack won't own it any more.'

'I doubt if he wants to. You can leave that part to me. Jack should end up with a quarter of the shares. Maybe a bit less. He'll still be laughing in two years when the company's been turned round.'

'Through the business you'll introduce?'

'Plus he'll be able to take on the new contracts he's been offered. Three years from now. . .'

'When we come back from Hong Kong?'

'If we go to Hong Kong.'

She looked up from what she was doing. 'How d'you mean?'

'Just that I've been thinking. I may even give up that job. Jack's going to need a lot of help pulling the company round. Perhaps I should be there doing some helping.'

'I see.'

Was there disappointment or just surprise in her voice? He found it difficult to gauge. 'It's only a thought. Either way we've got our money working for us.' He paused, regarding her earnestly. 'Nothing works harder than money, you know that? Not enough people do. But it's got to really work. Not just be passively invested in safe, remote public companies. Needs to be under your own hand. That's the way to get rich. I mean

39

very, very rich.' Again he paused. 'And remember, it's all got to happen before Fleur Grimandi gets too old and ugly to enjoy life at the very top.'

She half smiled, but his words had evidently not had the effect he had expected. 'Will it mean Jack has to work another three years?'

'Not necessarily. I might suggest he stays only as part-time chairman.'

'You have it all worked out.'

'Had something similar worked out, up to the time Mr Jarvas decided he wouldn't approve our marriage.'

'And now he's changed his mind. . .'

'It just depends on Jack, who should be here soon.' Jonas glanced at the time. 'Like my great-uncle. The message said he's coming by car. He should have told me he wasn't taking the train. Anyway, Jack's more important,' he ended brusquely. Oddly, the sentiment saddened Fleur.

'It's him, I told you. Standing there as bold as brass. Making as though we didn't know each other. Come to that, making as though I didn't exist.' Dick Clay took another mouthful of tea from the mug his wife had handed him. The two were together in the kitchen of the cottage that went with the job. It was a comfortable, three-bedroomed place in the same style as the Orchard, and standing at the far end of the hollow below the golf range. The workshop that housed the tools and estate machinery was close by. Dick usually came in for some tea around three-thirty.

'Fancy.' Mildred Clay was more than ten years younger than her husband – a buxom blonde, still with a good deal of animal attraction. 'Didn't expect to see him again. Not around here, anyway. Not ever really.' She had gone back to folding damp laundry after getting the tea, but her thoughts were elsewhere. There had been more speculation than surprise in her voice: it showed too in her eyes.

'And nobody'd be the worse off if he'd stayed away for ever.' Clay glowered into the mug. Then he pulled out a chair and sat at the table.

'He's here for the wedding, then? Talk was he was against it. Stopped her money, or something.'

'Well, I expect he's changed his tune. Must have done. Hardly have turned up otherwise.'

'How did he look?' She applied herself to the damp clothes with more energy. It helped her pretend the question was casual.

'Bloody old.' He glanced up sharply as he spoke. 'Like you'd expect in a worn-out, randy jail-bird.'

She sniggered, but just to please him. 'It was only three months he got. And that was a long time ago. Must have got over it long since.'

'It wasn't just the three months. Anyway he only served two. It was the bloody disgrace. That's what did for him. And a good thing too.'

'But it wasn't for anything really bad. We read about it. At the time.' She'd been getting out the ironing board. As she'd bent down to unfold it her ample breasts seemed on the point of popping out of the bulging, button-fronted dress she was wearing. 'Not really bad. Was it, love?' She'd settled herself and begun the ironing, knowing where his eyes had been. She undid another button of the dress. 'Phew, but it's hot working.'

'Fraud, it was.' His tone had lost its aggression. 'Accessory to an insurance swindle. Ruined him. Must have been seven or eight years ago. Heard nothing about him since.'

'Excepting the gossip that's come down from the manor. Lately, that is. Over the wedding. Interesting.'

'You fancy him still, then?'

'Don't be daft. I never fancied him.'

'Yes, you did. Didn't fool me either.'

'Well, you're wrong. Anyway, you don't half talk nonsense. Me with a grown-up daughter.'

'Reckon you were the same age as our Rose last time you set eyes on the high and mighty Mr Jarvas.' He'd got up and walked around the back of her. 'Bit of all right you were then. Bit of all right you are now.' He bent down and slipped a hand

41

inside her dress.

'And that's enough of that, Dick Clay.' She slapped his arm. 'For now anyway.' She gave him a knowing look. 'Later, love. We've both got work to do. Leastways, I have.'

It was not until after he'd left that she paused from what she was doing, staring thoughtfully in front of her. He'd got it wrong. She'd been eighteen at the time: Rose was nineteen now.

# CHAPTER FOUR

Rose Clay smiled demurely at Treasure from behind the reception counter at the Orchard. If her mother was well preserved and still coarsely attractive, Rose, with the same build and colouring, had the looks, the just ripening figure and the healthy complexion of a stunning country girl.

'You and Mrs Treasure have Room Five, sir. First floor. Just at the top of these stairs.'

'Good. That's the one we had last time. Two years ago. You weren't here then.' Treasure was signing the register.

'At college, I expect, sir.'

'Graduated, have you?' asked Molly.

'Not quite. It's a technical college. I'm hoping to qualify in Hotel and Catering. Doing my "practical" here. Mr Shannon's my sponsor. My father's been head gardener here a long time.' She reddened a little.

'Then I know him,' said the banker. 'Remember him well. Didn't he work for Mrs Figgle when she lived in Sussex?'

'That's right, sir. Shall you want help with your bags?'

'No, we'll manage. Where are you putting our friend Mr Grimandi?'

'I too can carry my own bag.' Silvano pointed to the medium-size suitcase which comprised his total ensemble. 'So, young lady.' He advanced to the desk beaming.

'I'm afraid all the single rooms are on the second floor, sir, and there's no lift. You're in Number Nine. It has a lovely view.'

'Is worth the climb, I expect,' the old man nodded. He too

43

signed the register, then followed the Treasures.

Some moments later Kit Jarvas strode into the hall from the big sitting room. 'Filling up, are we, Rose? From what Mr Shannon told me we'll have to share rooms by dinner time. No hardship in some cases. You on the second floor too, my dear?'

The girl reddened again. 'I don't sleep in, sir.'

'Too bad. Still, as they say in *The Mikado*, "What tho' the night may come too soon, We've years and years of afternoon". Motel owners' theme song. What?' He put his hand out to hers which was resting on the open register. She drew it away quickly. 'I missed you when I came down earlier,' he went on, without indicating he'd noticed her action. Coolly he swivelled the book around to read it. 'I gather you're off from two to four.'

'Yes, sir.'

'If I'd known, we might have had a spot of tea.' He paused. 'In my room. It's very comfortable. Perhaps. . .'

'All the rooms are nice, sir,' she interrupted. 'Is there anything you wanted?'

He looked up from the register. 'Well now, that's a very dangerous question for a lovely young woman to be putting to an unattached gentleman.'

This time she felt the blush burning her face. She swallowed. 'I meant. . .'

'Mr Shannon said you could let me have a set of golf clubs.' Suddenly he was talking much louder. 'Hello again, Mrs Shannon.' He greeted the stocky woman in the red jumper and dark blue trousers. She had appeared from the basement stairs behind the main staircase – head down and moving fast. He had been briefly introduced to her – also, as it were, at the gallop – when she had passed through the hall at the time of his arrival. Then she had been making in the opposite direction.

Myra Shannon gave a shifty smile. 'With Mrs Figgle, Rose. Back in twenty minutes,' she uttered without interrupting her determined progress towards the main door. When the obtaining, preparing, and serving of food wasn't occupying her whole existence, it was pre-occupying it. It was her cuisine that filled the hotel with guests, and kept bringing them back. The pleasantries of social intercourse she left to her husband. She threw another surreptitious glance at Jarvas. It wasn't that she'd forgotten who he was: his identity hadn't registered with her in the first place.

'Clubs for hire are kept in the locked lobby by the hall, sir. Over there. I'll give you the key. There's only a nominal charge.'

'That's what I like to hear from ravishing young women. Now, come and show me.' He had finished examining the hotel register. 'I see the Treasures have arrived. Old acquaintances of mine. Mr Silvano Grimandi, he'd be fairly elderly? An American, I believe. . .'

'My great-uncle. So he's made it,' came the voice of Jonas from behind.

This time Jarvas had been taken unawares. He quickly let go the receptionist's hand which he had grasped when she proffered the key, and which she had been trying to pull away. 'He's in Room Nine. That's opposite mine, old chap.' He smiled at Jonas expectantly.

'Jack Figgle's back,' said the younger man. He glanced deliberately at Rose before continuing. 'I've given him the . . . the envelope. .I'm to say you're cordially invited to dinner . . . and . . . and a chat before. Would six-thirty suit?'

'Admirably. We're not dressing? I didn't bring a dinner-jacket.'

'It's informal. Oh, there's also the question of the wedding rehearsal. It's in the church at five.'

'Which you'd like me to attend, of course.'

Rose had turned about and was busying herself with something at the back of her small domain. Jonas still led the other man aside. 'There's been no discussion yet, you understand? No chance,' he said quietly. 'Bit awkward really.'

'You mean before the treaty's signed?' Jarvas gave a flicker of a smile, then lit a cigarette. 'You have any doubts in the matter?'

'Not really.'

'Good. I'll be in the church at five.'

'OK. Could you excuse me now? I must find my great-uncle.'

'Naturally, dear boy.' And, as Jonas bounded up the stairs, Kit Jarvas went back to the reception desk, turning his whole attention to the altogether captivating back view of Rose. 'So what about our promised expedition to the locked room?'

It was ten minutes later when Mark Treasure reappeared in Room Five. He had been to reconnoitre. 'I've ordered tea downstairs now. There'll be plenty of light for nine holes of golf afterwards,' he announced, full of bonhomie. 'You're not still unpacking?'

'No, I did that some time ago. For both of us.' Molly gave an indulgent smile. 'I've also changed,' she added pointedly. She held up her small jewellery bag. 'Should I give this to that nice Rose at the desk? To put in the safe?'

'Shouldn't bother.' He hesitated. 'No, come to think of it, you'd better.'

'It's a bore extracting it every time I want a bauble. Wouldn't think anyone'd pinch anything. There are no locks on the doors. Always a good sign in hotels. Don't know why. Promotes confidence, I suppose.'

'Until something's nicked. I'd think the staff totally honest. Wouldn't vouch for all the guests. One in particular.'

'Someone we know? Now why did I say that?' She frowned, shaking her head.

'Someone who knows us. Or claims to. Kitson Jarvas, encountered in hot pursuit of the comely Rose. They were emerging from that little room where they store golf bags. She in some disarray.'

'You don't say? Was it deliciously embarrassing?'

'Not for Jarvas. He immediately grabbed my hand. Said how good it was to see me again, and how were you. Insists we met years ago. Didn't specify where. Suppose he's giving the bride away.'

'Meaning he approves the marriage after all. You didn't

46

ask?'

'Couldn't really. Any more than you could press old Grimandi more than you did.'

'About the timing of the wedding? He did clam up a bit on that. Is he having tea with us?'

'No. Gone to rest. Probably scared you'd third degree him again.'

'Nonsense. Poor little man's just tired out. Fancy his being an osteopath.' Molly rubbed the back of her neck involuntarily.

'Retired chiropractor.'

'Same thing.'

'Not quite. Anyway, for heaven's sake don't press him to do anything about your bent vertebrae.'

'I wouldn't dream of such a thing.' She smiled winsomely. 'At least, not till I know him better. Anyway, you told him about your tennis elbow.'

'That was quite different. Just polite conversation. You had the poor chap prodding your spine from the back seat while you were driving. Could have been dangerous.'

'A tiny, diagnostic feel, that was all. He has the touch though. You can tell. Anyway, it's nice to know there's an osteopath in the house.' She caught her husband's warning look. 'In an emergency,' she added. 'Funny, he certainly gave the impression the wedding was timed to defy Jarvas.'

'But wouldn't be drawn on whether Fleur's having a baby? Question is, how do you defy Jarvas by giving him ten thousand a year? Doesn't fit.'

'His being here doesn't fit.' She closed some open drawers. 'There, I'm ready.' Suddenly her expression changed. 'You don't suppose he intends getting up to protest. When the priest says the bit about if anyone can show cause why they can't lawfully be joined together in holy matrimony?'

'I wouldn't put anything past Jarvas. But he is dining at the manor tonight.'

'Oh,' said Molly walking through the doorway, clutching her jewellery bag. 'In that case there's nothing pending for the

47

popular press.'

'So let's be thankful for that,' said her husband.

Except as things turned out, they were both wrong.

'Choir dismissed. Kindly don't be late tomorrow. Robed in the vestry by twelve forty-five hours. Organist can stand down for five minutes.'

The Reverend Greville Sinn was a tall, ramrod straight figure with a beakish nose. His short black hair was brushed flat and parted in the centre. He was dressed in a belted cassock embellished over the left breast with two sewn-on rows of medal ribbons. All his cassocks as well as the black stole he wore for services were similarly adorned. He had trumpeted his instructions in a clipped tenor from the centre of the chancel where he had been conducting choir practice. It was nearly five o'clock.

The four small boys, three slightly older girls and five adults dispersed down the nave. It was an impressively large church choir for a small village. Sinn was proud of it.

He had entered Holy Orders early in life but had come much later to parish work. For twenty-five years he had been an army chaplain. The army had suited him. The commitment to defend Queen and country had first bridged a gap when he had realised – too late – his religious commitment was too slim to be sustained.

At the start he had struggled with the problem of retrieving his faith, but not for long. He was equipped for the physical not the mental fight: feats of human endurance came easier to him than metaphysical wrangles.

It did occur to him to resign his ministry and do something else. But he wasn't trained for anything else. In any case, he liked the job – and in the outward context he was good at it. The men respected him. He was popular with his fellow officers. Those who spurned religion often found him especially companionable since he never tried to alter their attitudes on Christian belief – a curious, even irrational commendation for basic ineffectiveness.

But Sinn was a padre who never caused embarrassment with Holy Joe behaviour in the mess, or anywhere else – an estimable virtue which commended him quite as much to the godly as the ungodly.

He was also considered by all to be a damned fine soldier.

Gradually, and through a process of sublimation which he could scarcely explain since he certainly didn't understand it, Sinn had emerged as a convincing, respected promoter of the Crown and Realm, the time-honoured values of truth and decency, and the virtues that had made the Old Country great.

Fortunately, most of those to whom he ministered found his simple doctrine entirely digestible and actually more logical than even drum-head Christianity. There were no lurking pacifist hang-ups with Sinn; no bomb-banning justifications tabled or entertained. Superficially what he taught was a goodliness so fashioned as to seem hardly distinguishable from godliness – a highly appropriate faith for serving soldiers, and thus popular with those set in immediate authority over them.

So it was that quite early on, Sinn had been able to forget about bridging his commitment gap: the gap just disappeared. True, he never became a ranking luminary in the corps of army ministers of religion. Regimental colonels might have approved of him, but succeeding Chaplain Generals found him lacking in some not quite definable respects. Even so, after retirement from the service at fifty-five, he had found no difficulty in securing a living exactly to his tastes. It was a Field Marshal who had interceded on his behalf with Jack Figgle who appointed the incumbent at St George's, Much Marton. The gift of the living was entailed with ownership of the manor.

After two years in office the new Vicar had endeared himself to the parishioners and somewhat increased the numbers who came regularly to Matins – summoned by bugles as well as bells, the wind instrumentation provided by members of the resuscitated Boy Scout troop. The cross of St George was hoisted and lowered daily on the tower, with proper ceremony. Larger church attendances were recorded on the Sundays next to the Queen's Birthday, Trafalgar Day and on Remembrance Sunday than Sinn's predecessor had logged for Easter or Christmas Communions.

The congregation had soon got used to a somewhat attenuated list of hymns. *I vow to thee my country, Fight the Good Fight* and *All hail to the Power* turned up with regularity, along with a few others whose first lines could be announced with enough jingoistic fervour to keep minds bent, throughout the subsequent rendering, on what the Vicar considered prime purposes. Monotony was avoided since Mrs Sinn, the organist, produced countless elegant variations on the tunes while showing a stark incapacity to play those attached to hymns her husband regarded as 'wishy washy', and which she consequently rarely had occasion to practise. The National Anthem was sung whenever justification arose – and often when it didn't, for instance to mark the birthdays of some of the Monarch's most obscure, distant and, in otherwise fallow periods, even foreign relatives: Sinn kept lists of them.

'Greville, is there time for a cup of tea?' The deep-throated appeal came from Penelope Sinn as she pushed back the organ curtain. She was a jolly, straightforward, God-fearing person, and not so perceptive that she had ever fathomed that her husband's goodness didn't stem from quite the same base as her own.

Penelope was a big, ample woman with a rich contralto voice, easily adapted to something deeper if need arose. Her wardrobe was made up almost entirely of what she termed 'scoops' from charity jumble sales. She was in two such items now – a green cardigan intended for an even larger woman, and a tight crimson skirt in a thickish material with six inches of multi-pleated hem: it was a garment conceivably designed with winter *thé dansants* in mind. The hem went into a flourish and ripple as Penelope swung herself off the organ bench.

The keyboard with the pipes above it was in a pointed archway in the north wall of the tower. The working chancel was the area beneath the high, three tiered tower. It extended eastwards under a transitional Gothic arch, but there the

50

building, though long, was also narrow – not wide enough properly to accommodate choir stalls, nor high enough for good vocal amplification: with the sanctuary beyond, this original chancel was Norman, and the oldest part of the building. Looking westward, the nave was the same age as the tower, much higher than the chancel and twice its length, with a clerestory: there were aisles both sides, and a south porch. Today the normally light and airy church seemed lighter still with wedding flowers everywhere and the atmosphere heavy with their scent.

'Wedding party due, my dear,' had been the Vicar's response to the plea for refreshment. 'Still, shan't really need you on the organ. Who chose the hymns?' he asked guardedly.

'You did, Greville. We just practised them. Before the Sunday lot. *England Arise!*, *Eternal Ruler* and. . .'

'*Hail to the Lord's Anointed*. Of course. Very suitable.' The last one he regarded as a loyal tribute to the sovereign and adaptable for all occasions. 'And both the Elgar voluntaries?' He preferred the British composers.

'Yes, Greville.' It wasn't that Sir Edward Elgar only wrote two pieces suitable as organ voluntaries: Penelope could only play two. 'I could probably manage *Jesu Joy of Man's Desiring* instead. Bach,' she offered tentatively, and with a 'nothing ventured' air.

He shook his head. She might just as well have suggested *Smoke Gets in Your Eyes*. 'Ah, here comes the happy couple, stepping lively,' he announced, inaccurately.

Amanda Figgle and her former husband, Kit Jarvas, had encountered each other at the church door. They were coming down the aisle at breakneck speed because Amanda expected Jarvas to drop back, and Jarvas was taking a perverse pleasure in keeping up.

'My mistake,' said Sinn squinting over his glasses as they came closer. 'Afternoon, Amanda. And you, sir, must be the bridegroom's father?'

'Wrong again, old dear. I'm the bride's father, actually. Come to study the form. What?'

51

'I see,' answered the Vicar, except he didn't at all. 'My name is Sinn.'

'How very original.'

'Please don't be facetious, Kit, for God's sake,' his ex-wife exclaimed before making towards Mrs Sinn. 'Penelope, are the flowers OK, d'you think? I haven't had time to get over again till now. I waited for Robin from school. Then I got caught on the 'phone, so I sent him on alone to choir practice. The pinks and the blues will come out in the bride's bouquet. . .'

'You've been introduced to my father, Vicar?' This was Fleur, looking determinedly un-bridal, the old sweater now tied around her neck. Behind her came a group of young people. Without waiting for Sinn's affirmation she went on, 'Jonas you know. These are Sara and Alexi Bedwell. They're the bridesmaids.'

'Eyes in the boat, Vicar,' Jarvas cautioned inappropriately, and with a look perhaps intended to be merely jocular, but which surfaced more as a lascivious leer.

The exceptionally pretty sisters – they were auburn-haired twins – presented hands for shaking, and giggled in unison too. They were a little younger than Fleur, whom they'd met at an Oxford secretarial college, and decidedly more attractive in a physical way. They were not especial friends of the bride's but had been invited because they were decorative, and likely to make themselves available at short notice since they enjoyed being pictured in the society magazines – there being a dearth of classy weddings in October.

The Bedwell father was rich. His daughters had nothing to do between their seasons at St Tropez and St Moritz except go back to secretarial college for 'refresher' courses in aptitudes they'd not developed in the first place.

'Best man. Name of Plimpton, Noah. How d'you do, sir.' The young man who emerged from between the sisters was of middle height and a bit overweight, with a moon-shaped face. His hair was the colour and nearly the texture of straw, except at the front where he was balding prematurely and where what growth remained comprised an isolated quiff of whitish fluff.

The heavy spectacles he pushed up the bridge of his nose gave his already serious appearance an extra touch of gravity. He was soberly dressed in a worn blazer, shiny grey trousers, white shirt and black tie. He had wrinkled his forehead twice while shaking hands with Sinn, who knew an undertaker who did the same thing. 'Don't panic. I have the ring already,' Noah Plimpton added a quiet assurance, giving the Vicar's hand an extra shake before letting it go.

'Noah's a well-known lawyer,' offered Fleur unexpectedly. The twins giggled again.

Noah looked slowly from side to side, considering the point. He glanced down at his shoes which were shabby brown suede. 'Oh, I don't know.' The spectacles were pushed up again, the eyebrows arched. 'I'm seriously contemplating ordination.' He paused. 'Only because the money's better.'

'I don't believe. . .' began Sinn.

'It's either that or marry both the Bedwell sisters. They're inseparable, you know,' the other concluded wanly.

'Noah, you are the end,' said Sara Bedwell.

'The end,' echoed Alexi Bedwell. Both sisters reverted to normal giggling.

'I'll take one of 'em off your hands, old dear. Just to help out. What d'you say, Vicar?' joked Jarvas, leering again at Sinn, despite the almost frozen frown of disapproval.

A middle-aged couple had now joined the group at the chancel steps. They had been conversing in whispered but penetrating Italian until Fleur began talking to the woman who then responded nervously in penetrating English. Jarvas had turned to engage both Bedwells – with total success.

'Can we get on, Vicar?' demanded Jonas, for some reason appearing embarrassed.

'Most certainly,' replied Sinn, conscious he had lost command.

'Glad you can dine tonight, Greville. Informal.' It was Amanda who startled Sinn by speaking into his ear after coming upon him from behind. She and Penelope had returned from examining the flowers in the sanctuary.

'Thank you, yes.' He answered through the general conversation and which he had been just about to quell.

'Let us pray,' uttered Noah Plimpton loudly, with a grin at the Vicar. Everybody shut up.

The Bedwell sisters exchanged surprised expressions, making 'ooing' shapes with their lips.

'Bride and father back into the porch, please,' ordered Sinn briskly. 'Groom and best man take up positions in the first pew there. Will everybody else kindly sit down. Oh, yes' – four limpid Bedwell eyes were fixed upon him – 'you two belong with the bride, of course. Organist ready?'

'Greville, you said you wouldn't need. . .' Penelope's disembodied voice came from the vestry. She and Amanda had gone there to count the service sheets.

'Well, just play a few bars of . . .'

A man's angry voice roared from the porch. This was followed by a muffled protest, also male. Then came the noise of scuffling. A girl screamed. Everyone at the front looked around in time to see Jarvas stagger backwards into the church and crash on to the tiled floor.

# CHAPTER FIVE

'So it's all square with one hole to play. Is that right, Silvano?' asked Molly brightly. She flashed a smile first at Silvano Grimandi, then at Byron Ware. 'How exciting. Except you gave me far too many handicap strokes, Byron.'

The quaint trio moved off the eighth green in the direction of the ninth tee. Unencumbered, Molly strode ahead in light tweed knickerbockers, jaunty tweed cap, and bright red shirt and stockings. Her opponent followed close behind, pulling his golf-trolley. The non-playing Silvano brought up the rear, with Molly's bag slung over his shoulder.

While Ware was dressed for golf, Silvano was still soberly suited – though he looked a good bit slimmer having shed one of the suits and his excess underwear.

Molly had collected the others along the way. Her husband had left her following an urgent summons from Jack Figgle. Silvano had been in the hall of the hotel, and had eagerly volunteered as caddy. Ware had been about to play by himself when the others had come upon him at the first tee, where introductions had been effected. Despite his curiosity over Jarvas, Ware had left the manor before Figgle had returned home: several new guests had arrived whose continued company he decided he could best avoid on the excuse he needed exercise, and after establishing they none of them played golf.

'I wish you'd let me carry my bag now, Silvano.' Molly turned about as she reached the tee.

'No, no. It's a pleasure . . . Molly.' He was still shy about using her name. Both Americans had insisted she should address them by their first names. She had agreed on condition the compliment was reciprocated.

'This is where we head for unknown territory,' remarked Ware. 'Last time I played here the ninth fairway dog-legged up toward the hotel.'

'Me too,' smiled Molly. 'Temporary green's straight ahead beyond the gap in those trees.'

'They have rings for fairies on the regular green. Mr Shannon is telling me.' This was Silvano. He shrugged. 'In America. . .'

'I expect they'd call them rings for something else,' Molly put in firmly. 'I must say, Tim Shannon keeps the course in impeccable condition.'

'And only one man on the permanent staff,' agreed Ware. He read the yardage figures on the hand-stencilled tee-board, then took an iron club from his bag. 'Guess that gap's about a hundred and eighty yards. Pretty narrow. Best to play up to it, not through it.' All this came more as speculation than plain statement.

'With everything to play for we're not giving any free advice, are we, Silvano?' Molly joked in answer. The two had settled themselves on the white-painted bench beside the tee. There had been similar benches on all the other holes. It was one of Tim Shannon's prouder boasts that the golf course 'furniture' was hand-made on the premises. This included the boards, the benches, the wooden waste-bins, and the moveable pairs of tee markers – the last being painted metal spikes, two feet long, with regular golf balls driven into one end and neatly painted with the relevant hole numbers, green numbers for the men, red for the ladies.

Byron Ware carefully placed his ball in line with the markers, then hit it straight down the fairway to within a few yards of the gap. Molly did the same from the forward tee.

'Does Jonas play golf, Silvano?' the other man asked as they all set off again.

'Very humble background. Not much leisure education. I

56

guess he doesn't get to play golf. Not yet,' Silvano replied, half in apology.

'He didn't play at school, you mean? At university, as they say over here?' This was Ware again. 'Say, which one did he go to?'

'I forget. He did well though,' said Silvano loyally. 'In America I help with the costs. Is the least I can do. *Per la famiglia*. For the family. You understand?'

'He didn't get a scholarship?'

'Maybe. Except I don't think that kind of school.'

'He didn't go to Columbia?' Ware sounded surprised. 'Or New York University?'

'No. Good school though. I forget the name.'

'And the young couple are very happy,' said Molly. 'I gather they're making quite a sacrifice to get married now,' she added in a tone that did nothing to imply a well-nurtured ulterior motive.

Silvano beamed. 'Is to show they do this for love. Is not because he cares about her money.' The unexpected but firm assurance had come with surprising promptness.

So now it could be told: Molly wondered why it had taken so long. 'Very commendable,' she remarked. 'Oh dear, I appear to be in a tiny hole.' She had stopped beside her ball.

'Then allow me to provide relief,' said Ware. He rolled the ball, with the club he was holding, out of the divot mark and on to a healthy patch of grass.

'Aren't you gallant. But I mustn't be allowed to cheat like that.'

'You didn't. I cheated for you.'

'So you did.' Her protest had in any case been rhetorical: she was already preparing to chip the ball the sixty yards to the temporary green. 'Rescued me from the consequences of my folly,' she remarked, almost to herself, then hit the ball. It sailed high through the gap and bounced on the green.

'Well played!' cried her chubby caddy.

'Nice shot,' confirmed Ware automatically, his mind pre-occupied with something else – and not just his own ball which

57

he even so sent accurately on its way. He too had been impressed with Silvano's easy revelation. More, he was longing to know how his granddaughter was to be rescued from the consequences of *her* own folly. For it was clear to him that Jarvas's appearance signalled his approval of the marriage after all. Silvano no doubt knew as much – possibly learned it from Jonas since his arrival – and got permission to admit Jonas's earlier virtuous attitude. Simply, Ware wondered what self-aggrandising scheme Jarvas had now invented.

Byron Ware loathed Jarvas. From the start he had been certain his ex-son-in-law had opposed the marriage so he could improve his own income. It followed the son-of-a-bitch now had a better idea. Ware seldom used such language, but it sometimes featured in his thinking.

It puzzled him too that a boy as bright as Jonas had been out to prove that his love for Fleur transcended money. Byron Ware was a realist. He accepted true love ideally took precedence over all other considerations, not that it eliminated them. A baby on the way could have been an understandable reason for a hasty marriage. This other explanation didn't fit his assessment of the characters involved, unless. . .

'Whoops, that was close,' cried Molly, rousing her opponent from his ruminations.

The three had just reached the green when a golf ball thudded into the ground only a few yards short of where Molly was standing. The ball had evidently been hit from the driving range above by someone who couldn't see the players.

'Dangerous, that is. Someone up there not reading the notice, I expect,' called Mildred Clay who had heard the thump of the ball. She was hurrying past on the path from her cottage which ran parallel to the fairway and some yards below it, crossing with the path up to the hotel further on at the tree line. She waved to Molly. 'Good to see you again, Mrs Treasure. Heard you were here.' Molly waved back as Mrs Clay went on. 'I'll give a shout when I get up there. Anyone practising ought to be hitting well over there to the left, where it's wider.' She pointed behind her. 'This is the long way round for me. Quicker up the slope. My husband makes me come this way for safety. I ask you! Mr Shannon gets that angry with people who don't read the notices.' All this had been delivered without the speaker breaking her stride. She had on a formal black dress, low cut at the front. Silvano seemed fascinated by her, and had forgotten about the golf ball until another landed close by.

'That does it. Let's call it quits, Byron,' said Molly, picking up both their balls and stepping off in the direction taken by the other woman. 'Come on, Silvano, we're not standing here to be bombarded.'

But Silvano was already following in the wake of the voluptuous Mrs Clay, even though her silhouette – as good as any he'd seen in Palermo in the old days – was fast disappearing in the gloaming ahead.

'That's the receptionist's mother. They look very alike,' said Molly.

'Ah, such a beauty,' chanted her caddy, not making it clear whether this was a collective compliment, and if not, which one of the female Clays he had especially in mind.

'Pretty girl,' Molly resolved the point. 'And so's your granddaughter, Byron. Can't wait to see her in her wedding gown. A splendid adornment for your family, Silvano.'

'*Si*. We are all proud they fell in love. Gino and Teresa, that's his momma and poppa, they'll tell you. They're here already. They stay at the manor. Right now they're at the church. For the rehearsal.'

'How did Jonas and Fleur meet?' enquired Molly.

Silvano shrugged. 'This I don't know for sure.'

'Goes for me too,' said the other man. 'Got the idea maybe it was through Noah. Could be wrong. You met Noah Plimpton? He's the best man. He's at the manor too.'

Molly shook her head. 'Haven't met him yet.'

'You will tonight. Nice young fellow. Guess he was pretty sweet on Fleur, too. One time, that is.' Was there regret in the voice? 'Kind of looks out for her. Protective. Struggling lawyer.

Case of the best man losing, you could say.'

Molly frowned. 'Poor Noah Plimpton. Such a nice name.'

'Nothing broken, Mr Jarvas, I can assure you of that. Jaw'll be a bit painful for a day or two, of course. The swelling should have gone by the morning. Smoke do you? Thank you.' Dr Handel Ewenny-Preece peppered his speech with nervous expressions of gratitude when he was attending fee-paying patients – or those from whom a fee was a reasonable expectancy. He stretched to offer the cigarette pack to his temporary patient who was sitting, half clothed, on a chair set to the right of the roll-top desk. The offer was accepted.

The purple-faced, multi-chinned, small Welsh doctor lunged over the side of the desk with a burning match clasped between nicotine-stained fingers. He let Jarvas light his cigarette, then, falling back into his seat, and breathing heavily, lit one for himself.

At the first inhalation Ewenny-Preece was consumed by a frightening fit of coughing. 'Oh dear. That's better,' he said, when it stopped. He returned to scribbling on the printed file card in front of him. 'Let's see now. Blood group I've got. Any heart trouble ever? No? Thank you. Wouldn't have thought so by the look of you. Can't always tell though. Water-works all right?' He looked up again and got a nod from the other. 'Thank you.' He put a tick on the card. He was squinting through his left eye because the smoke from the cigarette clamped in his lips had effectively shut the right one.

'Is this absolutely necessary, doctor?

'Not sure. Best to be on the safe side, though. You can put your clothes on. Thank you. No venereal diseases?'

'Certainly not.' Jarvas was doing up his shirt. This was the most untidy consulting room he'd ever been in, and one of the most confined. There had been nowhere to hang anything.

'Thank you.' Without looking up Ewenny-Preece volunteered, 'If you're looking for your tie you put it by the *Gray's Anatomy*. Bookshelf behind you. People always use that. Woman left her knickers there once. Would you believe?' He made a tutting noise. 'Sort of thing could get you in trouble. With the BMA or something. Thank you.' The cough was less sepulchral this time. 'If you did decide to sue, like you said when you came in, I'd have to prove the examination was thorough, you see?' The doctor brushed the cigarette ash off the card. It fell on to his trousers. 'It was my wife who found the knickers. Dusting.'

'Shoulder's bloody painful still.'

'Where you fell on it? Would be. Got that down earlier.' He turned the card over to check. 'Yes. Thank you. Might be worth some physiotherapy. Don't go to hospital for it, though. Little enough between any of us and sudden death these days without tempting providence. Don't know a hospital that isn't crawling with dirt and disease. And rife with incompetence. If aseptic surgery doesn't get you, the food poisoning will. Terrible. Scotch and water all right for you? It's all I keep in here. I'm parched.'

'That's very nice of you.'

The doctor produced a bottle, two glasses and a Thermos of cold water from the cupboard in the left pedestal of the desk. 'Thank you,' he wheezed as he poured the drinks. 'Marvellous cure-all, alcohol. Kept me out of trouble, I can tell you. In moderation, of course. Wouldn't credit I was fifty-seven, would you?' He looked much older. 'Six years older than you, that is.' He glanced at the card again. 'Yes. You could try an alcohol rub on that shoulder. Thank you,' he added as he stretched to pass Jarvas his glass. 'You knew Dick Clay from before, then?'

'Employed him and his wife years ago. Only for a short time. Gardener and housekeeper at our place in Sussex.'

'Indeed? Living in, were they?'

'There was a cottage.'

'Lucky.'

'It was when Mrs Figgle and I were married. They never suited really.'

'Not surprised. Chap's Bolshie, seems to me.'

'And crazy with it. Is he a patient of yours?'

61

'Probably. Have to ask my wife. She keeps the books. Never comes to see me. Clay, I mean. Nor the daughter. Wife comes. Big, handsome woman. Very handsome.' The words were redolent with recollection: pleasing recollection. 'Gall stones. Avoided operation. Thank God, or she might not be here today. Thank you.'

'So there wouldn't be any conflict of loyalty if you had to appear for me in court?'

The doctor's glass was arrested in transit and held just short of his own open mouth. 'You did say you were consulting me as a private paying patient?' He watched for the nod of assent, then took a large gulp from the glass. 'No conflict whatsoever,' he offered with assurance. 'Did you fetch the police?'

'No. One didn't want to make more fuss than was necessary at the time.'

'Quite so. Steer clear of them whenever you can. Swear black is white for tuppence, they will. Local lot are all right, I suppose.' His eyes indicated his thoughts had strayed. 'These drink and drive laws have got completely out of hand. Take my case. . .' He paused, then decided not to offer it after all. 'Plenty of witnesses, you said?'

'Yes, to an unprovoked, inexplicable case of unjustified assault.'

'And battery. Thank you. Know how you feel. Terrible thing, a sense of injustice. Gnaws at your very vitals.' He nearly went back to an account of how he had been wrongly accused of 'driving while under the influence' in Cardiff, after a Rugby football match, then thought better of it: again. He had been fingering a sample pack of a new drug for relieving anxiety and left him by a pharmaceutical company salesman that morning. 'These might be some use to you,' he said, without great conviction. He handed the packet to Jarvas. 'They say they're very good if you can't sleep. Might need one tonight. With an Aspirin for the pain. Another drink?'

'No, I'd better be off.'

'Thank you.' The doctor rummaged under the pile of letters, leaflets, other samples, plastic probes, empty cigarette packs and instrument boxes that littered the desk. It was the draught from an especially breathy cough that eventually revealed the edge of a blue-covered receipt book. He pulled it out from under a metal implement for syringing ears. 'Here we are then.' He cleared his throat. 'That'll be . . .' He gave a meaningful look at the other's empty glass. 'That'll be twenty . . . twenty-five pounds, if it's by cheque. I can give you a receipt.' The book was open, pen poised to show willing. 'If you like.' He looked up through the smoke. 'Cash would come a bit less. No administrative expenses.'

Jarvas proffered three five-pound notes. The doctor accepted them without demur. 'Receipt not required then,' he said. 'Better to get these things settled straight off, I always think.' The conviction strengthened. 'Especially where you might be suing for damages. Thank you.'

'Mr Clay could have knocked him out,' said Robin Figgle, aged eight and a half, only son of Jack and Amanda, and half-brother to Fleur.

'Killed him. Like as not. It was a heck of a punch,' Stephen Watkins replied: he was a few months older than Robin, but smaller, and dark where the other boy was fair. Stephen was the youngest of the local postman's four children.

After choir practice, the two boys had been playing at snipers behind the gravestones. They had been 'picking off' everybody entering the church and had witnessed the assault through the open door in the porch. Now they were in Robin's big dormer room at the manor.

' "Haven't learnt your lesson yet, Mr High and Mighty Jarvas. Going to learn it now." Then whang, bash, he went. It was like TV, wasn't it?' Robin had mimed the action with the words.

Stephen jumped up from the floor where they were both kneeling. He put his hands on his hips. ' "Just you leave my Rose alone".' It was a better treble imitation of Clay's voice. Then the boy turned about and stalked across the room, swinging round again to add in the same voice, ' "Should have

63

made it worth being fired the last time." ' Stephen rejoined his friend again on the rug. 'What d'you think he meant by that?'

'Dunno. Except he worked for my mother. Hundreds of years ago.'

'When she was married to Mr Jarvas, you mean?'

'Probably.'

'Your sister didn't half scream.'

'She's not my sister. She's my half-sister.'

'Full sisters are worse.' He had two. 'And the school gave you the whole weekend for her soppy wedding?'

'Till Sunday night, as usual.' Robin was a week-day boarder at a preparatory school, but not far away: he usually came home by bus at lunchtime on Saturdays. Stephen went to the church school in the next village.

'I got an afternoon off for my grandad's funeral last year. There was a smashing tea after. That's what your marquee's for. They always have smashing teas after weddings and funerals.'

'It's called breakfast after a wedding.'

'In the afternoon? Breakfast? With Shredded Wheat, and bacon and eggs? Don't be daft. You think this Mr Jarvas has been having you-know-what with Rose?' There was no pause or warning about the subject change.

'Expect so.'

'My dad says she's a sex kitten. What about the bridesmaids then? Better than this one.' They had gone back to turning the pages of a year old and very dog-eared copy of *Playboy*. In case of sudden interruption, this was camouflaged inside a newer issue of *The Economist* – demonstrating a sound sense of precaution but poor judgment on what adults would deem convincing leisure reading for the under-nines. ' 'Course, you can't tell with their clothes on.'

'Can with them off.' Robin rocked backwards and forwards, arms grasped around bent knees.

'Go on? When?'

'Just when I got home. Before practice. Up here.'

'Both of 'em?'

'Only one. She's in the bedroom next door. Didn't know I was here. Door was open.'

'Naked was she?' They both cringed involuntarily.

'Not all over.'

Stephen looked disappointed, then calculating. 'How much?'

'Topless.' There was more cringing.

'Anyone with her?'

'Yes.'

'Who?'

Robin told him.

'Go on!'

There was a sudden noise from outside in the corridor. Stephen pushed the magazines under the bed, while Robin jumped to open the door. Palmerston bustled in, staring around, it seemed reproachfully, through the hair that covered most of his eyes.

## CHAPTER SIX

'Good of you to come over like this, Mark. Didn't mean to trouble you with my business affairs. Stopped your golf too. You'll apologise to Molly?' Jack Figgle sounded genuinely sorry.

'My dear chap, we can play golf any time. I just wish you'd stirred me up earlier. At the office. I really hadn't appreciated things were in quite such bad shape. Should have though.' Treasure shook his head. 'You know I never read that report? Not properly. Just the summary.'

'Why should you have done? Anyway the Grenwood, Phipps's recommendations were clear enough. It was putting them through in time that caused the problems.' He pointed to his companion's whisky glass. 'Ready for the other half?'

The two men were in Figgle's study, a large, square, mahogany-panelled room, occupying the north-east corner of the building. It was reached through double doors on the left after one entered the house through the big hall.

There was very little conventional furniture in the room – an escritoire and chair in one corner, a drinks tray nearby, and a pair of button-backed leather armchairs, in which the men were sitting, before the carved fireplace on the south wall. Otherwise the room was given over to Figgle's collection of antique armour and weaponry.

Surrounding the mantel was a large geometrical display of shields, swords and scabbards, while a similar but less complex arrangement of breastplates, helmets, pikes and lances filled the entrance wall. Between the windows on the other walls were glass-encased examples of muskets and matchlock, wheel-lock and flintlock rifles. The centre of the room was given over to free-standing display cases housing crossbows and a variety of conical and cylindrical bored pistols, with powder boxes, samples of shot and other paraphernalia. It was an examination of these cases on a previous visit which had convinced Treasure that up to the mid-seventeenth century small arms must have been nearly as dangerous to fire as to face.

'May I help myself?' He crossed the room and poured a finger of Scotch and a lot of soda into his glass. 'Jarvas insists you sign the contract letter before the wedding, of course.'

'I haven't seen him yet, but yes, that's part of the message he sent via Jonas. You think I shouldn't sign?' Figgle looked down at the document in his hand. Treasure had just read it. 'It's pretty straightforward.'

'Oh, it's an example in brevity and clarity. It commits you totally, with no one else obliged to do a damned thing.'

'Jarvas says he'll give Fleur away.'

'Provided he does he can't pretend later he didn't approve the marriage. I think that'd hold up in law, certainly. Secures Fleur's inheritance. By itself it does nothing for you. Incidentally, I'd still rather Fleur had a letter from Jarvas giving his categoric approval.'

'I'll ask him for that after dinner.'

'No: demand it.' The banker was pacing slowly between the display cabinets. 'Get it in exchange for signing the letter. If you're determined to sign it.'

'What else can I do?'

'Depends on how surely you trust Fleur's intention, as propounded by her fiancé. The letter commits you and any future owner of your company to employ Jarvas as a corporate affairs executive, whatever that means, at twenty thousand a year for ten years, and a half pension afterwards. There are virtually no grounds on which you could fire him.'

'If we ever went into liquidation. . .'

'Under the rules of voluntary liquidation, of the type you've

67

been contemplating, that letter could constitute a charge on the company.'

'I'd have to pay him off? Like a preferred creditor?'

'Not quite, but not far off. It'd be different if he'd demanded to be made a director. But he's too smart for that. Even so, if the company folded, the pension commitment wouldn't be worth much.'

'So obviously he, at least, believes in Fleur's intentions.'

Treasure stopped pacing and considered the exhibits in one of the display cabinets. 'Seems so. You're confident young Grimandi can deliver those contracts?'

The other man shrugged his big shoulders. 'I think so. Even if he didn't, with a million in fresh capital we can become a going concern again.' He was leaning forward in his chair, his massive hands both clasped around his glass. Now the bushy eyebrows lifted. 'But yes, I think Jonas will deliver.'

'And you've no misgivings about Fleur's inheritance being sunk in the company?'

Figgle said nothing for several seconds. 'You've hit the nail on the head, of course, Mark. I have grave misgivings . . . except . . .'

'Except it'll give her legal control, and the assets are actually worth much more than the price she'll be paying for the shares. Except also she's a good deal richer than she would have been if you'd spent her income on her upbringing instead of investing it. And, as you say, that piece of her estate won't be put into the company.' Treasure's brow lifted in approbation. 'I think you can face your conscience clearly. The question remains, can you afford to allow your part of the bargain to be signed and delivered tonight? It leaves you beholden to Jarvas, while everyone else is simply honour bound to act as promised.'

'I'll make Jarvas write that letter.'

'Which gets us some of the way. I'll draft it for you. You trust Fleur. . .'

'Of course,' the other cut in sharply.

'I was going to say Fleur and her husband. To keep their

68

end of the deal? Tomorrow your step-daughter could effectively be endowing Jonas Grimandi with all her worldly goods,
which from the moment of her marriage will be greatly
enhanced.' The banker drank from his glass, then walked back
to his chair. 'How well d'you know Grimandi?'

'Not well, but well enough, I think. Of course, they've not
known each other that long. You've not met him yet?'

'No. Only his venerable great-uncle who speaks highly of
the boy. But then, he would do.'

'Are you suggesting. . . ?'

'I'm suggesting you let me have a word with these young
people this evening. In default of there being any legal
sanction you could or would want to apply, I'd like to be sure
they know what they're letting you in for.'

'To employing Jarvas ahead of Fleur getting control of the
company? Jonas seemed well aware of that.'

'Fine. Let's be sure Fleur is equally aware of it.' Treasure
slowly blew out a deep breath. 'It's all a bit loose and verbal,
Jack.'

The other smiled. 'But surely you City chaps do all your
dealing . . . ?

'Not with people like Jarvas we don't. And with respect, not
with Johnnie-come-lately, prospective sons-in-law either.'

Figgle hesitated. 'You spoke of legal sanctions?'

'Which I don't think you'd care for. For instance, it'd be
possible to have an agreement drawn tonight for Fleur to sign
in the morning committing her to the investment.'

'No, I wouldn't care for that,' Figgle put in promptly.
'Jarvas is one thing. Fleur's quite another. We're not that
close, but I've worked hard for what respect she has for me.
This step-father relationship can be a very delicate one. She's a
sensitive girl. Easily upset . . . or she can misunderstand motives. I'd like her to believe I trust her in this.'

Treasure nodded. 'Your motives do you credit.'

'Never earned me any, though. You're probably thinking
it's my sloppy ways that have brought me and the company to
the present impasse.'

'Probably, but I'd guess you've always slept at night.' Both men smiled as Treasure went on. 'So, we'll leave it that I'm allowed gently to remind Fleur and Jonas of the gravity of things, and you'll get the wedding consent from Jarvas. In writing.'

'That you can count on. I've no illusions about his probity.' Figgle put his glass down, then regarded his open palms, allowing his thumbs to rub the sides of his forefingers. 'If he let Fleur down I think I'd exterminate the perisher.'

Mildred Clay had reached the hotel well ahead of the golfers and hurried through the kitchen entrance. Whoever had been on the practice range had left. She had looked, but she hadn't wasted time going over to check more closely: there were other things on her mind.

It was nearly six-thirty. Mildred was due at the manor shortly. She was to help serve drinks and dinner. Her regular job was doing bedrooms at the hotel: mornings only. That was part of the arrangement when Mr Shannon first took Dick on – that his wife did three hours a day at the Orchard. She did waitressing by arrangement on an hourly basis, at the hotel and the manor.

She was always glad of extra cash, which she kept for herself: her husband wasn't over generous with their official joint income. He wasn't mean exactly. It was just that he seemed to resent the amount she spent on clothes and make-up. But he expected her to look nice: wanted it all ways.

The kitchen was crowded when she went through. Mrs Shannon was in the centre of things, getting some ducks ready. Everybody was busy at something. Mildred didn't greet anyone in particular or call attention to herself. Nobody who noticed her would have found her presence unusual. In passing she checked on the guest list, with room numbers, kept by the door to the stairs. Rose wouldn't be at reception. By now she'd be helping Mr Shannon with the bar. But it wasn't Rose she'd come to see.

70

When she reached Room Nine, she knocked on the door, then straightened her dress and patted her hair. There was the sound of movement from inside but no voices.

'Who's there?'

He'd called out after she'd knocked a second time, just as she heard someone starting to open the door of the room opposite. It was what she hadn't wanted to happen: for someone to see her up here, going into his room. She made up her mind quickly: she had to. The next moment she was inside with the door closed behind her. 'It's Mildred. I'm ever so sorry.'

Dick had been right: he did look older – and worn. But the face hadn't altered that much. And those eyes – the way they bored into you. She used to say she always felt naked when he looked at her: they were those sort of eyes.

All he had on, by the look of it, was a blue, spotted dressing gown. You could see it was worn, but it was silk all the same.

'Mildred?' he said testily, and with no sign of recognition.

'Mildred Clay.'

'Mildred Clay!' he hissed. Now he knew who she was. 'Well, for God's sake keep your voice down.'

She advanced into the room towards him. 'Oh Kit, I'm so ashamed. About Dick. Did he hurt you? It's so good to see you. I'm . . . I'm ever so sorry,' she repeated, feeling foolish. Now she wondered why she'd come, what good she'd expected to do, why she'd pushed in.

'I'm alive, as you can see. Your husband did his best. . .'

'It wasn't over Rose, you know that?' She interrupted. 'I don't believe it was anything to do with Rose. I don't think she'd said anything out of the way. About you, I mean. It was me he was angry about. I could see it when he came in for his tea. He's always suspected us. He's said so, ever so many times.'

'I don't know what you mean,' he answered quite loudly. 'Unless it was part of a trumped-up reason for his taking a poke at me. He's a madman, and he'll be lucky if I don't sue, I

71

can tell you that. Now, I think you'd better go, don't you?'

'I don't have to. Not for a minute. Nobody knows I'm in here.' She noticed the bottle of gin on the tray. There was tonic water too, and ice. 'You haven't said how I look. It's been a long time.' She moved closer to him. He was standing at the end of the bed. The cover had been disarranged, the pillows pulled out. He'd been taking a nap.

'You look very well. Fine.' He reached for a cigarette packet and lighter. They were on the table beside him, with the gin. He still hadn't moved from the end of the bed. It was where he'd been standing when she came in. The bathroom door to his left was closed.

She was disappointed he hadn't known who she was at first; but she supposed it was understandable. It was more than eight years since they'd been in touch – sixteen since he'd seen her: since they'd been lovers. She'd worked it out. It meant a lot to her that he should know she still cared: that she was still worth caring about.

'The money I sent. After you wrote. After you came out of . . . you know. Did you get it all right? It wasn't much.' It'd been all she had.

'I got it. I'm sure I wrote.'

'I knew you had. Letter got lost, I expect. Shocking, the post. Really it is. I was sure you'd written. Then someone said you'd gone to Kenya. Nice there. . . I'm sure.' She knew she was talking nonsense. 'Could we have a quick drink, love? For old times' sake? You are pleased to see me, Kit?' If only he knew how she felt. That he was still the most exciting man in her life. Whatever his faults, he had class and style. He'd known how to treat a woman all right. She'd probably never see him again. If he'd just put his arms around her once: give her a kiss: say something she'd remember – something to keep the memory alive.

If only she'd told him all those years ago. It might have been different if . . .

'It's not wildly convenient, Mildred. Not at this very

72

moment' – and that, he thought, must be the biggest understatement he'd make for some time. He drew on his cigarette, wondering what he had to do to get rid of her, short of physically thrusting her out the door. It was embarrassing – even by his standards. Keeping their voices down had done no good at all. 'I've still got to bath. Change for dinner. Perhaps we shall meet later. I'm here for the whole weekend.'

'No. There won't be another chance. Not like this. I know it. Oh Kit. Hold me, love. Just for a minute. You don't know what you've meant to me. Mean to me. After all these years.' Impelled, she closed the gap between them, throwing her arms around his neck, thrusting her whole substantial body against his.

The momentum had been heavy and unexpected. 'My God, my back!' he yelped. The discomfort was genuine as he fell on to the bed with Mildred Clay on top of him.

She leapt up. 'Oh love, I'm sorry. I'm ever so sorry. . .'

'Courtesy of your bloody husband.' He started to rub his shoulder.

'Let me massage it for you. You used to say I was good at that. Remember when you twisted . . .'

The dressing gown had fallen open. She was advancing again. By the way she was looking – and where she was looking – she'd have it off him in two seconds. The whole charade was out of hand. The scenario he had planned had taken a preposterous, nightmarish twist. 'Get out, Mildred,' he ordered, teeth clenched. He stood up, pulling the gown around him.

'Yes, love. I'm sorry. . .'

'Stop being sorry. Just go.'

'I'll straighten the bed for you.' What if anyone saw her leaving and then saw the state of the covers? She pushed past him to the far side of the bed. It was when she bent over that she saw the shoes. They were a new pair: white court – with fancy gold bars on the front. They'd nearly taken them back to the shop because of a slight scratch on one of those bars. There

73

was no mistaking that scratch.

She stood up, holding the shoes. 'You dirty swine,' she uttered slowly, the loving tone entirely gone. 'You dirty filthy swine.' Then raising her voice she cried, 'Rose, come out of that bathroom.'

# CHAPTER SEVEN

'And it's time the musical establishment recognised the quality of British composition. One asks what happened to Edward Elgar, Arnold Bax, Vaughan Williams?'

'They died?' Noah Plimpton pushed his glasses along his nose, and adopted a suitably mournful expression. 'Called to their rich rewards, Mrs Millant.'

Treasure suppressed a smile. It had been his misfortune to be cornered alone by the garrulous and over-earnest Mrs Bunty Millant. Noah had just come to the rescue.

Those who were dining at the manor were disposed in groups around the drawing room. Drinks were being served. There were a number of people the Treasures were meeting for the first time. Mrs Millant was one of these: a gaunt, lean woman of sombre countenance and disposition – impressions both matched by her appearance. She spoke softly in a conspiratorial strain, cultivated to command attention before unwary listeners concluded there was nothing being said that rated it. Like others practised in the same strategy, she continued to hold conversational sway through the careful avoidance of eye contact.

A widow, Bunty Millant had been introduced – then promptly abandoned – by Amanda, and named as one of the hostess's oldest friends. The implication that the two had been girlhood contemporaries Treasure found it only just possible to credit.

'Works by English composers are so seldom included in our concert programmes,' continued the lady, pulling what looked like a shawl in grey candlewick more tightly across a flat upper torso shrouded in even greyer crêpe-de-chine. Her gaze was focused, through a pair of immense, round, gold-rimmed spectacles, on the centre of Treasure's tie. It had been dwelling on that spot for some time. She appeared not to have heard Noah's contribution – or chosen not to have done so. 'Music acceptable for British consumption must be made on the Continent or in America, it seems, like. . .'

'Wine?' Noah put in promptly, and this time with more vigour.

Mrs Millant answered quietly and with disarming meekness. 'Do you suppose that is a fair comparison? My husband was an artist, you know?' She shot a gauging glance at the speaker.

'A composer?' asked Treasure. 'That would account. . .'

'A photographer. Very gifted but not given the celebrity he deserved in his all too short lifespan.'

'Did he make money at it, though?' This was Noah, undefeated and genuinely interested: he owned a camera.

She shook her head. 'But it gave me great consolation that he never had to compromise his artistic integrity with commercial considerations.'

'Well, that's a blessing. He was wealthy?'

'No, Mr Plimpton. But I am,' came in a breathy undertone – a privileged communiqué and not a boast.

'Your husband specialised, perhaps?' began Treasure. 'I understand the more esoteric. . .'

'He specialised, yes.'

'Let's guess. Images of social history? Relics of industrial Britain?' Noah offered. 'Stark shots of grim satanic mills. Abandoned coal-mines. Winding wheels silhouetted on the dawn skyline. . .'

'The female form.' She risked a pause after such a successful interjection. 'In all its aspects. Mostly the nude. I was his favourite model.'

The younger man swallowed slowly.

'Indeed,' said Treasure, compelled minutely to study the

empty glass he was holding. 'How very interesting. For both of you.' He cleared his throat. 'Tell me, how long have you known Amanda?'

'More than twenty-five years. Since well before she married Kitson. That was a mistake, of course. However, for a time, as couples, we were inseparable. We were close neighbours in Sussex. It's where I live still. And we often holidayed together. Until the divorce. Our loyalties lay with Amanda over that, as you'd assume. My husband died soon after. In an accident. I don't see so much of Amanda nowadays. Not as much as I'd like.'

'But you've made the effort for the wedding. Ah, have you met the Vicar?'

It happened that Greville Sinn was standing some feet away with his back to the group, but Noah's loud pronouncing of his title prompted him to turn.

'Vicar, d'you know Mrs Millant?' Noah followed through fast.

'Indeed I do. How very nice to see you again. Are you quite well?' Sinn came over, penetrating with platitudes. 'Splendid, splendid.' He approved the reply to his enquiry before it was uttered. 'Family all right?'

'Mother died since I was last here,' Mrs Millant half whispered.

'Splendid, splendid,' repeated Sinn with more gusto. 'I remember we once discussed the great contribution Sir Arthur Bliss made as Master of the Queen's Music. Some strident tunes.'

Treasure withdrew gently to another part of the room.

'And I gather Jonas has this marvellous job in Hong Kong?' Molly Treasure beamed approvingly at the bridegroom's parents. She had come upon them standing alone looking well pressed, Southern European, and thoroughly uncomfortable.

'He's doing well,' agreed Gino Grimandi, whose Italian accent was stronger than his Uncle Silvano's.

'We don't help so much. Not with the money.' Teresa Grimandi was short like her husband, and inclining to stoutness. They both seemed to be surrendering to middle-age without a fight. 'We had six children to bring up.' But over this she was on the defensive. 'The café, it don't make so much money.'

'We do our best,' interrupted her husband.

'You live in Glasgow? I believe the Scottish educational system is quite excellent,' said Molly.

'There we have been lucky. Two children in university now. The youngest also. At a polytechnic,' the man continued. 'But it still takes money to feed and clothe everyone. In Jonas's time, he's the oldest, we couldn't afford. You understand? It's why he leaves school. . .'

'Are my parents pressing you to visit their restaurant, Mrs Treasure? I don't suppose you get to Glasgow much. Their place is a bit off the beaten track. Still, if you're ever in the vicinity.' Jonas had joined them somewhat abruptly.

Molly judged a smile of good intention about fitted such an oblique invitation. 'You're not having a stag party tonight?' she asked.

'That was last Saturday. In London. But after dinner Noah's organising the younger element up at the Orchard. There'll be wine and dancing. All very decorous, I assure you. Bed by twelve-thirty.'

'We went to the wedding rehearsal. Such pretty flowers. Such a pretty church.' This was Mrs Grimandi.

'We're Catholic.' Her husband looked at their son, then shrugged. 'You can't have everything. She's a lovely girl. You know, when Jonas was sixteen. . .'

'Excuse me, Poppa, Momma, I have to take Mrs Treasure to meet someone over there,' Jonas interrupted. 'Don't move now. I'll be back.' He grasped Molly's arm and steered her away. 'You were just about to get the boring story of my life,' he confided, while glancing speculatively about the room. It seemed there was no one in particular he was taking her to – nor did he evidence any intention to return to his parents.

'. . .but he hit Mr Jarvas right on the chin,' Alexi Bedwell was recounting to Penelope Sinn in another part of the room.

'On the chin,' confirmed her sister.

'And there was I shut up in the vestry missing the action,' declared Penelope, at lower than fortissimo and with only a formal attempt at showing interest. She flicked a bit of cocktail biscuit off the pink taffeta dress snapped up at the last 'War on Want' jumble sale. It had been a bargain *and* her size. Even so, it clashed with her only lipstick, seldom worn but, when it was, always applied too generously.

'Oh, we saw it all. We were on our way back to the porch. . .' Alexi began.

'We heard what the green-keeper said, and everything,' her sister continued.

'His name's Mr Clay.'

'He positively roared at Mr Jarvas.'

'Then he hit him.'

'Then Mr Jarvas fell right back.'

'Nearly into us.'

'And Mr Jarvas says he didn't even know who Mr Clay's daughter was.'

'She works at the Orchard.'

'But he hadn't. . .'

'Done anything to her.' The duet was arrested with the participants exchanging meaning looks.

'Well, he'd only just arrived, hadn't he?' Penelope lowered her voice still further to a mid-bass response with unimpaired resonance. 'Dick Clay's a bit hot-headed. Actions speak louder than words. That'd be his motto. Hope he's done no real harm.'

'Shouldn't think so.' Byron Ware sounded pleased. He was the fourth member of the group which he had joined after earlier escaping from Bunty Millant's near soliloquising. 'Anyway, I guess Kit Jarvas will be keeping away from Miss Clay from now on. Yes sir.' From the corner of his eye he saw a bottle poised for pouring, and absently held out his glass. 'This champagne is excellent. Say, do you have a headache, Mrs Sinn? Can I get you something?' he enquired solicitously, then, looking up, he nodded warmly at the woman who had been

79

standing beside him with a tray and bottle for the previous few seconds. He realised too late it was Mildred Clay – also why Penelope Sinn had been screwing up her face at him as if consumed by agonies.

Amanda Figgle was standing near the fireplace. She was dressed – her mother privately felt unsuitably dressed – in an elegant black silk trouser suit. There was a log fire burning, largely in deference to hints from Mrs Ware. The evening was especially warm even for October. 'We're eighteen for dinner. I just don't know how Myra Shannon copes,' said the hostess to those standing beside her, which included her mother and Silvano Grimandi. 'They're full up at the Orchard. She's doing the wedding catering tomorrow, and she just asked me if we need dinner brought up here tomorrow evening too.'

'Some of the guests eat here tonight. Like me, yes?' Silvano beamed across his champagne glass. For his part there had been no difficulty in identifying the blonde and Rubenesque Mildred who had recently refilled it. He was still savouring the innocent pleasure provided by the close proximity: such dignity she maintained – in all circumstances.

'Doesn't mean we get another dinner later at the Orchard, you know, Silvano,' joked Treasure, who had just joined the group. He regarded the other's substantial figure with great amiability. 'Why d'you look different tonight?' he enquired, a split second before wishing he hadn't: the answer had suddenly become obvious.

Silvano broke into a coy grin, then patted the top of his head. 'You notice? Look younger, huh? Is the rug. The toupee,' he added since the first description brought several blank looks. 'You take me for my nephew, Gino? Or Jonas, maybe? I wear for special occasion. Is expensive,' he ended bashfully.

'Makes you look even more handsome,' said Treasure, like the others, now overtly inspecting Grimandi's nicely contrived accoutrement. At the same time he wondered why the owner only produced the thing as an occasional adornment – whatever the cost. 'If you'd had it on since you arrived, we'd all have taken you for forty-five.'

'It's really a very good one, Mr Grimandi,' volunteered Mrs Ware. 'They're quite normal in the States, you know?' she continued, then looked confused. 'I mean, everybody wears them, even . . . Oh dear, am I saying all the wrong things?'

'No, no, Signora Ware . . .'

'Please call me Harriet,' she pressed, desperately trying to assuage.

'OK. Harriet. You mean even classy people wear rugs these days? That's right. But Silvano Grimandi wears only sometimes. Like the special tie. The good suit.' With flourishes both hands flicked at his lapels. 'It's for the occasion. Not to make the lie. You understand? Is not so you think I'm forty-five.' He bowed to Amanda. 'Is because you know I make effort when I come to your beautiful house.'

'That's a charming compliment . . . Silvano,' said Harriet Ware.

'Is the truth. To lie is not for me. I hope for no Grimandi.' His tone had become solemn.

'It's hot in here.' Fleur, who had just appeared, impulsively linked her arm in Treasure's and drew him aside. 'How d'you get on with Bunty?'

'A worthy lady.'

'It's sad. She should have remarried. She's let herself go. In every kind of way.'

'You mean she was once even better than worthy?'

'Physically not so much. But she was great fun. I remember as a kid. And her husband, Basil. Wow!'

'Wow what?'

'Adonis type. Terribly masculine and athletic. Women used to drool over him.'

'When did he die?'

'Eight – no, nine years ago.'

'You were very young. He must have made quite an impression.'

'He was marvellous with children. I adored him. So did Mummy.'

'Photographer?'

'Mmm. Not that serious – or good. I mean it was a means to an end, if you follow.' She noted the puzzled frown. 'He did nudes. He had a studio. It was littered with beds and couches.'

'You mean he was a lecherous nude photographer?'

'Lecherous and licensed.'

'His widow told me she was . . .'

'His favourite model,' Fleur broke in nodding. 'Also his meal ticket. In his definitive book of photographic nudes, the one he never actually finished, there were plenty of shots of Bunty. She'd probably show them to you if you asked her nicely. I've seen them. Often.'

'You mean she'd have them with her?'

'Could be. Honestly.' Their perambulation across the room had brought them to the door to the tented corridor. The curtains had not yet been drawn. They stopped. She sighed at the sight of the marquee. There was just enough daylight left to see. The place looked stark and uninviting despite the hanging flowers. The colouring of the drapes was not distinguishable.

Treasure felt the girl give a shiver. 'Getting cold feet?' he asked lightly. 'It's not uncommon.'

'Not that. At the start it was all a gesture.'

'Of defiance? Independence?'

'Both probably. Now it's just a deal.'

'Oh dear. Did I overdo it?'

'In what you said to Jonas and me, in front of Jack? No. I understand Jack's putting a lot at risk. You were right to rub it in.'

'So that bit aside, it's all better than a deal. You love each other, after all. As for the business part, it's going to help Jack. A worthy cause.'

'I suppose so. You approve what my father's cooked up for himself?'

'With safeguards. For Jack.'

'You don't think I need safeguarding?' Her questions had

come swiftly and nervously.

'I assume your high-flying bridegroom knows what he's about. Of course, when you effectively control Jack's company he won't have much at stake. It's the immediate future . . .'

'Just so my father doesn't go back on approving the wedding? Hardly anyone trusts him. You can't blame them, I suppose. Had he really been groping Rose Clay?'

'Her father evidently thought so.'

'That was pretty embarrassing. In the church, I mean.' She took her arm from his and turned about. Her gaze sought out Mildred Clay who was well out of earshot. 'Not that peaches and cream Rosie is any kind of an innocent. She just trades on a virginal image. Ask anyone in the village. It was still vile of my father to behave quite so much in character.' She paused. 'Jonas blames Rose. He takes the tolerant view of Kitson Jarvas. He's the only one. Oh God, his parents are marooned again.' She made as though to go towards the couple, then stayed where she was, looking relieved.

'Good old Noah to the rescue,' said Treasure, because as Fleur had spoken, Noah Plimpton had gone over to the Grimandi pair.

'Jonas is positively neurotic about them,' Fleur went on. 'And the feeling's pretty mutual. They think they're letting him down, being such proles, I mean. He thinks they're having a hard time keeping up. That they should have made an excuse not to come. Or come tomorrow. They're obviously loathing every minute. But they do rather wallow in putting themselves down. And Jonas with them. He's so sensitive about what they say to people. I'm doing my bit, but it's hard-going.'

'Noah doesn't seem to think so. He's got them in stitches.' It was true. They could see the couple were now shaking with laughter.

'Noah's just a marvellous person.' There was a wholly uncharacteristic note of wistfulness in the voice.

'He's Jonas's closest friend? They don't seem to have a great deal in common.'

'Noah's my friend. Jonas hardly knows him. They met professionally. Sort of. Noah was involved in some legal job for Jonas. Something needed signing. They'd arranged to meet in a pub. In London. In July. I happened to be with Noah. And that's how I came to meet Jonas.'

'Who swept you off your feet?'

'Something like that. Look, there's Jack and my father, at last.'

'Mr Jarvas doesn't seem any the worse for wear.'

The two men had entered together. Jarvas was over-ebullient. Figgle looked worried and was promptly waylaid by Greville Sinn. Jarvas made towards Amanda who was still standing near the fire talking to Byron Ware and Molly Treasure.

'Sorry to have monopolised the host.' Jarvas mingled deftly. His smile was nothing less than gracious. The joints of his body never stilled as he dispensed too much unction. He was over-energetic, over-demonstrative. His feet were dancing. His elbows were bent inwards, the forearms up. Both hands were busy – the left massaging the twisting wrist of the right, while the right clawed the air for effect. 'Molly, you're even more devastating than before.'

'Before what?'

'And witty with it.' He grasped her hand in both his, then kissed her on both cheeks. 'Saw your powerful husband earlier. So exciting to meet again.'

'I'm sure it will be.'

The agitated performance and verbal effusions went on through other salutations. The enigmatic substance in Molly's responses was missed – or ignored. Mrs Ware's blurted enquiry as to the state of the Jarvas chin was cleverly parried without prejudice to litigation. Even Jonas's parents were received with warmth, albeit that they had to be brought forward by Noah, and suffered a somewhat short audience when Jarvas distracted himself with more engaging people.

At one point the man whisked a glass of champagne from Mildred Clay's tray with an aplomb that, knowing the circumstances, even his worst enemy might have grudgingly admired. The tray was moving at the time, and heading out of reach. Its bearer had no intention of stopping, or of changing direction for Kitson Jarvas.

'And you're here to give the bride away, Kit?' The question came quietly from behind him.

He spun about, his face wreathed in an ecstatic smile evidently intended to surpass the ones that had gone before. 'My darling Bunty. The journey's been worth it for you alone. You look quite ravishing.'

This frenzy of hyperbole seemed to make the right impression on the dowdy Mrs Millant. Encouraged, Jarvas drew her to him and planted a more than formal kiss on one cheek. By failing to present the other cheek for similar treatment it was clear the lady was showing a nice confusion rather than diffidence. In the end she was kissed twice on the same place.

'You haven't answered my question,' she said in a tone of almost coy reproof.

He let her go gently. 'My dear girl, there's a positive queue to hand Fleur down the aisle. I should be honoured, of course, but. . .' The arms were moving again, less actively because there was a glass in the right hand. But for once the shrug of the shoulders was more than meaningless affectation.

'Surely, the privilege is yours?' Molly enquired deliberately.

Conversation elsewhere in the room had tailed away. Most heads were turned toward Jarvas – along with some questing expressions.

'But am I deserving of it? Have I nurtured the lovely Fleur? Protected her as a father should all these years?'

'No, but. . .' Amanda began.

'It's all buts, you see. Times and conventions change. Jack and I have just been talking about it. I really feel the honour should go to him.'

'And what does Fleur feel?' asked Treasure from where he

85

was standing with the girl.

'That nobody cares a damn,' snapped Fleur. And she didn't burst into tears as many expected, nor did she run from the room.

It was Noah's voice that broke the silence. 'Wish someone would give me away. D'you think anyone'd take me?'

# CHAPTER EIGHT

'Not sorry that's over,' said Molly Treasure, unzipping her dress.

'The burglary made it eventful,' her husband answered. He had taken off his jacket and tie, and was slipping a woollen sweater over his shirt.

It was just before eleven o'clock. The two had returned to their room at the Orchard and were preparing to go down again.

'One quick view of a fleeing thief doesn't make up for two hours at dinner between somnolent Jack Figgle and solid, reliable Gino Grimandi.' She stepped out of her slip, then considered the line of clothes hanging in the wardrobe. 'And Silvano's such a sweetie. He was miles away from me. So was that nice Noah. I had Mrs Millant opposite – and the Vicar. Couple of weirdoes, if you ask me. It was a rotten seating plan.'

'You can hardly grumble at being sat on the host's right.'

'A penance not a privilege since he wasn't uttering. Which made two of them.' She took a pair of trousers from a hanger. 'You were surrounded by gorgeous young women.'

'Not as captivating as you with nothing on.'

'Aren't you gallant – and why am I feeling self-conscious? Stop staring. I do have something on.' She wrinkled her nose. 'I noticed the Bedwell twins never stopped drooling over you.'

'Really? Imagine they'd strip down nicely. And quickly. Well, everybody's good at something.' He was transferring things into the pockets of his golf jacket. 'Jack wasn't sleepy.

More likely preoccupied. Upset over Jarvas's deviousness.'

'You don't believe Jarvas will give Fleur away tomorrow?'

'I think he will. In the end. He's being foxy about it to avoid signing that letter.'

'The one you drafted saying he approves the marriage? Does it make that much difference?'

'It could.'

'Even if he actually leads his daughter to the altar?'

'Legally his consent would be a lot more binding if we had it in writing. There's a good deal of money at stake. He's playing a brinkmanship game with Jack, who I've just advised again not to sign that contract letter till Jarvas signs the other one. Somehow, though, I don't think Jack'll hold out. Jarvas won't be at the church unless he's got his contract, of course.'

'But he'll be there if he has?'

Treasure hesitated. 'Yes. Pretty certainly.'

'Then from what you've told me, I think Jack should sign and risk it. We'll all be at the church as witnesses, for heaven's sake. What about the bit in the service where the priest says "Who giveth this woman?" '

'To which there's no required verbal reply. Have you never noticed? Fathers don't have to answer "I do" or say anything. It's all done with gestures.'

'Are you sure?'

'Quite. I looked it up before dinner. So I doubt what happens constitutes a commitment. Only implies one. And I think Jarvas takes the same view. There could be another commitment he's avoiding too.' He looked at the time. 'Tell me, are you going like that?'

'Very funny,' said Molly who still hadn't decided which of the six available sweaters she should put on. 'I suppose we do have to go?'

'Not if you don't want. It's only for an hour though. I think it's rather a compliment. We've been included amongst what Noah calls the young. It's quite warm out. Tim Shannon's arranging a wine bar on the terrace in front of the pool. There'll be dancing. You enjoy that.'

'Well, I'm not swimming.' She glanced at the swimming trunks he was holding.

'Neither shall I probably. Indoor pool though. Water's kept at eighty-two.'

'Then I'll content myself watching you cavorting underwater with the Bedwells.'

'Except you'll be too busy being lionised for taking on the burglar single-handed.'

'By mistake,' Molly laughed. 'I mean it was largely unintentional. As I told the policeman, I was first out of the dining room, and went into Jack's study, thinking it was the drawing room. The burglar saw me and fled. It made me sound so heroic to the others.'

'But you did give chase.'

'I gave a sort of whooping noise, and advanced thinking there'd be others behind me. Then I walked into the display case. He was through that window like a shot. Sort of reaction that gets a girl bad notices.' She pulled a multi-coloured Dolman-sleeved sweater over her head. 'I should have gone for the light switch, of course. If I'd seen his face I could have picked him out in the Rogue's Gallery, or whatever they call it.'

'If he'd looked around again. Didn't you say he was wearing . . .'

'Jack's duffle coat. They found it outside on the drive. He had the hood over his head, of course, so I might not have got a proper look at his face.'

'What's surprising is he was working in the dark. He must have put the lights out. Jack says he left them on before dinner. He and Jarvas both remembered.'

'But Jack didn't leave the window open?'

'No. And it wasn't forced from outside either. Chap probably came through the open drawing room window, then went through the hall to the study.'

'What a nerve.' Molly was tidying her hair at the dressing table. 'I mean busting in when the house was full of people.'

'All more or less in one place. It's quite common. Bet he

intended to do all the bedrooms too, after he'd gone through the wedding presents which he thought would be in the study. That was your policeman's theory.'

'But the presents . . .'

'What there are of them. All in Fleur's bedroom. He never reached it, thanks to your intrepid intervention.'

'Nonsense.' Molly smiled all the same. 'I'd think he just got the timing of dinner wrong. He must still have got away with a lot from the study. I mean he had quite a large bag. I did see that. Did Jack say what was gone?'

'Still checking when we came away.'

Molly made a tutting noise. 'I should have run after him properly.'

'Glad you didn't.'

'Well, someone should have. There's too much crime.' She frowned severely into the mirror.

'But nobody knew till you ran back to the dining room. Amanda was seeing to the coffee. The other women seem to have gone upstairs in a body. . .'

'And the men were guzzling port.'

'All except the Vicar who'd gone to the loo. So had old Ware. Straight after the pudding. But he hadn't come back. Jack had gone for something. Brandy bottle. Someone wanted brandy. I suppose any of them could have run into the thief. Or heard your whooping.'

'Well, if they did, they didn't do anything about it.'

'The cloakroom's on the other side of the hall.'

'Well, they couldn't all have been in it. Not at the same time, surely? Anyway, if the thief wasn't in a car, and nobody heard one . . .'

'Probably had it parked on the main road. Got to it across country. It's not far.'

'What I mean is, six or seven able-bodied men, spread out, could have caught him. Some on foot, some in cars.'

'Sounds obvious after the event, I agree. We didn't think quickly enough. Most people staying in the house went to check their own rooms pretty smartly. Anyway, it's only supposition the man didn't have a car on the spot somewhere. It might not have been heard.'

'Little Robin Figgle says he didn't hear one, but his room's on the garden front. Wasn't he sweet when he came down? All packaged in his Jaeger dressing gown?'

'Sent to bed early to be fresh for tomorrow but still awake reading in bed. The family's fearless watchdog illegally sleeping in his room too.'

'So not everyone was in the same place. I'm glad that thief never got to the bedrooms. Despite the dog. Those kind of people can be quite ruthless, especially if they're panicked.'

'Should have thought of that when you started giving chase.'

'D'you think I did? Sort of subconsciously?' Molly sighed, and stood up. 'Well, what are we waiting for?' she demanded accusingly, strutting toward the door. 'On with the dance.'

'I don't care what anyone says to the contrary, that Jarvas is an absolute outsider. Belongs to a type the world would be better off without.' The Reverend Greville Sinn was standing before the uncurtained window of the vicarage kitchen in his shirtsleeves, applying polish to an already shining pair of shoes. He could see, and be seen by, passers-by outside where a lamp illumined the junction of the village street and the manor drive. He regularly performed his menial domestic chores on this spot so that parishioners could witness that he undertook the humblest tasks, and with proper zeal. His wife was preparing the hot chocolate drink they took each night before retiring.

'That's not a very Christian attitude, dear,' Penelope replied, but more in question than reproach. She was watching the milk in the saucepan to see it didn't boil over. At the same time she was preparing to swot a wasp. Greville liked the milk just under boiling, so as not to destroy the goodness. She had put a butcher's apron on over the pink taffeta, in case of splashes. Combined with her Wellington boots – she had just been out to lock up the chickens – the lipstick, and the leather-handled fly swatter, she was close to a Max Ernst print of an aging participant in a Thirties German cabaret.

Sinn looked at the time, and ignored his wife's irrelevant observation. 'You know the bounder should have done military service when he was eighteen?'

'Everybody did in those days, Greville.' Now she was poised on one leg like a Raphael nymph – swatter at the ready.

'Not Mr Jarvas. He bragged to me – bragged! – he got a false medical certificate from some crook in Harley Street. Never did a day in the Service – nor a day's work in his whole life from what he says. Drone. Parasite.' The Vicar's brushing had reached a frenzied pace. 'You know he's been in jug?'

'Somebody had the charity to remind me. Yes.' The milk had reached crisis point. Quickly she lifted the pan from the cooker. The wasp dived straight into it and promptly expired in the scalding liquid. 'Some kind of fraud, wasn't it?' She glanced around to make sure Greville hadn't witnessed the fatality. He was facing the other way. She extracted the dead body quickly. He was difficult about germs.

'Yes. And you know something else?' He'd looked about sharply. She froze with the wasp on the end of the long cooking spoon. 'Oh, good shooting, old girl. With a spoon, too.' He nodded approvingly, looking at the time again, before returning to the point and the polishing. 'According to Ware he could stop the wedding still. Remember we heard he didn't approve in the first place? Thought it fishy, his turning up at all. Jack's in a state about it all. Explained when he came in before. . .'

'But Fleur's of age.'

'Nothing to do with age. Money. Family trust. Ware hasn't got the details clear.'

'If it was after dinner, Mr Ware was a bit drunk.' She stirred the chocolate in the cups.

'If he hadn't been, he wouldn't have been so forthcoming. Jack's in deep trouble with his business. Didn't realise till tonight he's going bankrupt.' He snorted. 'All to do with unfair foreign competition.'

'Did Mr Ware say that?'

'No. I'm saying it. Obvious anyway. He's motor trade. Been ruined by Japan and France. Why can't people buy British?' He hadn't mentioned Germany. He always stretched a point over the Germans, whom he rather admired.

'I don't quite see how that's affected by the wedding. Want a biscuit, dear?'

'Well it is.' He waved away the biscuit tin as he went to wash his hands at the sink. 'Seriously affected. Jack implied as much. Ware confirmed it.' He sat down at the table with Penelope and began eyeing the top of his chocolate. She looked across surreptitiously in case there was anything like a dead wing floating on it. 'Meant to corner Jack again before we left.' So he was cogitating not scrutinising. He looked at his watch. 'Shouldn't have left a friend in trouble – comrade in arms – not without offering help. Trouble was he had Jarvas with him. We gave him marching orders over Dick Clay. Then I left them. Couldn't stick his company. Jarvas, I mean.' He was breathing deeply. 'Jack was decorated for bravery. In the war.'

Penelope concluded that outrage was upsetting the order of his thoughts. 'Not really our business, Greville,' she offered soothingly.

'Pass by on the other side, you mean?' He never felt quite right about calling up scripture – at least not in private. 'Friend in need is a friend indeed,' he added. That was better. 'Think I'll go back now.'

'It's quite late.'

'Wouldn't say that if you knew something tragic might happen.'

'Oh dear. D'you mean . . .?'

'Didn't like the look of Jack all evening. From the moment he came in with that toad Jarvas. I tell you, he reminded me of Percy what's-his-name. That young adjutant. When I was serving in Cyprus.'

93

'The one who committed suicide?'

'That's him. He looked the same way Jack did tonight. In the mess. The night he took his life.'

'But his daughter wasn't getting married next day.'

'Percy didn't have a daughter. Did he?' The Vicar frowned. 'Don't think so. He wasn't married.'

'Well, stop talking rubbish. I'm going back to help old Jack. He'll still be up.'

Penelope smiled and watched him leave. It was at times like these she admired the brightness of his Christian thought and action. In fact he was thinking darkly about Renault and Toyota – and Kitson Jarvas.


'I'm asking you for the last time, Rosie, what happened in that room before I got there?'

Mildred Clay was standing, arms akimbo, in the doorway of her daughter's bedroom. Rose was moving quickly about the room snatching the articles of clothing she intended to wear from drawers and shelves. 'And for the last time, Mum, I'm telling you nothing happened.'

'So why d'you have to lock yourself in the bathroom? Why were your shoes off by the bed? What else did you take off? You went in that bathroom to dress, didn't you? You'd been acting like a slut, hadn't you?' Fury showing in every expression and movement, Mildred advanced further into the room.

The girl flushed. 'That's a lousy thing to say. It's not true and you know it.'

'How do I know it?'

'Well, for a start I'd only been there a couple of minutes. I couldn't have left the bar for long.'

'Why d'you leave it at all?'

'Because evening room service for drinks is part of bar and reception duties. Ask anyone. Ask Mr Shannon.'

'So Jarvas told you to bring up a bottle of gin and two glasses? Two glasses to his single room? And you did it?'

'He rang down with his order like anyone else would. Yes,

94

he asked for two glasses. Plenty of guests have other guests in their rooms for drinks. He could have been asking Mr Grimandi from the room opposite or. . .'

'Oh, he could have been asking the Prince of Wales. But he wasn't, was he? He was asking you.'

'I don't drink gin.'

'He wasn't to know that. So why didn't you just take in the tray and leave? And how long's a couple of minutes, I'd like to know?'

Rose stopped what she was doing and faced her mother across the bed. 'Long enough to apologise. That's how long it was.' She bit her lip. 'To say I was sorry for mentioning to Dad. . .'

'That Jarvas had had his dirty hands on you?'

'For mentioning he'd made a play for me. Harmless. In fun. To say I was sorry my father had gone spare about it. Hitting Mr Jarvas and everything.'

'And that's when you started undressing?'

'I didn't, I tell you. He was ever so nice about it. Oh, Mum, I was so ashamed, I was crying.' And tears were welling up now in her eyes. 'He told me to sit down.'

'On the bed?' The mother's tone had not softened.

'There wasn't anywhere else. You know the size of those single rooms. He said to dry my eyes. To have a drink before I went back.'

'He would. And the rest.'

'I'd been on my feet since four. Those shoes were killing me. They're ever so tight. I kicked them off. Sort of without thinking. Then you knocked. I didn't know who it'd be. My face was such a mess, I dashed in the bathroom.'

'And now you're off duty you're tarting yourself up to go back again and meet him? You just wait till I tell your father all this.'

'I'm going back because Noah Plimpton kindly asked me to join the late party. Mr Jarvas won't even be there. But I don't feel like it any more. It's something I've been looking forward

95

to all day. Why d'you have to spoil it over nothing?' Now the tears were streaming down her face. 'Oh, Mum, why are you being so rotten to me? Why did Dad act like that at the church?' she sobbed. 'Mr Jarvas isn't so terrible. I've had much worse from other guests. And told you. And Dad. And we've all laughed about it. You know I can look after myself.' She slumped on to the bed, drying her eyes. 'I'm not a child' – even though at this moment she looked like one, and one deserving of understanding.

Mildred Clay walked around the bed and sat next to her daughter. 'Listen to me, love.' Her tone was now quite different. She put her hands on Rose's shoulders. 'Your Dad and me have known Kit Jarvas for a good many years. He's a bad lot. Always has been. Specially with young women. We're only protecting you.'

'I can protect myself.'

'Very likely you can. You know your Dad saw red when you told him what happened? I felt the same when I caught . . . when I found you were in that bedroom. But it's over now.'

'Not if you tell Dad.'

'About the bedroom. I won't. Not if you promise to stay away from Jarvas.'

'All right, Mum. But he is. . .'

'Romantic looking? I know.' Mildred's thoughts were twenty years away as she spoke: her eyes betrayed it. 'But do it for me. There's a special reason. Honestly.' She smiled: her gaze becoming alert again. 'And I want you to go to that party. So get dressed for it. I've promised Mr Shannon I'll give a hand clearing up there later.' She saw the doubt on Rose's face. 'Don't worry, I won't be snooping on you. And I won't embarrass you either. I'll be in the kitchen mostly. I can use the extra money, love,' she finished, half in apology, half in defence.

Rose threw her arms around her mother's neck. 'Oh Mum, you couldn't embarrass me. And I wish you didn't work so hard.' She paused. 'I'll keep clear of Mr Jarvas. I promise.'

Dick Clay hadn't waited to hear the last part of the

96

conversation. Earlier he had been standing downstairs in the hall of the cottage after entering without being heard. He'd spent most of the evening in the village pub. He'd listened to the exchange between the two women with mounting anger. Now he blundered away from the building telling himself he had to control the fury he was feeling – or else.

# CHAPTER NINE

Alone now in his room, Silvano Grimandi had not been invited to the young people's party for obvious reasons. Even so his great-nephew had troubled to explain them again before he had left the manor, to be sure there would be no offence. So why should he be offended? Worried he certainly was, but not offended. Reasons and attitudes had changed a lot from what he had expected – especially Jonas's reasons and attitudes.

A month ago this Kitson Jarvas had been the one spoiling everything. Silvano had given advice on what should happen, and Jonas had accepted it: so had Fleur, according to Jonas. The old man had been flattered. They wouldn't let the money rule everything. That was as it should be. That was the honourable way – the way that made Silvano proud of Jonas.

But earlier today Silvano learned things had changed. The bad Mr Jarvas was – all of a sudden – a good man after all. He had come to the wedding. He would be giving his daughter away. Fleur would be getting her inheritance. Everything was wonderful: Jonas said so – but it was not the same Jonas.

In the past the boy never seemed to hold anything back. For instance, he hadn't been ashamed to tell his problems ahead of borrowing money from his great-uncle. And while his great-uncle wasn't so rich, lending the money had been a pleasure. It had been in a good cause – first so the boy could better himself: then to keep up appearances with the family of the girl he loved. That was all good. But when Jonas had told the news about Mr Jarvas, that all was well, the boy hadn't been so open. He hadn't offered the details like before.

Now, tonight, the picture had changed again because what Mr Jarvas intended could be switched again. This would make Fleur unhappy. Maybe her father wouldn't give her away because Mr Figgle, this time, wouldn't play ball over something. Maybe she wouldn't be getting all that money for ten years. That was like before: not so terrible – except now Jonas was pretty mad with Mr Jarvas.

And another thing: Jonas, who had told Silvano many times he was proud to be a Grimandi, had treated his parents tonight like he was ashamed of them. It wasn't right a son should make it so plain his hard-working momma and poppa were some kind of an embarrassment when they came to his wedding.

Dully the old man reasoned the changes in Jonas matched the vacillations of Mr Jarvas. The more he thought about it, the more it seemed Mr Jarvas was behind every problem.

He peered through the small dormer window of his room. The party below had been in full swing for some time. The music was quite loud, but it would stop at twelve-thirty, or soon after: this had been promised. The view from the window did not take in the floodlit terrace below, nor the golf range which he knew was also lit up. There was a full moon in a cloudless sky. He could see the church and the roof of the manor below it clearly enough. For the rest, the window was set back too far into the roof. He could probably get a sighting if he leaned out, but this might be perilous: it could also advertise what he was doing to everyone below.

Silvano gathered the equipment that had taken up so much precious room in his case. He opened the door of his room a fraction, and listened. Satisfied there was no one in the corridor, he crept out and made for the landing. Next, instead of going down the main stairs, he turned to the narrow circular stairway opposite which wound round inside the turret – the architectural solecism so conspicuous from the outside of the building. He had made a reconnaissance of the feature in daylight, after his afternoon rest. That had been mainly out of curiosity, to find out what happened at the end of the stone steps.

Slowly he trudged to the top. There the door opened outwards into the small, empty chamber with the window to the south. He realised too late that he should have brought a chair. His grip wasn't nearly as firm as it used to be. It would have been better if he had something to steady his aim.

'Men who dance well are automatically and deservedly suspect,' shouted Noah Plimpton to Molly Treasure in an authoritative voice, and over the noise of the music. He continued with his emulation of someone strenuously climbing a very long rope and facing one way throughout. From time to time he did a deep knees' bend – the only variation in his dance routine, which, judging from his expression, was executed in a state of near trance. There was no rhythmic movement involved – or if there was, it was unrelated to the prevailing tempo of the music. 'Actually I'm better at the cheek-to-cheek stuff,' he added, giving his spectacles a push, and before reverting to his hypnotic kind of stare.

'Good,' replied Molly with feeling. Although she liked Noah, she was bored with finding new ways of dancing attendance around a partner rooted to one spot. 'Don't suppose you get much chance to practise your dancing.'

'Oh, quite a lot, as a matter of fact.' The possessed expression changed briefly to one of mild surprise. 'This step is very serviceable, don't you think?'

'Could we stop for a bit? I'd like a drink if . . .'

'Delighted,' answered the amused stranger Molly had addressed by mistake. Noah had done his knees' bend, and her comment had gone over his head to the rugged young man dancing behind him with Fleur.

'Noah doing his hornpipe, is he?' called Fleur. 'This is Jeremy. Come on, Noah, Molly wants a drink.'

They all four went over to the trolley bar where Tim Shannon was presiding. 'Wine only. Red or White. Compliments of the house,' snapped the beaming hotel proprietor, coming down so hard on the 'white' that Molly took it as an

100

injunction and automatically picked up a glass. Shannon took her picture with the Polaroid camera he had hanging around his neck. 'Famous actress imbibes at fabulous hotel,' he announced. 'Or the other way round.'

'Blinded by the flash but not the booze,' commented Noah.

There were some thirty people on the terrace, dancing to the music amplified by the portable 'discotheque' unit. Some of the dancers were dressed in towel gowns over swimsuits. There was a great deal of noise coming from the pool itself, where the sliding glass windows had been opened to the terrace. The whole area was ablaze with lights.

'It's so warm. I'm overdressed,' said Molly, eyeing the Bedwell sisters at the bar who were hardly dressed at all in the briefest of two-piece bikinis.

'We haven't been in the water yet,' giggled Sara Bedwell.

'Not yet,' agreed her sister. 'We're waiting for some others.'

Molly looked about her. 'Are all these people staying here, Mr Shannon?'

'Only a few. And a few from the manor. The rest are locals.'

'All friends coming to the wedding,' said Fleur. 'No more boring relatives yet, thank God. They're mostly coming tomorrow. Hundreds of them.'

'Relatives are so often boring,' pronounced Noah. 'One wonders why Einstein invented them.'

'Blood's thicker than water, you know.' This was Tim Shannon.

'And much nastier,' Noah came back promptly.

'Noah's being facetious.' Fleur turned back to Molly. 'Jeremy you've met. He farms near Worcester. He's brought Claudia and Giles. They're over there.'

'And Tina and Keith and Wendy, in the Land Rover,' said Jeremy. 'More the merrier.'

'Where's Jonas?' asked Molly.

'Counting the muskets again with my step-father,' Fleur answered. 'He should be here soon.' There was irritation in her voice.

'D'you know what was pinched?' This was Treasure who

101

had joined them with Rose Clay: the two had been dancing.

It was Noah who replied, pulling a piece of paper from his trouser pocket. 'Matching pair of flintlock pistols, late eighteenth century. Pride of the collection apparently, but not signed by the maker. Also a three-hundred-year-old powder flask, a fishing crossbow, about 1820 vintage, quite valuable, and an early Colt, double-action revolver.' He looked up at the others. 'A selective steal, it seems.'

'You mean he picked good stuff?' asked Treasure.

Fleur nodded. 'Some of it. And Jack says all very saleable items. Seems he should have had a permit for the revolver. May mean trouble. It works. So do the pistols, but they don't count. That's what I heard the copper say.'

'How exasperating to be robbed, and then to be prosecuted,' remarked the banker.

'We'll try to get round that. It's why I have the list.' Noah gave a modest smile. 'I'm giving the matter my full attention.'

'My hero!' cried Fleur, giving him a too generous kiss on the lips.

Noah looked agreeably surprised, then blinked earnestly several times. 'I think all antique guns bought as curios are exempt under the Firearms Act. I'm checking it in the morning. With my legal adviser,' he ended, with mock seriousness.

'That Colt is a very impressive curio. I was looking at it today,' Treasure said thoughtfully. He drew Noah aside. 'There was a bullet on show in the case with it.'

'That's gone too, I'm afraid. But we haven't bothered telling the police.' The younger man made a face.

Suddenly the music stopped. 'Hear this. Hear this. There'll now be a novelty golf competition on the driving range,' Tim Shannon announced over the loudspeakers, with his customary bits of emphasis. 'As many entries as you like. Entrance fee a pound a ball. Six balls for a fiver. Nearest to the hole wins a magnum of champagne. Profits for the church organ fund.'

'Religion again,' exclaimed Noah. 'Is nothing profane?'

'Where's the hole, Tim?' asked Jeremy.

'Temporary ninth. Below in the dip. It's floodlit.'

'It may be, but you still can't see it from up here.'

'That's the idea. Blind shot, and no peeking. Gives everybody a chance.'

'Don't think that follows, but here's my money,' said Treasure, proffering a five-pound note.

'Then you get numbers one to six, Mr Treasure.' Rose Clay was helping Shannon. She took the money and handed Treasure a box of six balls from the pile of similar boxes on the bar. 'Each ball has a sticky label with a number on. There's a choice of clubs here.' The implements in question looked distinctly elderly.

'Thanks, I'll get one of my own. My bag's in the car over there.'

'Unfair to beginners,' moaned Noah. 'Anyone want a half share in my ball? Only seventy-five pence?' he added optimistically. 'Well, I'm not the one who'll be hitting the wretched thing. I don't know how to.'

'Could you get me my seven iron from the car, Mark?' called Molly. 'And lend me a fiver?'

'A box here please, Rose,' demanded Jeremy.

'And one for me,' added his friend Giles.

'There's obviously money in farming,' Noah complained, while waving aloft a single pound note.

It was then that the hairy object fell to earth at Molly's feet. 'Ugh!' she cried, jumping to one side.

'It's Silvano's toupee,' said Treasure, picking it up, and searching the upper windows for signs of the owner. 'D'you suppose he's hanging upside down somewhere?'

'More likely he's washed it and hung it out to dry,' suggested Noah, while absently feeling the front of his own balding pate.

'I'll give it him in the morning.' The banker carefully put the toupee in the pocket of his golf jacket.

By the time the music started again, more than a dozen competitors had assembled at the designated spot on the golf range to the right of the terrace. As many people again had

103

come to watch.

That the green really was out of sight, in the hollow below, didn't seem to bother anyone. Shannon several times pointed out the correct line for the shot. 'Measured distance to the hole, one hundred and twenty yards. Or thereabouts. Give or take an inch,' he announced, beaming at all contestants.

The competition lasted longer than expected. Knowledgeable participants took a good deal of time preparing each shot: so did Noah, who was eventually persuaded to hit the one ball he'd paid for himself. It went like a bullet in the right direction across the ground, but without ever appearing to leave it.

'Hope there were no floodlit golfers down there,' joked Molly as she and her husband came back to the terrace arm in arm. They'd been putting away the clubs they'd used.

'Bit late to think of that,' commented Treasure. 'Of course, the lights are not for golfing after dark. They're to show up the hotel from the main road. Want to dance? I say, those two look a bit miserable on their wedding eve.' He nodded to their left. Jonas, whom he hadn't noticed earlier, was walking with Fleur away from the crowd. The girl was gesticulating – it seemed angrily. Then, confirming this impression, she stopped abruptly, stamped a foot and thumped her fiancé on the chest with a clenched fist. Then she turned about and stalked away from him back to the party. Jonas looked around, evidently anxious to establish if anyone had been watching the unseemly little tableau.

'Any more entries for the golf competition?' called Tim Shannon into the microphone, after arranging a break in the music. 'Looks like no more takers,' he remarked to Rose Clay a few moments later. 'Shall we go down and measure up the winner?'

'Been inspecting the scene of the crime. Sorry, I thought you'd be in here.' Byron Ware had moved back sharply, almost guiltily, from the display case he was examining as Jack Figgle entered his study followed by Palmerston. 'Been out?' Ware continued. 'You look a bit puffed.'

104

'Am a bit. Strange, I could have sworn I saw you coming down the drive a minute ago. Moonlight playing tricks,' said Figgle, smoothing the dog's head. 'Needed air. We've had a brisk turn. In the grounds. I'd been closeted in here with Jarvas since the police left.'

'Know what you mean. He crowds me too. Always has done. Did you. . . ?'

'Sign his wretched contract? Yes. In the end. Went against the grain, I can tell you. He wouldn't sign the letter Treasure put together for me. Jonas was here. At the beginning. Did his best to persuade him. Left when he failed. Possibly thought I'd do better on my own on that one.'

'And you didn't?'

'No. Jarvas insists the thing's unnecessary. Says he won't sign anything he doesn't have to. Never again. Not since he was wrongfully convicted over something he was tricked into signing.'

'You believe that?'

'That he was wrongly convicted? No. I can understand his caution though.'

'Well, I can't figure it. Not unless there's a reason we don't know about.'

Figgle shrugged. 'We just have to hope he's as good as his word tomorrow. His word! Fellow's what they used to call an unmitigated cad.'

'There are even more appropriate names.' Ware paused. 'Well, I suppose you know what you're about. Burglary couldn't have come at a worse time, I guess. See they've been looking for fingerprints.' Deliberately he rubbed at the powder on the glass-top in front of him. 'Any luck, d'you think?'

'Doubt it. Police didn't seem very hopeful. Routine sort of crime these days, apparently. Routine sort of investigation too, I'd imagine. Damned nerve of the fellow. Took my coat and put the booty in a hold-all he pinched from the lobby.' He looked around the room. 'Didn't break anything, though. Considerate sort of thief.' He laughed bitterly.

'I gather the collection's insured, at least.'

'Yes. Not for enough, I'm afraid. Only the brace of pistols run into a five-figure valuation. The other stuff was good, but not in the same class.'

'Curious he didn't take other pricey stuff. I mean, if he knew enough to value the pistols.'

'The rifles would've been more difficult to transport. Then again, he was surprised.' Figgle grimaced. 'Damned stupid of me not to have a permit for the Colt. Never thought of it. Not that anyone's going to use it to rob a bank. It's so evidently a collector's item.' He dropped into one of the armchairs. 'Have some port. Decanter's over there. Pour me some as well, if you would.'

'You haven't brought Amanda in over the deal with Jarvas? Any special reason?' Ware asked as he filled the glasses.

'Yes. She made it plain today she wanted nothing to do with anything involving him.'

'Even though it's aimed at keeping your family business alive?' He handed his host a glass, then took the chair opposite.

Figgle paused over his reply. 'As Amanda's father, perhaps you understand her better than I do. When it was simply a matter of both Fleur's parents approving this marriage, so Fleur would inherit, Amanda did all the right things. But she predicted Jarvas's opposition. Said her support was academic.'

'And now he's co-operating, on his own terms?'

'And since he's turned up in person, she's been edgy about him. Not just nervous. More like frightened.'

'And you've no idea of the reason?'

'None. Have you?'

It was the American's turn to pause. 'No, none at all,' he replied eventually, avoiding Figgle's gaze by fixing his own on the liquid in his glass.

'Judge's decision will be final. Mr Mark Treasure appointed official photographer,' announced Tim Shannon, to the few within hearing, as he strode down the slope toward the temporary ninth green. There were only three others with him.

Most people were dancing or else had joined the now quite large contingent of swimmers. 'Pity I didn't stop your father dressing the green after play today, Rose. Never thought.' He smiled at the girl beside him. 'That peat's dirty stuff. Stains material. Those shoes linen? Shouldn't wear them on the green. He's so thorough, your father.'

Treasure listened to the remarks as he prepared Shannon's camera to take a flash picture. He wondered if the compliment was meant as a pointed, gratuitous mark of confidence for transmission through daughter to father – an indication that Clay had got away with hitting one of the hotel guests without spoiling his standing with his employer.

'Those lights are blinding,' said Noah, the fourth member of the group, shading his eyes from the glare of the two big spot lamps on the far side of the dip: one was immediately behind the green.

'After you get over the crest they are. Lovely effect from the road, though,' Rose offered. She was carrying a large cardboard box. She intended to collect up the balls, knowing it might otherwise be something left for her father to do in the morning.

'Some people didn't get very far,' said Treasure. He had joined the others after losing his dancing partner to one of the young farmers. He kicked a ball lying in front of him.

'No knocking balls on to the green before we get there,' Shannon warned officiously.

'Not unless you see mine. It was Number Twenty-Seven,' pleaded Noah hopefully, squinting ahead. 'Look, there're hundreds on the green. You're right. Looks uncommonly dirty.'

'Autumn turf dressing. Very nutritious,' advised the hotelier.

'Is someone measuring already?' This was Noah again.

All four were now approaching their goal at an angle that cut out direct glare from the spotlights. 'There is someone down there.' Shannon's tone reflected the apprehension they all felt quite suddenly. He broke into a run. 'Hey, you all

107

right?'

The others were close behind him. 'He couldn't have been there during the barrage,' said Noah uncertainly. 'Perhaps he's ill.'

'Hope it isn't my Dad,' uttered Rose with more feeling, and quickening her pace.

'Go round the green not across,' shouted Treasure instinctively. They all obeyed, as he stopped and, on an impulse, took a picture of the scene.

A man's still body was curled up on its left side near the middle of the green, just beyond the hole. It was fronted by an eddy of golf balls. The right arm was pulled in. Both legs were bent. The left arm was stretched along the ground, pointing directly to the flag. But what fixed every gaze was the bloody, ragged star-shaped fracture in the side of the face, centred an inch above the right ear. Above that, massively raised bruising had distorted the scalp, making the sight as grotesque as it was obscene.

'Quite dead, I'm afraid,' muttered Shannon, on his knees.

Rose Clay dropped the box, as her hands went to claw the sides of her face. She let out an agonised whimper, then broke into a moaning repetition. 'Oh, no, no, no,' she sobbed.

# CHAPTER TEN

'Internal rupture of the middle meningeal artery. That's my guess. Didn't stand a cat in hell's chance, poor sod.' Dr Handel Ewenny-Preece stood with the others, on the path below the green, watching the ambulance drive off with the body of Kitson Jarvas.

'What's the point of rushing him to hospital if he's dead?' asked Dick Clay.

'Mortuary not hospital,' answered the doctor, coughing harshly, and squinting through the smoke from his cigarette. 'Hospital's where they go when there's any spark of life left. Where they can guarantee to put an end to it.' His chest heaved again. 'Sorry. Bad taste. Life was extinct when I got here at eleven-forty. Some minutes before, I'd say. And I was well ahead of the ambulance. Couldn't do anything, of course.' He inhaled deeply. 'Yes, middle meningeal haemorrhage is what they'll find. Probably copped it about eleven-twenty, just after he left Mrs Clay. Doesn't take long.' He closed his bag. 'Examined him this evening, too, after the er. . .Yes. Coroner will want my report on that.' He made a tutting noise, looked narrowly at Clay, then looked away again quickly. 'What happened to Fleur?'

'Her fiancé drove her back to the manor,' said Treasure.

'That's where I'll go next, then. Thank you. See she's all right. Want me for anything more, Alwyn?'

The dark and youngish police sergeant glanced up from his notes. 'Not now, doctor, thanks. You won't be doing the death certificate?'

'No. That'll be for the coroner, I expect. There'll be an inquest after the post mortem, no doubt.'

'But it was an accident, doctor?' This was Clay again. He was standing with Rose a little apart from the others. He had been on his way back from the manor when he'd seen the ambulance arrive.

'What else? Golf balls don't crash into people's skulls on purpose. Mark you, it must have been going a fair lick. God knows how many pounds of pressure it took to make that mess.' The savage cough was followed by a terrifying sort of wheeze. 'Oh dear,' he complained, putting the cigarette back in his mouth.

'Will this do, Alwyn?' Mildred Clay had appeared with a roll of tear-off plastic bags.

'Marvellous. Thanks Mildred.' The sergeant, who seemed to be well known to all the locals, accepted the materials and passed them on to the constable who had arrived with him in the police car. The other man had been depositing individual golf balls in evidence bags. 'We don't usually need this many bags. Must be more than fifty balls.'

'Fifty-eight, Alwyn,' offered Tim Shannon. 'That includes the twenty-two we've collected on the slope. They're here.' He held up the box Rose had been carrying earlier.

'Very helpful, Mr Shannon. We'll take those with us, just to be sure.' The sergeant looked at his watch. 'We ought to be following up that ambulance. Pity the ball didn't stay in the wound. Would have saved all this.' He, too, was now on his haunches examining balls one by one before putting them in separate bags.

All the balls that had been on the green had picked up some of the sticky, dark brown dressing: most were covered in it.

'Ball that killed him must have been one of those fairly close to the body,' Treasure ruminated aloud.

'That's right, sir,' the sergeant agreed. 'Or you'd think so. None of these looks any different from the others.'

'One will show human remains after proper examination.' This was the doctor. 'Don't lose any of that gunge that's stuck

110

to them. Well, I'm off.' He left, wheezing loudly.

'Right. Thirty-six balls in all, plus the ones in the box. That's the lot,' said the sergeant who'd been doing the counting. He gathered up the bags. 'Come on Derek. Time we delivered these. Don't forget the measuring tape. Could be we'll be back later, Mr Shannon.' He turned to Treasure. 'You did say you particularly noticed there were no footmarks on the green when you got here, sir?'

'We all did. There were none at all, except where Mr Jarvas had walked.'

'Bit different now, of course,' said the policeman, glancing ruefully at the way the turf dressing had been scattered about near the area where the body had lain. 'Still, I don't suppose it'll matter. Cause of death'll be clear enough. Thank you, everybody.'

As soon as the police left the lately subdued group of ex-revellers became suddenly re-animated.

'It was his own fault, wasn't it?'

'Everybody knew about the competition.'

'There won't be charges, will there?'

'When they know who's ball. . .'

'Did Fleur really pass out?'

'What about the wedding? Will it . . . ?

Some of the questioners looked to Treasure as the most authoritative of those present, but it was Tim Shannon who issued the directive. 'There'll obviously be nothing new till morning. If anyone not staying in the village wants to ring the hotel then, we'll be glad to supply a bulletin of what we get. Now I think it'd be best if we all went to bed.'

There was a general murmur of assent.

'Can't see how a lofted ball would have that much punch in it at the end.' This was Jeremy, the young farmer. He had been silent earlier.

'Neither can I, as a matter of fact,' agreed Treasure. He had watched Jeremy and his friend Giles play all their shots. Like the banker, they were better than competent golfers.

'You mean . . . ?' a girl's voice put in.

111

'That we all tried to drop balls on to the green from a very great height to stop 'em rolling when they landed. You don't use muscle over a hundred and twenty yards. You just go for accuracy and high trajectory.'

'Jeremy's right,' put in Giles. 'Nobody drove hard at the ball. Not so it'd be like a bullet at the end.'

He turned to Shannon. 'Did the sergeant keep the list of who had what numbers?'

'Yes. I had to give it to him.' The tone was slightly defensive.

'We'll never know who won,' said someone.

'One of us must be a big loser. The list'll show who hit the fatal ball when it's identified,' Jeremy put in solemnly.

It was at this point that Silvano Grimandi slipped away, back to the hotel. Nobody had noticed him arrive and he had contrived to stay in the shadows. He had listened carefully to everything that was said. He had seen Treasure pick up the toupee and had drawn back from view immediately after. They may not have seen him: maybe no one would figure what he'd been doing.

'*My* ball went like a bullet,' said Noah.

'Along the ground. I saw it,' said Treasure smiling. 'I doubt it reached the green. If it did it would have been going very slowly. Don't think I saw one ball, well hit or mis-hit, that looked likely to damage anybody at the distance.'

'Stranger things have happened in golf.' Most people had to turn to see the speaker. It was Clay standing at the back of the group. 'Could have been a ricochet off a tree. That can add power. Ball might have hit a stone at an awkward angle. Could be his skull was specially thin. We'll know in the morning. I'll say goodnight if that's all right, Mr Shannon?' At a nod from his employer he turned on his heel and made toward his cottage. His wife hesitated then followed. Rose went with her.

The others began dispersing up the grass slope in animated groups of twos and threes. The Treasures and Shannon walked the short distance to the gap in the trees. Molly wanted to follow the path back because of the shoes she was wearing.

112

'Ricochet?' said the banker doubtfully, looking along the line of oaks and horse-chestnuts.

Shannon shook his head. 'Only if it bounced off something extra resilient. More likely it was a freak shot. One no one noticed.'

'Did Mrs Clay know where Mr Jarvas was going?' This was Molly. The three of them had stopped in the gap and were looking back on to the green.

'I didn't hear her say. One supposes he was going to the hotel. Same route we're taking now,' said the hotelier.

'So why cut across the green?' Molly pressed.

'Just a whim, perhaps. Before he noticed the mucky dressing.' Treasure frowned before continuing. 'You know, he must have cried out.'

'And nobody heard above the racket of the disco,' Shannon offered.

'Would he have known about the golf competition?' asked Molly. 'We talked about it before dinner. I remember the Vicar being delighted. About the money for the organ.'

'I don't believe Jarvas was there then. Someone might have mentioned it to him later, of course,' said Treasure.

'But he couldn't have known the exact time. There wasn't one.' This was Shannon. 'I mean, what if he was coming along just before it started, and was hit by one of the first balls?'

'I hit the first six,' Molly observed stiffly.


'Fleur's quite adamant. She's not going through with any wedding tomorrow,' Jack Figgle stated without embellishment. It was well after midnight, and he had just entered the drawing room. 'Is that tea? Think I'll have a cup.' There was a tray of tea things, with biscuits, on the table in front of the fire.

Amanda Figgle and her mother were sitting side-by-side on one of the settees, Mrs Harriet Cartland Ware somewhat self-consciously enveloped in an elegant dressing gown; she had been preparing for bed when news of the accident had reached her. Byron Ware was occupying his favourite chair across the room. Bunty Millant and Greville Sinn were on the settee opposite the two ladies.

The Vicar, very upright, was holding a teacup but not drinking from it. He didn't care for tea, but since his arrival had been the excuse for making some, he had felt obliged to accept a cup – mindful, like many parsons, that the economy of Sri Lanka owes much to the high incidence of ecclesiastical house calls in the English towns and shires.

'Fleur will feel differently in the morning,' said Mrs Ware with confidence, and looking reproachfully at a fresh log that was refusing to take light in the dying embers of the fire.

'You . . . think so?' uttered Mrs Millant haltingly and in a whisper that everyone naturally strained to hear before wondering why. She was still in crêpe de chine and looking even greyer than before. When on her feet she had seemed unsteady. It was the general conclusion – matched by her own – that she had drunk too much alcohol in the course of a long evening.

'Fleur seemed very decided just now,' offered Figgle without enthusiasm.

'Then that's how she'll stay.' This was Amanda, a mother's tutored resignation sounding through every syllable.

'The proper course, I suppose. In the circumstances.'

'I don't agree, Vicar.' Mrs Ware had retorted quite fiercely.

'Misplaced res . . . res . . . pect . . . perhaps.' Mrs Millant faltered over the words, compounding an impression by failing to suppress a loud if lone hiccup.

'He was Fleur's father. . .' Sinn began.

'And a wholly irresponsible one.' This was Ware with greater feeling even than his wife's. 'Abandons his wife and child years ago. Re-appears to object to the marriage entirely for selfish and material reasons. Then changes his mind for more selfish and material reasons. Bunty and you, Vicar, may not know what the reasons were, don't need to, but you can take my word on it. Then, tonight, he was vacillating again. Playing ducks and drakes over a very important understanding with Jack. Isn't that right, Jack?'

'He was tending to run to form. Yes,' said Figgle, but

114

carefully.

'And probably wouldn't have shown up at the church anyway, letting everyone down, especially Fleur. In short, he was behaving like Kitson Jarvas always behaved. Now he's gotten himself killed walking into a golf ball . . .'

'He'd have given Fleur away.' Figgle interrupted Ware. 'There can't be any doubt he approved the marriage.'

'I thought you . . .?' Ware stopped in mid-sentence. 'Oh, I see . . . No doubt at all, you feel?' he finished uncertainly.

'Would it affect Fleur's inheritance one way or the other now Kitson's gone?' asked Mrs Ware.

Bunty Millant leaned forward. So did everyone else in the expectation she was about to say something. Instead she picked up her cup and looked to Figgle when he started to speak.

'I don't believe so,' he said, then paused, stroking his forehead. 'Kit never expressed disapproval in writing.'

There was silence for a moment while several present did some thinking. 'You won't need to send back the wedding presents,' Mrs Ware broke in with a practical observation.

'Not for a postponement,' her daughter asserted.

'Inconvenient for you I expect, Vicar,' said Ware, his usual equanimity recovered after the outburst.

'Not as much as for Kit Jarvas, perhaps,' Mrs Millant inserted unexpectedly, quite loudly and with laboured articulation.

'How sad to die with absolutely no one to miss or mourn you,' said Mrs Ware with extravagant assurance – or more of it than seemed entirely justified. 'Still, we shall pray for his soul. Gone to a better place, Vicar.'

Taken off guard at a late hour, Sinn looked mildly perplexed before stirring himself into registering professional agreement with this pious sentiment. While he was doing it, Dr Handel Ewenny-Preece came in.

'She'll be all right. Given her something to make her sleep. But there'll be no wedding,' said the newcomer firmly. 'Taken her father's death very hard, as I expect you all know. Didn't

115

realise they were so close.'

'They weren't,' commented Amanda drily.

'Tea, Handel?' enquired Figgle.

The doctor didn't trouble with a spoken refusal. 'Scotch, drop of plain water if it's handy, not if it isn't, no ice, thank you, very kind.' This practised recitation had been made curiously melodious by usage and the Celtic cadence. He produced a cigarette from a nearly empty packet, and lit it. 'Well, if it's not Mr Jarvas's death that's done it. . .'

'What else could possibly make her postpone the wedding?' Mrs Ware protested, while regarding the doctor's cigarette with evident distaste.

'Any . . . any number of things. She's a young woman with a mind of her own,' said Mrs Millant slowly. 'May I have some more tea, please? Then I shall go to bed.'

'You mean Fleur's been confiding in you, Bunty?' This was Amanda, penetrating, singularly alert and before doing anything about the tea. 'Was there something in particular?'

Mrs Millant looked straight at the speaker, then pointedly her gaze swept the others in the room, coming back to study the hands folded in her lap. If she was going to answer the question, her gestures indicated, it wouldn't be now.

'Excuse me, but I don't think Fleur's talking about postponement,' said the doctor, ending the embarrassed silence and accepting the neat whisky Figgle had poured for him.

'But you just said as much,' said Sinn, sounding irritated because he thought Ewenny-Preece was drunk again, as he believed he was most of the time, as well as incompetent, slack and a bad example.

The doctor wheezed, spilling some of his drink. The Vicar looked heavenwards with a quite prayerful expression. Mrs Ware registered greater disapproval, while her daughter got up to fetch some water to dilute the whisky.

'I didn't say she was postponing.' Ewenny-Preece breathed in deeply, making a terrible noise. 'Calling it off for good.

That's what she was saying to Jonas just now.' He squinted at the others. 'Thank you.'

'I agreed because I thought I was pregnant.'

'And if you thought you still were, you'd go through with the wedding. In any circumstances.'

'That's a lie.'

'But you don't hold with abortion?'

'So what makes you think I couldn't have gone through with a baby on my own? I never asked to marry you. You asked me. Remember?' Fleur was sitting rigidly on the edge of the armchair in her bedroom, her nails digging into the backs of her clasped hands, her dark eyes flashing anger.

'You've had a shock.' Jonas was standing quite still by the door of the room which earlier he'd been preparing to leave. He was doing his best not to appear as desperate as he felt. Taking the offensive hadn't worked: his last words were a first try at amelioration.

'I've had two shocks, to be exact. My father was killed. . .'

'That's to overdramatise. The accident. . .'

'My father was killed tonight,' she repeated more distinctly, 'and you didn't think it was a reason to call off the wedding.' She jumped to her feet. 'Well, out of common bloody decency, I did think it was a reason. And now I'm calling it off for ever because I think your attitude over everything is hateful. Especially over money. You've always said my money means nothing to you.'

'It means something to Jack Figgle.'

'Oh, very clever. Well, despite your concern, I can tell you he'll understand why I'm not marrying you.' She stamped across to a window, threw back the curtains and stared outwards with her back to Jonas.

'But you hardly knew your father. He really wasn't a very nice person.'

'You mean I didn't know him as well as you did? Not since the meetings you had with him? To work things out with that

117

not very nice person? To work things out with him for your mutual benefit?'

'For everybody's benefit. Especially yours and Jack's.' He moved back into the room towards her, but stopped some distance away.

'Except Jack and my mother weren't to know about the sordid little plot. The trick to make everyone think my father was against the marriage till the last minute.'

'So Jack wouldn't take for ever to decide to give your father that contract, and the rest of the. . .the deal.'

'Not so Jonas Grimandi would come out smelling of roses? Unaffected by the lure of my money?'

'That's an unkind thing to say. You're not yourself.'

She swung round to face him. 'And I wasn't when I said I'd marry you. When we thought. . . Before I knew the fantastic education and that whizz-kid image were phoney. And that nobody else wanted the fabulous Hong Kong job.'

'None of that's fair.'

'Isn't it? Didn't you have to go to college in New York at Silvano's expense? Weren't you kicked out of school here for not working? Not qualifying? Didn't you go back to New York to borrow more money from him? You didn't go to be interviewed for that lousy job. The one you'd already been offered. The one you were going to pass up after the wedding.' She'd been watching for the look of surprise. 'It's what you were saving to tell me next, isn't it? That you'd definitely decided to join Figgle & Sons instead?'

'I don't know why you've suddenly come to all these bizarre conclusions. They're a travesty of. . .'

'Because I've talked to sweet, innocent Silvano. And your mother and father whom you didn't want at the wedding. Because I didn't like the way you avoided Mr Treasure's questions tonight. Because I've pieced things together. . .'

'I love you enough. . .' he tried to break in again, but she wouldn't be stopped.

'Well, I only thought I loved you enough to excuse the way you fantasise. To excuse the way you use people. The way you meant to use my money. To use me.' Tears of anger were now rolling down her cheeks. 'I don't love you at all, Jonas. Not at all. Do you understand that?' She threw herself face downwards on the bed sobbing.

He sat down beside her and tentatively smoothed her hair. 'You're overwrought, darling. Sorry I was insensitive about Kit Jarvas. About his death. You're wrong about me. You've misunderstood – a whole lot of things. I can explain. Tomorrow, when you're more yourself. No decisions tonight, eh? Not even about the wedding. In the morning things'll be different. The money isn't important to me either. I'm thinking mostly of Jack.'

She rolled away from his touch, pulling herself upright against the bedhead, clasping her arms around her legs. 'I understood everything. I'm not marrying you. I shan't change my mind in the morning. Now get out of my room. Go back to pawing Alexi Bedwell.' The tears had stopped. 'And don't think I haven't been watching you with her. Just get out of my life. If Jack needs my money I'll find a way to give it to him. We don't need you.'

Jonas waited for a moment then got up from the bed. He stood looking down at her, his handsome face a study in mute resignation. He made for the door, where he turned. 'Before you decide who gets your money, better make sure you're entitled to it,' he said.

# CHAPTER ELEVEN

Silvano Grimandi had walked more than a mile down the main road in the direction of Monmouth before he attempted to hail a lift. He had intended to call a taxi by telephone – but not through the hotel switchboard. He had remembered seeing a telephone box at the road junction, but when he reached it he found it was out of order. He had no idea about the frequency of pay phones on English country roads, but, after walking for twenty minutes without seeing another, concluded they didn't happen like milestones. He had tripped over the second milestone.

He was fit enough to walk all night, if necessary, even carrying his case, which wasn't heavy. He had avoided thumbing a lift to this point, in case he was picked up by someone connected with the hotel. He didn't want anyone to learn he had left – not till he was out of the country.

His plan was to pick up the rented car from where he had left it with Mr R. Jones on the outskirts of Monmouth. The car was ready. There had been a message that Mr Jones intended driving it over in the morning. Once he had his own transport again, Silvano was going straight to the airport and catching the first plane available to New York. He wasn't sure whether his special price return ticket was transferrable: if it wasn't he would gladly pay for a new ticket, just so he could get out of the country quickly.

What else could he do, he kept asking himself? There was no going back – he had to get out. He waved at a second car: like the first, it didn't stop nor even slow. Maybe people didn't give lifts to strangers in this country on deserted roads after midnight: so who could blame them? He wouldn't have picked up someone escaping from the police. Except he didn't look like someone the police would be after: in the daylight that would work for him. Maybe he should find shelter of some kind and sleep for a while – till dawn? Again he worked out how long it had taken to drive from the airport and decided he couldn't afford the time to sleep.

People might start wondering where he was around nine, maybe ten in the morning. Would Mark Treasure bring him his toupee before then? It had given him away once: now it might do it again. It would never have blown off: the top of the turret window had brushed it off as he'd brought his head in. Then he remembered he'd promised to take a walk with Gino and Teresa at ten-thirty. Probably he had till then before anyone found his belongings had gone. He could be airborne by ten-thirty, beyond the reach of the British authorities.

He was a first generation, legal US citizen. So he wasn't qualified to be President, but he didn't believe he could be extradited either. He wasn't absolutely sure on the last point, but if there was to be any argument about it he needed to be in America to be arguing to any purpose.

The unmarked, light van drew up beside him with a screech of brakes. He hadn't waved it down nor been aware of its approach, being momentarily preoccupied with his thoughts.

'Want a lift, Dad?' called the man in the passenger seat. He was wearing dark glasses and a khaki linen cap with a big peak pulled low on his forehead.

'Is very kind,' said Silvano. 'I go to Monmouth. . .'

'Great place. That's where we're going.'

'I get in at the back?'

'No, hop in here.' The man had already climbed over the seat and settled himself on the floor behind. 'Give us your case back here, Dad. More room.'

Silvano gratefully did as he was told. The driver had on a woollen hat that covered his ears and a good deal of his face. The van was old. There were no lights inside.

'Come far?' asked the driver, moving the vehicle off as promptly as he had stopped it. He was young, like his companion.

'From New York,' said Silvano, then wished he hadn't. He was a very inexpert fugitive. 'My car, it's broken down today. I go to collect it. In Monmouth. Mr R. Jones.' He added the address which he'd learned by heart, before remembering he shouldn't have done that either.

'Easy,' said the first man. 'We go right past there.'

Silvano looked around. 'You sure? I wouldn't want you to make a detour for me. It's late to work. You're very kind.' He figured he'd been lucky to fall in with such a helpful pair. Who said the young weren't ready to help the old these days? He smiled over his shoulder. Dimly he could make out that the man who had given him the seat was re-arranging things on the floor at the back.

'No problem, Dad. Where you going after? Back to New York? To the airport? Got your ticket? Got your passport, have you?'

'*Si*. Yes. Thank you.' He didn't mind being called Dad.

'Looks like he's got everything, don't it, Dave?'

'You're right,' answered the driver, whose name wasn't Dave.

'OK for money are you? To pay for the car like? Can be expensive. Repairs.'

'Sure. I'm OK, thanks.' Another fine example yet – offering to lend a stranger money. Did he look that poor, he wondered? 'I got plenty thanks. English pounds.'

'Great,' said the driver, swinging the van down a side road. 'Got to make a delivery down here.'

'Short cut to Monmouth,' said the other man almost simultaneously.

Silvano thought it late to be making deliveries. But then, it was late to be collecting a car.


'Curious thing is. . .' Treasure took one more deep breath, then let it out slowly, completing the cycle of Canadian Air

Force exercises he did most nights and every morning.

'I can't wait,' sighed Molly looking over the top of her reading glasses. She was already propped up in the four-poster bed with a copy of George Eliot's *Middlemarch*.

'The only ball I saw hit that could possibly have ended up doing that kind of damage. . .'

'Was Noah Plimpton's? I thought the same thing, except you said to him. . .'

'It wouldn't have made the distance.' He was now speaking from the bathroom. 'Had to say something reassuring. Chap was turning a shade whiter at the time.' There followed a muffled snort. 'No scales in here.'

'Then we'll have to guess your weight for two days, or find you an all-night chemist.'

'Very droll. You know Noah doesn't play golf?'

'Mmm. He can't dance either. It was a lucky shot.'

'Unlucky if it killed Jarvas. It was going like hell.'

'But close to the ground. No loft to it.'

'Wouldn't have needed loft once the ground fell away. If it kept the momentum, after a hundred and twenty yards it might have been head high and still shifting.'

Molly laid her book flat on the bedclothes. 'It must have been one of the early balls that did the damage. Jarvas wouldn't have knowingly walked into a rain of balls. Noah hit directly after me.'

'And none of your shots made the green.'

'How d'you know?'

'You were underclubbed with that seven iron.'

'That's your opinion, except for once I don't mind your being right.'

'I am right.' He came out of the bathroom looking for his pyjamas. 'I saw three of your six balls in the box the police took away. Remembered the sequence of numbers. Began with thirteen.'

'That's right.'

'I've no doubt the others were there too. All picked up short of the green. Very short.'

'Wish you'd told me.'

'I just have, allowing a proper interval for concern, so you don't get the idea your underclubbing is a virtue.' He frowned while trimming a toenail with the scissors Molly had left on the dressing table. 'D'you think this toe's broken? Been hurting all week.' He put one foot on the bed, wiggling the member in question.

'If it was broken it wouldn't do that. You've dropped something on it, I expect. Anyway, please take it away. I could never develop a fetish for feet. Not even yours. So when do you suppose we'll be told which ball killed Mr Jarvas?'

'First thing, I'd guess. No reason why not. That's assuming it was one of the balls they took away, which I doubt. And if the post mortem shows he really was killed by a ball.'

'It could have been something else?'

'Certainly. And if it was, there'll be more than two uniformed bobbies wandering round that green before dawn.'

'You suggesting someone did him in? On purpose?'

'Plenty of people had reason. And that's only counting the group gathered here together for holy matrimony.'

'That's another bit from the Prayer Book,' she said, while considering something else. 'Your penchant for suspecting foul play doesn't fit with the facts though. Mr Jarvas was dropped by a missile, fairly obviously a golf ball. The only footmarks were his. You said any others would have shown. There weren't any.'

'Unless he'd been carried to the spot when already dead, and whoever deposited him on the green walked off it backwards in the same footmarks.'

'Imaginative, if not wildly likely. Anyway, Jack wouldn't kill anyone.'

'To be strictly accurate, Jack's killed dozens of people. He was decorated for it. In the war.'

'That's quite different. I meant. . .'

'I know what you meant, and I suppose I agree. But you're assuming Jack's the only person around who might have had it in for Jarvas. Byron Ware loathed him too. Makes no bones

124

about it. I don't know how young Grimandi felt about him. Not at the end of the evening.'

'But we know Dick Clay tried to lay him out at the beginning of it. And Mrs Clay had a bust-up with him in his room. When she found Rose was there.'

'When?'

'Before dinner. Didn't I tell you? Silvano heard it all. He has the room opposite. It got so noisy at one point he was afraid to come out.'

Treasure got into bed, lying back against the raised pillows with his hands behind his head. 'What was Rose supposed to be doing in the room?'

'Well, she wasn't counting the towels.' Molly sniffed. 'For that matter, what was Jarvas doing at the cottage? Presumably Mrs Clay told the policeman.'

'The Clays go back a long way with Jarvas – and Amanda.'

'So, I gathered, did Bunty Millant. With all of them.' She arched her eyebrows, staring at her husband over the glasses that were now perched on the very end of her nose. 'You do seriously believe there could be more to this than a golfing accident?'

'I think that could become the common view quite shortly. Country doctors and country policemen tend to lead sheltered lives.'

'And jump to the easiest conclusions?'

'Which could still be the right ones in this case. I'm sceptical, that's all. Can't credit a golf ball did all that damage. Especially a ball somebody might try to prove was hit by me.'

'Or me. Or poor Noah.' She picked up the book, then put it down again. 'They'll postpone the wedding?'

'Most likely. He was the bride's father after all.'

Molly drew up her knees. 'I thought Fleur's reaction very moving. Genuine, too,' she offered reflectively.

'If unpredictable?'

'No, I don't believe so. She's sensitive and nervous. Tense, too. Remember that tantrum on the terrace? Quite honestly, I don't believe they're awfully well suited. She and Jonas. I also think she knows it.'

'That she's making a mistake? I'm not impressed with Jonas.' He made a puffing noise. 'Poseur.'

'I thought the same. Doesn't deserve that cuddly great-uncle. . .'

'Nor the parents. They may be boring, but they've obviously done their best for him . . .'

'While he goes out of his way to disown them. Not nice.'

'It'd be interesting to know his real standing in his company. Jack reckons he's marked for top management. Blue-eyed boy.'

'Because Jonas has told him so? Didn't you say you knew his chairman?'

'Yes. But I can hardly ring him tomorrow morning to ask if Jonas Grimandi is all he cracks himself up to be. Anyway, it's a big outfit. Probably never heard of Jonas.'

'Not even if he's marked for top management?'

'You've got a point there. But it really is too late to be fishing for a character reference now. I should have got a run-down on him earlier. When Jack first mentioned he was marrying Fleur. I thought of it. But the Figgles were so certain of the chap's credentials.'

'And this business he's sending to Figgle & Sons?'

'Smells of graft. That's really why I've cooled on young Grimandi. Since Jack gave me the details this evening.'

'It's crooked?'

'Not exactly. Computer manufacturers farm out a lot of their components. It's usually done on tender. The sub-contractor who quotes the lowest price gets the work. Jonas guarantees Figgle's will get all his company's contracts for plastic casings. Over quite a long period.'

'That's dishonest?'

'Fishy. He must have done a deal with someone else in the company. Could involve a bribe. A kick-back.'

'To the person who approves the contracts?'

'Not necessarily. Could be just the man who opens the tenders when they come in. All he has to do is hold back the

Figgle tender till he's seen all the others.'

'Then make sure Figgle's is the lowest?'

'That's the game in its simplest form, yes. There are any number of variations. The thing is, these particular contracts are for very large numbers of components.'

'So you don't have to play the game too often?'

'Precisely. And now's the perfect time because the company's changing the cases on its equipment. So are a lot of other manufacturers.'

'Changing the styling?'

'No, the material they're made from. The latest thing is to add nickel dust in suspension into the plastic.'

'You've lost me.'

'It suppresses airborne interference.'

'That's important for a computer?'

'Very. They're very sensitive. The more you can protect them from being got at, by passing motorbikes for instance, the more reliable they become.'

'And Jack's company can make plastic cases?'

'For computers, calculators, electronic typewriters, the lot. He's got the basic equipment. It's just he has no entrée to the market. No track record. To date he's worked entirely in the automotive field.'

'So if Jonas brings it off?'

'There's no doubt it'd be a shot in the arm for the company. Whether his methods are ethical, and whether there'll be any profit short term. . .'

'Is there any point if there isn't?'

'There's every point. The way Jonas has arranged it, Fleur is getting control of the company at a knock-down price. She's buying the ordinary shares at far less than asset value. She's also putting up loan capital, but she'd get most of that back if the company was wound up for any reason. If it can keep going for a year or two, even on a break-even basis, with the car trade picking up, it ought to be worth a great deal more than she's paying for it.'

Molly wrinkled her nose. 'It's all in the family, of course.'

'I'm not so sure. It depends how Jonas is organising things. Jack's so trusting and Fleur's so untutored. Jonas could be planning to cut himself in for shares.' He pouted before continuing. 'Anyway, if they postpone the wedding, at least there's a breathing space. Which means we don't have to go on all night discussing Figgle & Sons.' He moved further down in the bed. 'Four-posters went out long before this house was built. Elegant though.'

'You've forgotten your pyjamas.'

'No, I haven't. They're over there.'

She closed the book without bothering to use the marker. 'That must be the third time I've got to page two of *Middlemarch*.'

'I'll bear in mind George Eliot is one woman not to be taken in bed. Molly Treasure, on the other hand. . .'

'You do say the nicest things.'


'Is that you, Greville?' enquired Penelope Sinn sleepily.

'If it wasn't, my dear, you wouldn't still be lying there. Would you?'

'Suppose not. You can put the light on. I'm awake.'

He did as she asked. Her white Grecian style nightdress had been a size too big for Amanda Figgle, which is why she had got rid of it. It was several sizes too small for Penelope. 'You needn't have put your hair rollers in. The wedding's cancelled,' said her husband. 'Jarvas was killed in an accident.'

Penelope sat up in bed blinking. She had wrapped a scarf over the rollers and tied it under her chin, but the knot had slipped over one ear. She might have been suffering a bad toothache. 'What kind of accident?'

He told her.

'You should have fetched me,' she admonished, removing the scarf. The rollers were in assorted colours.

'There was nothing you could have done. He was dead.'

'Did you see him?' In response to his pained expression, she had given a lively, two-handed heave to the bodice of the nightdress. Instead of a too generous display of naked bosom

128

at the centre, there was now a far greater quantity bulging at the sides. 'You weren't there?' she continued, reaching across for her bed-jacket and stretching the two sides of the bodice to endurance: they joined in one narrow piece down Penelope's cleavage, leaving everything else to look after itself. The effect was like something by Rubens, but not so nice.

'I got the news at the manor,' he answered with unnecessary brusqueness, observing these fresh dispositions with distaste.

'What time was that?' She was used to his brief flashes of acerbity.

'Can't remember.' He was emptying his pockets before undressing. 'After half past eleven I should think.'

'But you left here long before that.'

'Did I? Does it matter?'

'Only I waited up, thinking you'd be back.'

'Sorry, my dear. Got caught up with the family, I'm afraid.'

'How did Jack take things?'

'Very well. On the whole. Looked a lot less unhinged than he'd been at dinner.' He put the keys he had taken from one trouser pocket on top of the chest of drawers, along with his wallet and some loose change. 'No doubt Jarvas's death will ease life for most people connected with him.'

'Oh dear, that sounds awfully callous.' She caught sight of the contents of the other trouser pocket. 'You've found another golf ball. In the garden was it? Looks like a nice new one.'

# CHAPTER TWELVE

'Funny sort of burglar. Are you sure?' asked Stephen Watkins, the postman's son. He and Robin Figgle continued pushing their bicycles up the hill into Stingly Parva, a village three miles from Much Marton. The dog Palmerston was some yards ahead of them.

'Sure as sure,' answered Robin. 'I was doing the parapet. Not all of it. I was right over the study. You know?'

Stephen nodded. The intelligence about the parapet seemed to clinch matters when it came to burglar spotting.

It was six-twenty in the morning. They had met outside the Watkins' house at six, as they had done often during the recent summer holidays, for an early ride to Stingly Parva. Palmerston usually went with them. There was a municipal playground there on the village green. It had swings, a climbing gantry, a slide and a merry-go-round they could make go very fast indeed if the two of them pushed flat out before jumping on. There was no similar playground in Much Marton, but they had the Stingly Parva one to themselves if they went there early.

'What time was it?'

'Ten,' Robin said. 'Too early for late bird watching. I was doing a recce. For later. No good. The Bedwell birds had pulled their curtains. The other lot weren't supposed to arrive till this morning. Expect they'll cancel now.'

The parapet in question was a wide one that encircled the manor just below attic storey level. It was easily accessible from Robin's window. When Fleur had girlfriends to stay, he

130

sometimes clambered along it after dark on the chance of watching them disrobe. The forays were more in the nature of dares than salacious enterprises.

'Are you going to tell your mother?'

'No fear. Not supposed to go on the parapet.'

'You could have been looking out the window.'

'Not round two corners I couldn't. You'd never get into MI6.'

'Don't want to,' Stephen parried the snub. 'Beat you to the top.' It was still uphill, but not quite so steep. They mounted their bikes. Palmerston glanced around, then moved from a slow walk to a brisk one. He liked to stay ahead. 'Is the wedding off just for today?'

'For ever. You should have heard Fleur and Jonas. "Get out of my life," she said, terribly loud.' Robin's room was immediately above his half-sister's: if he listened carefully at the fireplace he could distinguish most of what was said there.

'Wonder what they'll do with the food? Was Mr Jarvas killed on purpose, you think?'

'Expect so.'

'By Rose's father? For doing it to her? Like we said?'

'Most likely. They had police.'

'Did they arrest Mr Clay?'

'Not yet. Insufficient evidence,' said Robin darkly and without a morsel of justification.

Talking ceased as they reached flat ground and both pedalled hard to be first at their destination. As they dropped their machines on the grass of the Stingly Parva village green, Palmerston was sitting waiting for them. It was then the dog opened his mouth and let fall a much-chewed golf ball. He'd had it about him since the previous night, waiting for someone to play 'throw and fetch'.

'Yes, terrible shock. We're all numbed by it still. Fleur especially. . .Oh yes, he was here to give her away. Completely reconciled to the match. . .Yes, it's some consolation. . .Good of you to be so understanding. . .We'll be in touch about the

131

new date. Goodbye.'

Jack Figgle made a guilty face at his wife as he put down the bedroom telephone, then looked at the time. It was just before seven o'clock. He had been phoning people for the previous forty minutes. He was fully dressed. Amanda had on a pretty blue housecoat that matched the negligee beneath it. He had a chair drawn up to the bedside table. She was curled on the bed with a pencil, their address book and the list of wedding guests. There was a tray of coffee beyond her feet.

'Is that the lot except for locals? The Thompsons were on the point of leaving. So were the Heyworths,' he said. 'Still feel a fraud not letting on the thing's off for good.'

'It may not be. You know how impetuous Fleur can be.' Amanda, cool and strangely relaxed, looked down the list in her hand. 'The Garretts are staying in Hereford. They'll be at the Green Dragon. I'll ring them, and any others left. In about half an hour?'

He nodded. 'I hope now she doesn't marry Jonas.'

'If it makes no difference to her inheriting.'

'Not when she's twenty-one, it won't.'

'So if, as you say, Jonas is still putting those contracts with the company. . .'

'I was thinking more of her happiness.'

She glanced up to see from his expression whether she was being rebuked. She wasn't: he was looking pensive. 'Very commendable, darling. You don't mind if I occasionally think of our happiness. One of us ought to,' she added, taking the offensive. 'The computer orders will make the difference?'

'Unquestionably. Strange chap, Jonas. I mean, by one o'clock this morning you might say he'd cut his losses over Fleur. He was in my study negotiating new terms to replace the Jarvas arrangement.'

'The one you signed after dinner? Pass me a cigarette, will you?' Amanda took a sip from her coffee cup. 'Kit's contract has to be replaced now he's dead?'

'Because if Jonas isn't marrying Fleur. . .'

'There's nothing in it for Jonas any more. Sorry, that's

obvious.' She inhaled deeply from the cigarette she had just lit, then blew the smoke out slowly. 'Unless she still marries him. Will that cancel out any new thing?'

'Partly, perhaps.' He looked mildly perplexed. 'The company will pay Jonas a commission, a consultant's commission, quite a small one, for any business he brings. It'll be a lot less than the salary we were going to pay Kit. In the long run. I mean, it'll be a one-off payment. Each time Jonas introduces an order.' He paused. 'He also wants an option to buy five per cent of the shares at the same price Fleur pays.'

'And you're giving it to him?'

'Don't want to. But we are rather relying on him.'

'He certainly seems prepared for every eventuality,' she remarked drily.

'It's a question of speed. Unless we work quickly we'll lose the business. If he and Fleur should patch things up, I daresay we'll make some other arrangement.'

'Like what?'

'Jonas was ready to pass up the Hong Kong job to be managing director of Figgle & Sons.'

'He hadn't mentioned this before?'

'Found it . . . er . . . inappropriate to suggest.'

'Until he'd produced the goods?'

'Something of the kind. To his credit, I thought.' Amanda wished he wasn't always so eager to credit people with unselfish, good intentions. 'He'd still do it,' her husband went on, 'but he seems to think Fleur would be against.'

Amanda dismissed the matter with a movement of her slim shoulders. 'What's important is, with Kit gone, you think the Jarvas trustees will advance money for the company. Against what Fleur will be getting anyway next year. That's whether she marries or not? I do have that right?' There was detectable anxiety in her tone.

'Not quite. My bank, or perhaps Grenwood, Phipps, will lend Fleur enough to do that against the expectancy. It wouldn't be for long. I have to talk to Mark Treasure about it this morning.'

'Come in,' Amanda called in response to the rap on the door, but Fleur was in already. She was dressed in an old shirt, jeans and tennis shoes but had made no real attempt to make herself presentable: her hair was unbrushed, accentuating the lacklustre appearance of the face – especially the drawn area around the eyes.

'God, what a night,' she said. 'I hardly slept. Are you both mad at me?' She looked from one to the other, then, without waiting for an answer: 'I still can't go through with it. I haven't changed my mind again. I thought I should come and tell you.'

'No, we're not angry with you,' said Amanda. 'We'd be glad of some help with the cancellations though.'

'And I'd like a word about some proposals from Jonas,' her step-father muttered.

'Which I know about,' Fleur answered quickly. 'They're fine with me. Well, acceptable anyway. My money can still go into the company if that's what you want.'

'It's what we both want,' said her mother.

'OK. And I think Jonas is good for those contracts. From his company. For making the cases. In other things he fantasises.' She looked at the telephone. 'Who'd you like me to ring?'

'A few locals, in a minute. We're saying postponement, not cancellation. For the moment. After your father's funeral. . .'

'Fine, Mummy. OK. Just give me the numbers.'

'Well, first, could you take Bunty a cup of this coffee? Heaven knows when anyone'll get breakfast this morning. Bunty's an early riser. Coffee will keep her at bay for a bit.'

'Morning, Mr Treasure. Sleep all right?'

'Good morning, Mr Shannon. Yes, thanks.' The two had met as the banker was coming down the stairs. Treasure thought he had also sighted Mrs Shannon rushing, head lowered, towards the basement – but he couldn't be sure.

'Breakfast doesn't officially start till seven-thirty in the dining room. That's in twenty minutes. If you'd like me to arrange something now? Or send something up?' The 'up'

134

came like a word of command to a well-trained dog.

'Certainly not. Came down early to knock a few balls about on the range. Then a swim, I thought.'

'Ah. Practice range closed. Sorry. Pool's all yours, though.' Shannon marked the querulous look that came after the one of mild surprise. 'Yes, police, I'm afraid. Haven't found that ball. So it seems.'

'I see. Uniformed police or plainclothes?'

'Uniformed. Not CID. Would you think . . . ?'

'They'd need detectives to find a lost golf ball? No, I wouldn't. Not unless it was one of mine.' He smiled wryly. 'And the wedding?'

'It's off, I'm afraid.'

'Thought it would be.'

'We're putting on a special buffet lunch here for hotel guests, and any others who come not knowing about the cancellation.'

'Lot of work for you and your wife. Mustn't hold you up. See you later, no doubt.'

Treasure let himself out on to the terrace, then down the grass slope towards the temporary ninth green. It was a promising October morning with a little early mist still lying in the hollow – but not so much as to make it difficult to discern the amount of activity going on there.

'You work long hours, sergeant,' the banker nodded at the policeman he recognised. There were three others – all constables – who hadn't been present the night before, and who were now diligently searching in the undergrowth some distance from the green.

'Been off duty since I saw you last, sir. Working the day shift this morning by request. Didn't expect to be back here though. Can't find that damn ball, you see.'

'The one that killed Mr Jarvas? There's no doubt . . . ?'

'No doubt about the cause of the accident, sir. Not even about the make of the ball. Different golf balls having different sorts of indentations.'

'But the balls we used in the competition were all the same.

135

They belonged to the hotel.'

'That's right, sir. PRO-TRUST they're called. And it was a PRO-TRUST that killed him. Pretty certainly. Got that from the micro examination of the wound at the post mortem. Thing is, seven of those balls we took carried traces of blood. None had hair or human tissue attached. They reckon the ball responsible is bound to have had more than just blood. There was quite a bit of blood on the ground, you see. Any ball that landed near the body could have picked up traces. That's what they reckon.' The sergeant had ended with the implication that 'they' could just conceivably be wrong.

'But as I remember there were fifty-eight balls used and. . .'

'Fifty-eight collected. That's right, sir. What we know now is there were other balls we could have picked up, thinking they'd been in the competition. Well, one anyway. This normally being part of the practice range, and the balls Mr Shannon hires out for practice all being PRO-TRUST. Well, it was a mistake easily made.' The strong tone of justification in the last phrase implied firmly that the person being held responsible for making that mistake was the sergeant himself. 'One ball didn't have a numbered sticker on it. Didn't have blood on it either,' he finished.

'So you're looking for the fifty-ninth ball?'

'We've found that. Nowhere near the green. And four others. Three of them are PRO-TRUST. But you can see where my men have been looking.' They were none of them closer than twenty yards to the spot where Jarvas had lain: two were twice that distance away. 'We've found nothing close by.'

'Then you haven't found the guilty ball,' said Treasure with assurance. 'The one that killed him must have ended somewhere near the body. Very near.'

'My sentiments exactly, sir. Got to be thorough, though. There'll be the coroner, you see.'

'What about him?'

'Sticklers they are for detail. Coroners. Fact the ball that did it can't be identified. Not definitely.' The policeman shook his head, leaving the dire consequences of coroners' sticklings to

Treasure's imagination.

'Perhaps they'll take a closer look at the blooded balls,' the banker remarked. 'Can't have had time for more than a cursory check as yet, surely?'

'No, they've checked properly, all right. Got the equipment, see?' said the other slowly. 'Seven had blood on. If it had been one. . .'

'Anyway, you say there's no doubt at all about how he died.'

For a moment the sergeant looked wary, perhaps regretting he'd vouchsafed such an explicit opinion earlier. 'Up to the coroner, of course, sir. But no. Seems it was a golf ball going a hell of a speed.'

'You play golf, sergeant?'

'No, sir. Never got around to it.'

Treasure wondered if whoever had done the autopsy would have given the same answer. 'Well, I'll leave you to your searches,' he said aloud. He nodded, and headed along the path leading to the Clays' cottage, which made a different route back to the hotel.

The cottage was further than he had expected – or what he could see of it to the left, behind a screen of apple trees and before the way divided. It was here he took the fork that bore half right to widen out and stop before a dilapidated, large red-brick outbuilding. It was single storey, but with a high-pitched slate roof and a loft hoist above the barn door in the gable-end he was approaching.

One half of the door was propped open. Outside on the concreted forecourt was a Ferguson tractor with a six cutter gang-mower attached. Behind that was a big turf scarifier with ragged saw blades and a towing bar. To one side was a hopper trailer half filled with a dark earthy material identifiable as turf dressing from the broken mounds of peat and sand, and the torn bags of phosphates and potash close to it. Against the near side wall was an untidy stack of empty oil drums, a wheel-less, up-ended wheelbarrow, and some rusting bits of old machinery with nettles growing through.

Inside the building Treasure could see a disordered

collection of smaller implements, and a long workbench which, like the shelves above and the space below it, was entirely occupied with tools and equipment, except for the small patch in front of the vice. Dick Clay was working at the vice. He was holding an electric drill with both hands.

'Good morning, Mr Clay.' Treasure stepped over the threshold on to the uneven brick floor.

Clay swung around swiftly, involuntarily, it seemed, bringing up the drill so that it pointed directly at the caller – like a gun-fighter in a Western movie. The implement looked not very different from a pistol. 'Morning,' he answered without enthusiasm and a look that was just short of threatening. He turned back to what he was doing.

There was a short burst of noise from the drill which its operator then set aside. He blew on whatever was in the vice, before taking up a hammer with his right hand and a slim, two-foot metal stake with his left.

'You're an early worker,' Treasure returned: he had suffered less promising starts to engaging conversations, but not many.

There was an uncomfortable silence for a moment. 'We keep farm hours here,' said Clay eventually, after giving the upper end of the stake a sharp tap with the hammer. He loosened the vice. What he was now holding in his left hand was the stake with a golf ball embedded in one end. The ball had a neatly stencilled figure nine on it.

'New marker for the ninth tee,' said the banker, conscious he was stating the obvious: Clay gave him a look that indicated as much.

'People collect 'em, it seems. Two missing yesterday. Vandalism, I call it.'

'May I see?' Treasure took the marker while Clay rummaged in a box for another stake. 'You're well prepared with replacement parts, anyway.' There was another box with balls in it, some already stencilled with numbers ranging from one to nine. Absently the banker swung the marker he was holding like a cosh, bringing the ball hard into his left palm. 'You always use PRO-TRUST balls, I see.'

If Clay had intended to answer he was forestalled by the sudden appearance of his wife. She in turn was briefly taken aback at the sight of Treasure. But what she had to say took precedence over conventional greeting.

'Heard the latest?' Mildred Clay demanded, her tone presaging disaster. She was drying her hands – or perhaps wringing them – in a tea towel, evidence, probably, that she had hardly stopped whatever she had been doing before hurrying to promulgate her news. 'Mrs Millant. Oh, dear.'

'Well go on, woman,' urged her husband.

'The postman just told me. Dead in her bed.'

# CHAPTER THIRTEEN

'Let's hope they don't come in threes, that's all I can say, Alwyn.' Dr Ewenny-Preece sniffed as he looked around the small guest bedroom that had been the last resting place of Bunty Millant. The body had already been removed to the same mortuary that had received the remains of Kitson Jarvas nine or so hours before.

'Well, it's the third time I've been called to this village since last night,' said the police sergeant, whose origins and accent were as Welsh as the doctor's. 'Here already this time, of course. Looking for golf balls.'

'But there's no hardship since you live here? At least you can pop home between fatalities like.' The doctor looked down at some notes he had made on the back of a very old envelope.

'And that's just what my superintendent probably thinks. District Mobile Patrol, not village bobbies, we're supposed to be. I'll be going then, Doctor. I've got the samples and the exhibits.'

'This'll be barbiturate poisoning, I should think. Self-administered. Or else a coronary. Or both. Poor woman. Not a bundle of fun, what I saw of her, but I wouldn't have classed her as an imminent suicide case.'

'Can't always tell.'

Ewenny-Preece's little eyes indicated that someone of his experience could tell better than just-promoted police sergeants, but he let the point pass. He quite liked Alwyn – not officious like so many policemen these days. 'If last night was typical, she knocked it back a bit,' he volunteered with a sternness that would have done justice to a spokesman from the League of Temperance.

'She drank?'

'Lethal combination, drink and drugs.' This awful warning was punctuated by a fit of raw coughing and the lighting of a cigarette. 'Lot depends on the constitution of the deceased, of course.'

'So it could have been an accident?'

'Depends on her medical history, and what they find in her stomach.' The doctor wiped his eyes. 'And what the coroner makes of that note. Pity we don't know how many capsules were in the bottle when she went to bed.'

'Strong, were they? The capsules?'

'Not very. Not according to the label. So it depends on how many she took. Sodium amytal. For sleeping.' He inhaled with a pained expression. 'Matter of fact, it was what I gave Fleur to take last night. Right for someone getting over a big emotional shock. Stronger dose, of course. Always carry some with me.' He turned to his medical case that was lying open on a chair, rummaged through the contents but failed to find what he was seeking. 'Here somewhere,' he muttered, nearly closing his eyes against the smoke spiralling into them. Then he snapped the case shut, remembered his stethoscope was around his neck, opened the case again and pushed the stethoscope into it.

'But you wouldn't think Mrs Millant had the capsules just for emergencies, Doctor?'

'Could have been a chronic insomniac. Her doctor will say. I can't.' He picked up his bag. 'Those tea-cup dregs will have a tale to tell, of course. If she emptied capsules into tea she was most likely over-dosing.'

'On purpose? To kill herself?'

'Usually the case. Gets a lot of powder down faster. Doesn't taste, so I'm told. Well, I'm off for my breakfast. If anybody else round here kicks the bucket in the next hour, don't send for me, there's a good chap. Thank you.'

'How d'you suppose Mrs Figgle's going to feel about it?' asked Mildred Clay across the kitchen table in the cottage. Her

141

daughter had just left for the Orchard. Her husband, whom she was addressing, had come in for his breakfast shortly after she had taken him the news of Mrs Millant's death.

'Depends on the state of her conscience,' said Clay darkly.

'And what's that supposed to mean?'

'What it says.' He turned over a page of the *Daily Mirror*. As usual the paper was propped against the milk jug in front of him. 'No love lost between those two.'

'That's not true. Who told you that?' There was genuine outrage in the question. 'They were best friends. Always have been.'

He looked across at his wife. 'Didn't need telling. Not anyone with eyes in his head. For best friends they haven't seen much of each other. Not for ten years, have they? Not since Basil Millant died.'

'You mean . . . ?'

'I mean Mrs Figgle, or Mrs Jarvas as was, dropped her best friend pretty sharp when Basil copped it in that accident.'

'They live miles apart.'

'Wouldn't have stopped our Amanda from going to have her photo taken every other week.'

'That was all above board. He did portraits as well as . . .'

'Dirty pictures.'

'They weren't dirty. They were artistic poses. He did exhibitions. In London.'

'I'll bet he did.' Dick Clay didn't smile much, but he did so now at his own barbed witticism. 'Asked you once, as I remember.' He stared hard at Mildred while he consumed a large mouthful of bacon and egg. 'Except Jarvas warned him off. Honour among thieves they call that,' he added, washing the mouthful down with a gulp of tea.

She felt the flush rising in her neck and cheeks. She hadn't been feeling well anyway: it was the general upset since yesterday – and Dick's attitude didn't help. She got up too quickly to clear the plates: the action made her slightly giddy. 'I didn't get photographed because you said not. You know that. He was going to pay me a fee, too.'

142

'And he'd have made you earn it. Slut's work, that was. You were too simple to see it.'

'It wasn't like that, I tell you. I could have been famous. Well, I might have got other modelling work out of it.'

'Don't you kid yourself. Not proper modelling work. Not decent work.'

'Anyway I don't know why you think Kit Jarvas had anything to do with stopping me.'

'Because we worked for him. Because he thought if you had any extra favours going, they belonged to him. He got 'em too. It was me who was too daft to see that. At the time, that was.'

'None of that's true, Dick Clay.'

'Isn't it? I think it is.' He pushed his emptied plate away and turned to the sports pages of the paper.

They didn't speak for a while, until Mildred said, 'Anyway, Mrs Millant came for the wedding.' She was standing at the sink, wishing he'd drop the bitterness. She swallowed against the feeling of nausea in her throat. 'Not so many were coming because of the short notice. Showed loyalty, I thought.'

'Except she's done herself in.'

'We don't know that for sure.'

'No, but we know it's most likely. And a nice show of loyalty that was, coming to a wedding and committing suicide.'

'By then she'd have known it was off.' She bit her lip. 'I think she was depressed over Kit Jarvas' – as Mildred was herself.

He stopped reading. She had said something that had given him pause for thought. 'You think there was ever anything between them?'

'Not like what you mean. They were old friends.'

He seemed not to have heard. 'I suppose he could have been getting his own back on Basil Millant. If he'd found out what his precious Amanda had been up to. Like I rumbled you and him. In the end.'

She didn't answer. He had made that charge so many times. He hadn't really found out: only guessed. There was no way he could prove anything: only she knew the truth. Was he going to bring it up again in future? If only Kit hadn't made that pass at Rose. If only Rose hadn't told Dick about it. Mildred went on rubbing at a perfectly clean plate in the sink, her thoughts racing and jumbled. It had all been something she could have handled better by herself, right from the start. Kit shouldn't have reacted the way he did after she'd sent Rose from that room: it was no wonder she'd been ready to kill him.

'Well, I think it was totally thoughtless of Bunty. She was always strange. Even as a young woman.' Harriet Cartland Ware was sitting bolt upright in a small armchair in the Figgles' bedroom. She was in the dressing gown again, and her coiffure was enveloped in voluminous silk netting – the 'meringue' had thus acquired a sort of candy-floss coating: it was a night precaution that took careful dismantling and she hadn't yet had the time for that. 'The note was insufficient explanation.' She went on. 'Bunty owed us more.'

'She is dead, Mother.' Amanda was not yet dressed either, but she had produced a fresh tray of coffee for her mother and father. Jack Figgle had left to telephone the remaining wedding guests from his study.

'And as for Fleur. The poor child.' Mrs Ware shook her head. 'Is there some sweetener?'

Amanda handed her mother a box of saccharin tablets. 'Fleur coped very well,' she said. 'Of course it was a shock.'

'Where is she now?' asked Byron Ware who had only just joined them. He was in day clothes.

'She's trying to avoid people, I think. Gone for a walk. Probably hoping Jonas and his parents will have left by the time she gets back.'

'And all Bunty's note said was . . . ?'

'It was hardly a note, Daddy. Jack gave it to the police. It just said "Amanda, I'm sorry" in that huge scrawl of hers. It was on the top sheet of the message pad by her bed.'

'She didn't sign it?'

'There wouldn't have been room. The bottom half of the sheet was torn off. Handel Ewenny-Preece thinks they'll say it was suicide while the balance of her mind was disturbed.'

'What by?' demanded Mrs Ware indignantly.

'She was very fond of Kit.'

'Tosh. She had some feeling for him. Lord knows why, after the way he treated you.'

'Bunty always said Kit and I shouldn't have married.'

'Only because she'd have liked him for herself. At the time, that is.'

'That could be true, Mummy. I've never really thought about it.' Amanda moved to the seat in front of her dressing table and began arranging her hair.

'Well, it was pretty obvious to everyone else. She got engaged to that other sponger, Millant, pretty soon after.'

Amanda stiffened for a second, then relaxed again. 'He was quite a catch. For Bunty. It's true he wasn't well off.' Her expression became pensive. 'Kit wasn't a sponger in those days. He had plenty of money.'

'That's true,' put in Ware, who was drifting about the room with his hands in his pockets. 'After all, we sent you over to your aunt for the London season to catch a rich husband. . .'

'To meet suitable young men of the right class and breeding,' snapped his wife.

'Amounts to the same thing. You fell in love with Kit. Your mother found him highly acceptable. His class and breeding were impeccable. So was his bank balance at the time. Or so he said.'

'I had some reservations,' said Mrs Ware defensively.

'I don't recall them, my dear. Except you were sore he didn't have a title.'

'Mummy's reservations wouldn't have made the least difference. I was crazy about him.' Amanda made a face at herself in the mirror, then began applying eyeshadow. 'Pity he didn't marry Bunty.'

'Maybe she was still aiming to be the fourth Mrs Jarvas.' This was her father. 'She didn't know he was coming to the wedding?'

'I don't know how she could. We didn't, after all,' said

Amanda. 'Jonas seems to have known, of course.' She blinked several times at her reflection.

'But if Bunty was setting her cap at him? With his dying like that . . .'

'Would have been pretty upsetting,' Ware interrupted his wife. 'Can't see it would have driven her to take her life though.'

Amanda paused in what she was doing to her face. 'I wonder? She did seem pleased to see Kit last night. Bit shy, perhaps. You don't think . . . ? Not after all those years, surely?'

'And the shock,' mused her father.

'She was drunk, of course,' said Mrs Ware firmly. 'When we all went to bed, somebody had to carry the tea she took to her room.'


'Fact is, I didn't see much possibility of breakfast at the manor,' said Noah Plimpton. He had come into the dining room at the Orchard a moment earlier.

'You know, my wife and I predicted exactly that as far back as lunchtime yesterday?' Treasure remarked, looking up from *The Times*. He was so far the only hotel guest in the room. 'Please join me. Molly doesn't take breakfast, so there's a free one going.'

'Are you sure?' asked the other, sitting down immediately. 'Bacon and eggs, please.' He beamed at the waitress who had appeared to take his order. 'Oh, and sausage . . . and tomatoes . . . and mushrooms, please,' he added, now reading from the menu which he had noticed just in time. 'Two eggs, if that's all right?' came after another look at the card. Then he turned it over in case there was anything on the back.

'To avoid fainting from lack of nourishment till that arrives, there's grapefruit, juices and assorted cereals on the table over there,' Treasure remarked lightly. 'Kippers are extra, but I'll stand you one if you want.'

'It's the country air,' Noah announced as he returned a minute later laden with a perilously balanced and more than

146

representative selection of everything on offer. He adjusted his spectacles and wrinkled his forehead several times while arranging this collection in a considered order for consumption. 'Mind you, I'm pretty hungry in town as well,' he admitted. 'Very decent of you, sir. One could have foraged for oneself in the manor kitchen, I suppose, but there's a limit to the bounds of hospitality.' So saying, he drained his second glass of orange juice before applying himself to half a grapefruit.

'The young women down there weren't coming to the aid of the party?'

'Fleur's disappeared. I doubt if the Bedwell twins know how to boil water. Anyway, one was having a slow bath and the other was having. . .' He paused, frowned, then changed the subject. 'Actually, it just seemed a bit unfeeling to be doing anything so frivolous as making breakfast. I mean with poor Mrs Millant being carted away and policemen and doctors all over the place looking grave.' He squinted at the ingredients listed on the single-helping pack of Bran Buds, compared these with the equivalent entry on the pack of Cornflakes, emptied the contents of both packs into a plate and glanced about for the milk and sugar. 'Suppose one will now have to consider heading for home.'

Treasure sensed the last thought fathered another – a consideration of whether the consumables to hand would provide adequate sustenance against the journey and whatever privations could be expected to follow. 'You came by car?'

'Got a lift from London with Jonas. Don't run to four wheels. Not yet.'

'Motor bike?' Treasure dipped into his single boiled egg.

'Bicycle, actually.'

'Marvellous exercise.'

'Is it? Yes, I suppose so.' He nodded seriously at the banker as though the information carried special weight coming from a Rolls-Royce owner. 'You see I'm not quite qualified. As a solicitor. I've done my articles and . . . er, taken the exams.'

'So what's left?'

'I didn't pass,' Noah announced flatly, then cleared his throat of Bran Buds residual. 'Not the finals. Took them again in July. Won't have the results till November. So I'm on an articled clerk's salary still. It's why I don't have a car, I expect.' He seemed uncertain. 'And why I never asked Fleur to marry me.'

'I see.'

'Do you? Good.' He helped himself to a piece of toast pending the arrival of the cooked victuals. 'Jonas didn't let her money come between them, of course,' he added, ruminating.

'One got the impression he was effectively spurning her fortune. That he has excellent prospects,' Treasure offered carefully.

'Very bad, I'd have thought,' Noah replied. The waitress, who had just returned, seemed about to protest. 'Not the eggs. They look fine,' he assured her warmly. The girl departed. 'Great romancer, Jonas.'

'You mean he's not being promoted. . .'

'To Hong Kong, you mean? Moved sideways. Thought everybody knew. It was that or be made redundant. Company's cutting back here. He's some kind of data processor. Whatever that means. Middle-weight computer wallah. Chap who works with him told me.' He finished chewing a piece of sausage. 'Mark you, he's a fixer. Wheeler-dealer. Trouble is, fixers need power bases. I think Jonas lacks a power base.'

'He's not an especial friend of yours?'

'Hardly know him. Nothing against him, but now he and Fleur have broken up I shan't be seeing much of him.'

'After he's driven you back to town?'

'Oh, he won't be doing that. It was Fleur's car. Jonas just borrowed it. Expect he'll leave with Alexi Bedwell. They seem quite . . . quite chummy.'

'Well, if you're fond of Fleur . . .' The stern advice just about to be offered was stemmed by the arrival of Tim Shannon who had hurried across to the table.

'Mr Treasure, could you possibly come to the phone? It's old Mr Grimandi. Silvano Grimandi. He won't talk to anyone but you.'

'Of course.' Treasure pushed back his chair and dropped his napkin on to the table. 'Is he calling from his room? Perhaps he's ill.'

'Actually he's calling from the Monmouth Police Station. Seems he's been detained there. Most of the night.' He glanced from Treasure to Noah. 'I suppose there can be no mistake. He's not in his room. The police say he's wearing two suits.' The emphasis on the last word was coloured with incredulity.

'Then there's no mistake,' said the banker, striding out of the dining room.

# CHAPTER FOURTEEN

'The duty inspector offered to ring you at two this morning, but Mr Grimandi here wouldn't hear of it, apparently.' The detective sergeant smiled benignly across the table of the interview room at the police station in Glendower Street, Monmouth. He was a heavy man, approaching middle age, with a face like a ripe peach. 'So he's been our guest here.'

Silvano was seated beside Treasure on the other side of the table. Noah, who had accompanied the banker on the fast drive down, was doing his best to look judicial at the top end. Mr R. Jones, Garden Machinery, Sales & Maintenance, was alongside the sergeant, a little awed but, in the main, enjoying the proceedings.

'Who wants he should get out of bed at that time? Better everybody sleep comfortable till morning,' Silvano reasoned unselfishly.

'But you slept in a cell?'

'Mr Treasure, they don't lock the door. That's different. Is very nice. Is a civilised country. Like America.' He ended with a patriotic afterthought.

'It wouldn't have been unlocked if we hadn't apprehended those two villains. They hadn't got very far. Trying to thumb a lift to Newport. They stopped a police car.' The sergeant shook his head over the ineptitude of the criminal classes. 'Very much the worse for wear they are still. And thick with it. They're in locked cells,' he finished pointedly, for fear the others might conclude there was no end to the soft heartedness of the Gwent County Constabulary.

150

Treasure said, 'So you opened the van door and threw one out over your shoulder?'

'He had my case open. The van was stopped. The driver, he was getting out anyway.' Silvano shrugged. 'I help him a little also.'

'Tipped him head first into an old quarry, where I expect they meant to push Mr Grimandi,' put in the sergeant. 'Then he jumps into the driving seat and leaves 'em to their fate. Fantastic. He should be on the Force. This morning, before you got here, he's been demonstrating that throw. From a sitting position. Incredible. You know he was a Black Belt?'

'First Dan only. Means first grade. Is a long time ago. Many chiropractors learn karate.'

'At first, we had to detain Mr Grimandi, of course,' the sergeant put in apologetically. 'Exceeding the speed limit on the A40 at one-fifteen this morning. Driving a van he didn't own, full of goods he couldn't identify. All stolen incidentally, as we now know. He insisted he was just looking for Mr Jones. Oh, and that he knew nothing about the death of Mr Jarvas. That was the gentleman who died in the accident at Much Marton. We didn't know that at the time either. And Mr Grimandi seemed to be wearing two of everything. Our patrolmen found that very suspicious.' He turned to Noah. 'You're a lawyer, sir, what else could we have done except detain for questioning?'

'Quite,' answered Noah, sounding fully qualified and deeply anxious not to say anything that could possibly jeopardise the client's rights.

'Bob Jones here turned out quick enough. Confirmed he had Mr Grimandi's hired car, like he'd said. But the inspector needed more corroboration and identification. Couldn't get that without disturbing you, sir, or Mr Figgle. You do understand, Mr. . .Plimpton?' The policeman checked the last name from his notebook.

'Quite,' repeated Noah guardedly, moving his glasses about with near abandon and frowning at everyone in turn to confirm he had considered all the alternatives. 'But Mr

Grimandi is, of course, free to leave. At will.' The confident tone suggested dire consequences for any who might now dare to challenge this fairly shaky premise.

The sergeant beamed. 'Perfectly free, sir, sorry as we are to lose him. My uniformed colleagues are overlooking the speeding offence. Letting him off with a warning.' A look of gentle admonition went in Noah's direction for forgetting the point, before the speaker turned to Silvano. 'If you could just sign your statement, sir. The typed copy should be ready.'

'Just one thing.' This was Treasure. 'There was a burglary at Marton Manor last evening.'

'We got the notification, including the list of what was nicked.' The sergeant glanced at Silvano. 'At first we thought Mr Grimandi might have been involved. Natural enough. Then, of course, the two real villains. But there was nothing in the van that's on that list. We'll be cross-checking fingerprints, naturally.' The sergeant paused. 'The Marton Manor job sounds like it was done by experts. Knew what they were after. The two jokers we've got here wouldn't know a Botticelli from a bus ticket.'

'Glad you've decided to stay on, Silvano,' said the banker a few minutes later, as he headed the Rolls towards Much Marton. Noah had gone with Mr Jones to collect the hire car and drive it back.

'Maybe it's better.' The reply was enigmatic. The speaker, despite his bulk and the two suits, seemed to have shrunk a little. He was holding himself very straight and had tightly buckled his seat belt.

'There's to be a lunch for disappointed wedding guests. You'll enjoy that. Tell me, whatever made you rush off like that in the first place? You mentioned Jarvas to the police? Did his death bother you in some special way?'

'Was accident, huh?'

'They think so, yes. He was killed by a golf ball. They've had a post mortem.'

'A golf ball hit by a golf club? Is possible to hit so hard?'

152

'Yes. But in my opinion none of the shots that were supposed to have done it were really hit hard enough. And that's not just because Molly and I hit a dozen of them. You have anything else in mind?'

'Mr Jarvas. He was not a very nice man.' The words came out as a statement, not a question.

'By some standards a perfectly obnoxious man.'

'You think anyone would want to kill him?'

'Wanting to do something, to kill someone, is a lot different from actually doing it.' Treasure gunned the accelerator so that the big car charged past a labouring lorry on a straight and clear uphill stretch of road. 'Even if the intention is there, you need opportunity. Like overtaking on narrow roads.' He reduced speed slightly. 'To answer your question, in the course of a pretty scandalous life, I think it probable Kitson Jarvas recruited whole armies of people ready to bump him off. You think someone did?'

'And killing him. It could be . . . justified?'

'Possibly before God, but definitely not before a British High Court. Did you kill him, Silvano?'

'No!'

'Well at least you've answered a direct question at last.'

'You believe me?'

'Sure. But if you weren't trying to flee the country for doing a murder. . .'

'How you know. . . ?'

'That you were on your way to the airport? From the drift of this conversation there's nothing else you could have been doing. Especially in all those clothes. So if you haven't done a murder, did you witness one? Did you actually see the Vicar do it?'

'The Vicar did it! No, certainly no?'

'Well, we seem to have established you saw someone. Or was it something? I've got your toupee, by the way. Were you leaning out the window when it fell off?'

'Kind of. Thank you.' Silvano blew his nose loudly. 'What I'm seeing. Is only suspect. How do you say, the *circostanze*?'

153

'Your evidence is circumstantial?'

'That's right. And could be like a red snapper.'

'Herring. Just a different fish. You mean you're not sure?'

'So if it was . . . how you say . . . *coincidenza*?'

'Coincidence?'

'*Si*. If it was coincidence, I make trouble only. For nothing. Maybe for innocent people.'

'That's if you tell the police.'

'Not the police.'

'How about telling me?'

'This is what I am thinking last night. In the cell. Is better to make confidence with someone you trust, but important, honourable man like you. Or else go home and have to live with the conscience if. . .'

'If it turns out not to have been an accident. Someone gets accused of murder. And you know he's innocent. Or you know someone else did it.'

Silvano visibly relaxed. 'We can have such a confidence? You and me?'

'For the reason these people are friends of mine. I don't relish having them investigated by the police. Not if we can head off the need for official enquiries before they start. But we shall need to be absolutely frank. You understand frank?'

'He's one of the friends?'

'No. Not a person. Frank means open. We've got to tell each other everything.'

'Like I said. OK.'

'So, could Mrs Millant have killed Jarvas?'

'Mrs Millant! Is a game you play? First the priest. Then. . .'

'I gather you don't suspect Mrs Millant? That's a pity in a way. She killed herself this morning. Overdose of sleeping pills.'

'I'm sorry. She seemed troubled. But it's a shock, huh?' He made the sign of the cross over his bulging lapels. 'Would be convenient if it was her, yes? I understand.'

'So why don't you tell me who you do suspect?'

'Is what I saw when I'm in the *torretta*.'

Treasure frowned. 'You mean the turret? The one at the hotel?'

'Yes. Is a room at the top. I go there after we come back from dinner.'

'What for?'

'To take photographs. Is a good view. Better than my room. I plan to make pictures of the wedding. Candid pictures. Also before and after the wedding.' He saw Treasure's frown. 'Nice pictures, but when people not . . . posing. You understand?'

'I think so. Good idea.'

'So, I have the special camera for night pictures. Very expensive camera. No flash. Natural pictures.'

'You were taking pictures of the dancing on the terrace?'

'Is right. Only from there . . . from the *torretta*, the turret, is a good view of the ground below the terrace.'

'The slope down to the green? The ninth green. Where you were with Molly earlier?'

'And Mr Ware. Playing golf. From the . . . turret you don't see the whole green. The left part you don't see.'

'That's where Jarvas's body was found.'

Silvano nodded vigorously. 'The rest you see. Also the path to the house of the family Clay. And the workshop.'

'And you were in the turret room when the dancing started?'

'Also before. When Mr Jarvas is going along the path.'

'Towards the Clay house?' He watched for Silvano's nod. 'What time was that?'

'Is difficult. . .'

'Well, what time d'you think it was? Molly and I brought you back from the manor at ten-fifty. I remember checking the time because the disco was starting at eleven. You went up to your room. You got your camera. . .'

'I did some things. Maybe in fifteen minutes I go up to the turret.'

'And that's when you saw Jarvas?'

'Yes. I'm using a telescopic lens. But it's too early for pictures. Not enough people below. I wait a while. Then I remember I need an extra filter, so I go back to my room to get

155

it.'

'But you went up again later?'

'Sure. Also this time I take a small chair to the turret. Is no furniture up there. I think I need the chair to steady the grip.' He shrugged. 'In the end the windowsill is best. But I kneel on the chair.'

'OK. So you go back at what time? Eleven-fifteen? Eleven-twenty?'

'Eleven-fifteen, I think.'

'Lots of people were dancing?'

'*Si*. You and Mrs Treasure were there then.'

'Was there anyone on the green below or on the path?'

'On the path. Mr Clay is coming from his house. He goes to the workshop. Soon he comes from there with a long pole. Is thin. Metal. Only I don't know what for.'

'A long pole? Was it a fishing rod of some kind?'

'Not fishing rod. On the end is something small. Difficult to see. I don't look through camera. I just notice. Is not important. Not then.'

'And where was he taking this thing?'

'He walks along the path below. He walks out of sight.'

'Past the green?'

'That's right.' Silvano paused. 'Then Jonas.'

'Jonas was on the terrace or below on the path?'

'He's a good boy. OK, he's not so important as he makes out. Not so caring for his parents, maybe. He has to use his wits. Is a shame you tell me the wedding is off.' The sentences came in rapid succession.

'Silvano, what was Jonas doing on the path?'

'He was going towards Mr Clay's house.'

'Did he have anything with him?'

He sighed. 'What you call . . . ? The tee marker.'

'You mean one of those spikes with a ball on the end?' He waited for a nod from the other. 'And what did he do with it?'

'He sticks it in the path where it makes two – one way is going to the house. . .'

'And the other to the workshop. I know. But why?'

156

'I think he finds it somewhere. Is on his way to the hotel, so he puts it where someone sees it, in the morning. Mr Clay maybe. Is sensible thing to do. He's sensible boy. Only. . .' Silvano had run out of words again.

'Only what? Did he pick it up again? The tee marker?'

'Is strong like a golf club, huh? Not to make the ball fly. To use like . . . like a hammer.'

'With the ball as the hammer head. It would take a hefty blow and a strong arm to do as much damage as was done to Jarvas. But, yes, it's as conceivable he was killed by such a blow as by one of the golf shots from the terrace. More conceivable, in fact.'

'These shots. I am watching them later. Like I watch Mrs Treasure and Mr Ware in the afternoon. Is all up in the air shots. Not for long distance. They drop gentle.'

'Not as gentle as all that, but you're quite right, Silvano. You wouldn't expect to do someone a grave injury with that kind of high shot. One or two people hit low by mistake, but they were bad shots anyway.' The banker glanced at his passenger. 'So, are you telling me Jonas picked up the marker again and went back along the path?'

Silvano hid his face in his hands for a moment. 'Jonas, no. Jonas left the marker where he put it. Then he walked back along the path. Later he joins the party. Like Rose a little before. I forget to say about Rose.'

'Rose came from the cottage before you saw Jonas? How did she get to the hotel? Did she walk up the slope or take the path past the green?' He set the direction indicators flashing and swung the car off the A466 on to the minor country road that would take them across to the almost parallel A465.

'Rose went up the slope, after the workshop.'

'Was this before the golf competition started?'

'Sure. Then came Jonas. Then Mr Jarvas again.'

'From where?'

'From the cottage of the Clays.'

'He'd been inside.'

'Is not possible to say.'

'Except Mrs Clay has said so.'

'So.' Silvano seemed to consider the fact. 'For me, not possible to see. In front of the house. . .'

'There are some trees. Apple trees. You couldn't see behind them? Not even from that high window?'

'That's right. So Mr Jarvas comes along the path like he's going back to the manor.'

'Did you see him again?'

'Not after he goes past the green.'

'You lost sight of him when he passed the right side of the green?'

The other nodded, but not with any satisfaction. His expression was more pained than Treasure had noted since the start of the journey. 'Then Mrs Clay comes. From the cottage.'

'She was on her way to the hotel? I saw her there later. She was helping with the disco party.'

'Like with dinner at the manor. A fine figure of a woman. Such energy. . .' Silvano ended wistfully.

There was silence between the two for some moments until Treasure asked: 'Mrs Clay, she took the short route up to the hotel, I suppose?'

Silvano sighed. 'When she came to where the path goes in two, she's seeing the tee marker where Jonas leaves it. She picks it up. Then she's looking along the path to the green.'

The banker smiled. 'You were watching her through that telescopic camera.'

'That's right, Mr Treasure. Also when she runs on the path after Mr Jarvas.'

## CHAPTER FIFTEEN

'No one found it because no one was looking for it, I suppose,' said Jack Figgle. 'Can't blame the police. Last thing you'd expect is to find the booty practically back in the house.'

Figgle and Mark and Molly Treasure were in the study at the manor. It was nearly eleven. The banker had returned to the hotel earlier with Silvano. Molly had left a message for him at the desk. The couple had been invited for coffee at the manor and she had gone ahead. Amanda had not yet appeared. When Treasure had joined the other two they had been exulting over a big canvas hold-all containing all the objects stolen the night before – all except for the Colt revolver.

'And it was in the marquee?' This was Treasure.

'Lying on the top table. Or what would have been the top table if it had ever been laid,' Figgle replied. 'Could have been taken for a bit of caterer's paraphernalia. Except it belongs to us. Lives in the lobby with the coats. It was Amanda who noticed it. Brought it in here brandishing the brace of pistols.' He made a guilty face. 'Imagine she ruined any fingerprints. We both did. Had all the stuff out to check in a flash.'

'I think the thief wore gloves,' said Molly.

'It's what the police thought,' commented Figgle. 'Anyway, I'm just glad to have the stuff back. It was under-insured. The only good news in a long time, except. . .' But he didn't continue.

'Police won't grieve if there's nothing to follow up. They have enough to do,' said Treasure. 'It may bother them the pistol is still at large. Less valuable but I suppose more useful to a villain than anything else in the haul.'

'Everything in the collection's in working order,' countered the collection's owner with some pride. 'See what you mean, though. We regard the Colt as a museum piece, but it's not that much larger than a Service revolver.' He had also recalled the stricture he had received the night before for not having registered the weapon. 'May turn up like the other stuff,' he added hopefully.

'Anything developed on Mrs Millant?' asked Treasure as he watched his host carefully replacing the exhibits in their allotted places.

'Yes. I was just going to say. Not local. I was on the phone to her solicitor in Lewes when Molly arrived. Haven't had a chance to tell anyone yet.' Figgle shook his head. 'Amanda had rung the solicitor first thing. Close friend as well. Of Bunty's, I mean. Name of Bryning. Amanda knows him too. That's why she had the number. He was very distressed when he first got the news. More composed when he rang back just now. Bunty had a heart condition. Pretty bad. Not operable. Result of having rheumatic fever when she was a child. Insisted on keeping it to herself. No one knew about it. Bryning did, of course.'

'Should her doctor have prescribed those sleeping pills?'

'He hadn't, Mark. At least not recently. Worst thing she could have taken, unless . . . Bryning says she must have . . . kept them by her.'

'In case of need,' said Molly quietly.

'Explains the suicide. Not wanting to end up an invalid. It could have come to that, apparently. Also accounted for the way she looked. And behaved. Shadow of her former self. I said so to Amanda when she arrived.'

'Explains the suicide, if not the time and place of it,' Treasure suggested.

'Could explain that too,' Molly countered. 'She'd had quite a ball last night. With her oldest friend. Could have been shattered by Kit Jarvas's death, another pretty old friend. She knew the wedding was off, so she wouldn't literally be a death's head at the feast. If she was thinking straight at all, in a way, this time and place for bowing out might have seemed quite appropriate.'

'Then I give way to the logic of your perception,' replied her husband – which was quite different from saying he accepted it.

'She left the bulk of her quite considerable estate, half to Amanda, in trust for life, and the rest to Fleur immediately.' This was Figgle. 'She made me joint trustee with Bryning. We have absolute discretion about how the capital is invested. Involves about two million after taxes. That's all confidential for the moment. Decent of Bryning to be so forthcoming, I thought.'

'And Amanda's half also goes to Fleur after her death?'

'That's right, Mark. It really couldn't have come at a more opportune time. Hypocrisy to claim anything else.'

'Mmm. Shall you let this affect any arrangement with Jonas Grimandi?'

Figgle continued to study the powder flask – one of the stolen exhibits – which he was holding in both hands. 'Have to see what Amanda thinks. Expect I'll call it off. Nearly did so earlier this morning.' Now he looked up at Treasure, measuring the reaction to the last statement – or perhaps its credibility. 'It wasn't right, was it? Different if they'd been marrying.'

'Not much. The basis of the deal was a bit . . . eccentric.'

'You mean the computer contracts? I agree. Made me very uncomfortable. And having Fleur risk so much money. So, feel in the new circumstances I should grasp the nettle. Go for voluntary liquidation. Should end up slightly better than even. Earlier that would have meant giving up this place, of course. Would have hurt Amanda a lot.'

'You mean the Millant bequest . . . ?' Molly began, then wished she hadn't.

'Oh, it makes all the difference in the world,' Figgle cut in without constraint. 'Source of a comfortable retirement instead of having to alter our life-style.'

161

'I still think we should be able to find a buyer for the company,' Treasure volunteered. He had the unjustified but nagging feeling he had let Figgle down over that. He had been inhibited about openly faulting the Jonas Grimandi deal, since at least it had promised to keep the business afloat. He was still relieved to know it would be abandoned.

'If Grenwood, Phipps could find someone to take us over as a going concern, even at liquidation value, it'd still be a load off my mind, Mark. There are jobs at stake. Good workers. I'd hate. . .' He was interrupted by a kick at the door which he hurried to open. Amanda appeared with a coffee tray.

'Sorry to be so slow. As if we haven't enough to contend with, Mrs Clay went lame on us.'

'Anything serious?' asked Molly.

'Haven't had time to find out. Just got a message. I'll try to drop in there later. So dependable usually.' She stood still for a moment after putting down the tray, then, in a characteristic gesture, allowed the slim, sensuous fingers of one hand gently to touch the perfectly groomed hair. 'You'd think a cancelled wedding would reduce work. It doesn't. The house is full of guests. They all need food and other home comforts.'

'Lunch is laid on for all at the Orchard,' said Treasure.

'But nobody here's had a proper breakfast. Mrs Clay was supposed to be coping with that before she started her other work. Frankly, I just wish the wedding guests would quietly slip away. Not you two.' Languidly Amanda focused a smile on each of the Treasures. 'Noah and Fleur have gone off somewhere in her car. He's so good with her.'

Not for the first time the banker pondered the anomaly of how such a serene woman had mothered a child as instinctively nervous and tense as Fleur. Jarvas, the father, had certainly burned up quantities of physical energy – but even he had not been mentally taut like his daughter.

'I'm just so dreadfully depressed, still, about Bunty,' Amanda added, though this pronouncement came without the deep-sounding conviction the speaker probably intended. It was almost as though she was lamenting the passing of

162

summer.

'Oh, Bryning rang back,' said Figgle. 'Apologised for being so thrown by your call. Terrible blow. Was for all of us of course. Anyway, he wanted you and Fleur to know about Bunty's estate.'

'What about it? She's left us something? How sweet of her.'

'Seems she's left the two of you everything.'

'I don't understand.'

Figgle explained the details. Amanda's first show of surprise quickly deepened into something much nearer incredulity. For some moments she was silent. Then, looking almost pleadingly at her husband, she uttered, 'My God, I had no idea.' And slowly – very slowly – her eyes were filled with tears.

The Treasures' departure on foot for the hotel took place ten minutes later. They had stayed less time than expected, a fact that was the unintentional cause of a small embarrassment. Figgle walked out through the front door with them just as Palmerston, outside it and just beyond the high portico, began barking loudly.

In the nature of things, Palmerston's bark was naturally penetrating. It sounded ferocious because it couldn't be made to sound anything else, even when it was part of his evidencing pleasurable sentiments, as was often the case. The bark was also usually set to endure, unless anyone the animal respected was around to shut it off.

'Quiet, Palmerston,' ordered Figgle.

The dog, sitting upright in the drive opposite the door, stopped making a noise, but continued flicking gravel about in several directions with his wagging tail. Now he extended his attention to cover the newcomers on the scene, without losing touch with those people and objects that were already engaging it.

Mr and Mrs Gino Grimandi were settled in the front seats of a small Fiat car with the engine running. Jonas Grimandi was placing luggage in the boot. It was this action which had prompted Palmerston's protest. He invariably registered his objection to the removal of property from the premises by non-residents – whether they were refuse collectors in lorries or disenchanted Italians in tiny four seaters, even though he was perversely aware the participants were friendly and authorised.

'My parents were just coming in to say goodbye,' Jonas claimed with nobody believing him.

His father stopped the engine, got out of the car, and with great dignity walked up to Figgle. 'Jonas said it was best to leave now. Without fuss. He thought you were too busy to see.' He half made to extend his hand, dropped it, then had to lift it again as Figgle put out his own.

'Sorry you're not staying for lunch. Sorry the two young people have decided not to. . .er. Well, there it is,' said the host as he warmly shook the other's hand. He then went round to the other side of the car to shake hands with Mrs Grimandi. 'My wife will be sorry to have missed you. Have a good journey.' He looked across at Jonas who was closing the car boot. 'You're not leaving too?' It was difficult to gauge which way his hopes were pointing.

'Not till after lunch.'

'Then we might have a word, if you've a minute to spare.'

When the Fiat had disappeared from view, and Figgle and Jonas had gone inside, the Treasures were still in the vicinity of the doorway. The banker was scratching Palmerston's ample and extended neck when Molly said, 'I've found a fortune,' and having said it bent to pick up the ten pence coin lying on the lower step. But as her fingers were about to grasp the piece it whisked upwards out of sight. Molly looked dumbfounded.

Peals of treble laughter emanated from the window above the doorway. Treasure chuckled too, and Palmerston, barking excitedly, began leaping up after the coin to no purpose.

'Not funny,' exclaimed Molly.

'I thought it was rather,' said her husband, still laughing. 'You should have seen your face.'

'It wasn't meant for you, Mrs Treasure,' came breathlessly

164

from Robin Figgle, who had tumbled through the doorway, followed by a less assured Stephen Watkin. 'It was meant for Jonas. Honestly.'

'Well, it would have been a pity to waste a good trick, I suppose.' Molly smiled. 'How was it done?'

'Sticky tape and black thread. This is Stephen. Quiet, Palmerston. Palmerston knows the trick. We do it to him with a tennis ball.' Robin took a breath. 'There aren't so many going to lunch at the Orchard. I'm still not invited though.'

'We're having a picnic here,' was Stephen's first contribution.

'Instead,' agreed Robin.

'Well, someone has to watch the place for burglars,' observed the banker lightly.

The two boys exchanged knowing glances.

'Did you hear Mummy brought back the stuff from last night? All except the Colt?' asked Robin.

'Clever Mummy,' said Molly.


A short time later Treasure stood musing at the edge of the temporary ninth green. It was too early for lunch. Molly had gone to call on Mildred Clay to see if there was anything she could do for her: she had promised Amanda she would.

The turf dressing, disturbed earlier by innumerable footmarks, had now been re-raked so that it was again spread in a more or less even pattern. This served firmly to re-establish in Treasure's mind that, apart from ball marks, the raked surface had been nearly intact the night before when he and the others had come down to judge the winning ball. The single intrusion had been the body of Kitson Jarvas which had lain forward and slightly to the right of where Treasure was now standing.

There was no reason to doubt the accuracy of his recall. Jarvas had taken three steps on to the green, then fallen in his tracks. The floodlight and the moonlight had illumined everything as bright as day – and Treasure, with an alertness born of foreboding, had missed nothing as he had prepared to take the photograph.

165

The direction of Jarvas's steps had indicated he had been making towards the hole. If he'd had a putter with him one would certainly have assumed he was putting out a ball. But he had been returning along the path from the Clays' – that much Silvano had vouched for: Silvano would have noticed a putter.

The tee marker – the two-foot spike with the ball on the end – was in Treasure's mind as he stood on the edge of the green. Even someone with very long arms could not have wielded a marker and struck Jarvas with it without also being on the green itself. What if someone had done this, then re-raked the green? Then the re-raked portion would have looked different from the rest. Earth dressings dry out very quickly: a patch of fresh raking would have been very evident.

Treasure turned about and stepped down to the path. It was some ten paces from the edge of the green, with the ground sloping quite sharply. A tall person, walking upright along the path, would just have a clear view of the putting surface: a short person wouldn't – nor a golfer stooped to make an approach shot to the green from the area of the path, and definitely not from below the path.

To test the last point, the banker took several paces backwards off the path. It was then the apple hit him. It was propelled by a device he could see when he looked up, waving about in the tree above.

> 'What wondrous life is this I lead!
> Ripe apples drop about my head,'

Treasure quoted aloud.

'Terribly sorry,' called Greville Sinn, peering over the top of an eight-foot brick wall and looking like God distributing manna in an Italian Renaissance painting. 'Did it really drop on your head?'

'No. Bit of Andrew Marvell seemed appropriate, that's all.'

'Glad you like poetry. So do I. Tennyson's best, of course.

Volleyed and thundered, rode the six hundred, and all that. Very stirring.'

'He also wrote some quite sensitive stuff,' replied Treasure absently, having, with some effort, remembered that the last line of the stanza he'd quoted went: *Ensnared with flowers, I fall on grass*. He retrieved the apple from amongst the rotting and wasp-ridden windfalls.

'Can't get the top ones with this step-ladder,' said the Vicar, swaying a bit. He was also doing his best to guide and control the fruit-picker Treasure had noted at the start – and which was basically a slim, nine-foot aluminium pole: probably the one Silvano had described. It had a two-part metal ring-grab fixed to the far end. This was actuated by a wired lever near the handle. Once the two halves of the ring-grab were around the fruit, the grip could be tightened by the mechanism at the handle end.

'Your fruit-picker isn't quite perfect, either.'

'Sound principle though,' said the other defensively. 'Doesn't damage the merchandise.'

'If you operate it fast enough.'

'A mistake can happen, of course, as it did just now. In theory, though, once you get the fruit, any fruit, inside the ring it's held there. Even a plum. Needs practice, naturally. Want to see?' He handed down the pole over the vicarage wall.

'Very sturdy, certainly.'

'Wouldn't bend easily,' agreed the Vicar, swaying some more. 'It's not mine. Step-ladder's mine. Needs repairing. Clay lent me the picker. To finish off this tree. Should have Laxton Fortune cropped by the end of October.'

'Is that the name of the apple?' asked Treasure, pocketing the one that had hit him and dropping the grab over a smallish and unripe windfall. He closed the grab tightly over the apple then, after a few swishes of the pole in the air, brought the end down with a splutter of apple as he hit the captured fruit against the top of the wall. 'You're right. Holds up pretty well.'

Sinn had now come through an iron gate set in the wall.

167

They both looked down at what was left of the apple. Half of it, the undamaged half, was still held in the grab. The leading half was pulped. It was not unlike looking at the hole in Jarvas's face: the Vicar hadn't seen that, but he seemed to be reacting as if to something unpleasant all the same.

# CHAPTER SIXTEEN

'It's not like me. Not like me at all. I just hope Mrs Figgle understands.'

'I'm sure she does, Mrs Clay,' Molly Treasure affirmed with extra conviction. As she recalled, Amanda had not been brimming over with sympathy when she had announced Mildred Clay's defection earlier.

'I'll be all right after lunch, I'm positive. All right now, really.'

'If the doctor told you to rest up for the day, I should do just that.'

The patient smiled weakly. 'Poor man thought I might be the third death in the village.'

'I'm sure he didn't say so.'

'He looked it though. Anyway, I feel so daft lying in bed like this. It's ever so kind of you to drop in. Friendly face. My Rose, she's good as gold, of course, she'll be down at two.'

Molly had earlier elicited that Mildred Clay had fainted, and made things worse by hitting her head on the kitchen sink as she fell. Fortunately her daughter had returned to the cottage soon after to get something she had forgotten. Dr Ewenny-Preece had been summoned and hurried over from his house, filled with extra foreboding.

'You've been overdoing things, by the sound of it,' said Molly.

The other nodded, then winced with pain. Her hand went to the lump on her forehead made to seem even larger by the dressing over it. 'The wedding meant a lot of extra work. But it was the mental strain that did it, I think. All the fuss yesterday. My husband and Mr Jarvas. Then I had a row with Rose over Mr Jarvas. Then both deaths. . .'

'Well, don't fret about it all again now,' said Molly gently.

'I shan't any more. Got it in focus, like, lying here this morning.' She hesitated. 'Years ago there was something between me and Kitson Jarvas. People have probably guessed since Dick. . .'

'You don't need to. . .'

'I'd rather talk about it. To you. He was a bad egg, all right, was Kit. There was something you couldn't resist about him though. Not ever. I was like the rest. Trouble was, Dick got it fixed in his head, one time, that Kit could be Rose's father.'

'I see. He wasn't, of course.'

'Tell you the truth, I've never been sure. I don't think so. You won't tell anyone that?'

It seemed somewhat late to be begging the confidence: Molly had put the astonishing revelation down to the effects of concussion. She eschewed ever admitting to herself it was her sympathetic aura that regularly invoked embarrassing confessions. She smiled understandingly. 'You mean you and Kit Jarvas were having an affair?'

'Seemed just a bit of fun at the time. I was only eighteen, so you could say he was taking advantage. I was married, mind you. Sounds awful, I suppose, but Dick was away a lot.'

'I thought you worked as a couple for the Jarvases?'

'We did. We had a cottage in the grounds. Rent free. I worked in the house. Dick did the garden, but only part-time at the start. They had another gardener. Old man. He retired later. Up till then, Dick did long-distance lorry driving as well.'

'I see.' And if Mildred Clay had looked then anywhere near as attractive as her daughter did now, it wasn't surprising Jarvas had taken advantage of her while her husband was pounding up and down the Great North Road.

'They were all a bit loose in those days. Mr Jarvas wasn't the only one after me. Terrible really. Of course, I don't know

170

why they ever got married. Mr and Mrs Jarvas, I mean – Mrs Figgle that is now. Expect you know she was a famous beauty? But they never got on in bed. He told me.'

'Don't you think he might have said that anyway?'

'So I'd let him have his way?' She gave a guilty smile, absently picking at the lace top of her nightdress. 'He didn't need to. I think it was the truth. He said she was frigid – with him anyway. Not the same with Mr Millant though.'

'Bunty Millant's husband?' Molly was aware she'd got herself involved in a scandalous unburdening which she ought to terminate – soon.

Mildred nodded in answer to the question. 'Basil, his name was. Very thick with Amanda Jarvas. The four of them used to practically live together.'

'That was in Sussex?'

'Mmm. They had separate houses, of course. Officially.' Her eyes opened wide – full of meaning. 'They always had their holidays together. Rented huge villas in the South of France. Yachts too, some years. Shooting in Scotland in winter.' She sighed. 'They used to say Mrs Millant couldn't have children.'

'Who said that?'

'Oh, just gossip. No secret Kit Jarvas didn't want children. He told me so. Couldn't stand kids. Probably why him and his wife didn't click in bed. Too many precautions taken.' She sniffed. 'None taken elsewhere, I can tell you. Not by him. Every woman for herself in that quarter. And I wasn't bothering most of the time. It's really why I couldn't ever be certain. About Rose. And that wasn't the only. . .' She hesitated, then shook her head. Whatever she'd had in mind to say was left uncompleted.

'And you saw Kit . . . ?'

'He wrote to me. Eight years ago,' Mildred interrupted, misunderstanding the question. 'It was years since I'd seen him. He asked me to lend him money. I did, too. When he was on his uppers. Silly really. They say there's still money in the family. His family. But he couldn't touch it. Anyway, I sent him all I'd got. He never paid it back. It wasn't much.'

Molly smiled sympathetically. 'Actually, I meant you saw him last night. That he came here after dinner.'

'Oh, I see. Yes, that's right. I felt awful. I'd been such a fool really. You see, I'd never told him he could have been Rose's father. But she was in his bedroom. I mean . . .' She was blushing.

'I understand.' Incest was a delicate subject – even, as in this case, when it was inadvertent, probably avoided, and downright problematical.

'I just saw red. It was on top of him putting Dick in that temper. So I told him what I thought of him. That's after I'd sent Rose out of his room.'

'You told him then about his possible relationship with Rose?'

Mildred nodded, holding her head. 'He came later to apologise. Waited outside in the trees till I was alone. Dick had been in. And Rose. He could see. I hadn't drawn the curtains. Not till then. He promised he'd never touch her again. Not in that way. Said he'd like to help with her education. Seems he was coming into money. Someone else's I shouldn't wonder.'

'I think it probably was,' said Molly quietly.

'Oh, and he said he wasn't taking Dick to court. Not for punching him. Mrs Figgle had sent him to say that.'

'But surely Amanda Figgle didn't know about . . . ?'

'About the other business? About Rose? No. But she knew Rose had told Dick the truth. When she said Kit had been bothering her. Up at the Orchard.' Mildred blew her nose loudly. 'The last word he said to me was sorry. I think he was, too.' She touched her nose again with the handkerchief.

'When he left, someone mentioned seeing you leave quite soon afterwards.'

The other woman showed no surprise or curiosity. 'That's right. Not straightaway. I was ever so late though. Promised Mr Shannon I'd help with the party.'

'But you didn't go straight to the hotel?'

'Found a tee marker, that's why. Dick gets that angry when

people pinch them or move them around. It was stuck in the path. Belonged on the ninth tee.'

'So you went out of your way to go over with it? You really are conscientious.'

Mildred smiled. 'Dick's got plenty to put up with. And when I got to the tee, the other marker was missing.' She made a tutting sound. 'It riles him so, that kind of thing. Just makes work.'

'Obviously the accident to Kit Jarvas hadn't happened when . . .'

'When I went past the green? Couldn't have, could it? They hadn't started that daft competition. Music was going full blast though. In any case, I might not have seen him. If he'd been lying there already, I mean. You don't see from where I was. Not properly. Not that I'd have been looking. You have to watch your step on that path at night. I was hurrying too.'

'The floodlighting . . .'

'Doesn't light the path. Too low. Blinds you, though, in places, all the same.'

'Kit couldn't have been very far ahead of you.'

'That's what I keep telling myself. I never saw him though. Not after he left here.' She paused, then added reflectively. 'He had aged. Ever so much.'


'Lucky that finger's not broken,' said Ewenny-Preece.

'Well the Vicar's step-ladder is,' retorted Treasure with some sharpness. He was seated in the consulting room.

'Toe's all right, too.' The doctor frowned. 'How was your foot involved?'

'It wasn't. Some other occasion. Haven't consulted a doctor since. Thought it worth checking,' the banker explained somewhat brusquely, while putting on his sock.

'Quite so. Thank you. That fingernail will probably come off in time. False economy to use broken implements. Especially ladders. Damned nerve asking you to hold it.'

'I volunteered. There were just a few good apples at the very top of the tree. Seemed a pity to leave them. If I'd been quicker

I needn't have got my fingers jammed.'

'Hmm. Greville Sinn's all right, of course?' The disappointment he was anticipating came over firmly.

'Yes, he jumped clear. Landed like an athlete. He seems very fit.'

The doctor gave an unwholesome cough. 'Appearances can be deceptive.'

'Certainly one wouldn't have guessed Bunty Millant was about to take her life. Not last night. Have you . . . er . . . have you heard any more in that quarter? Jack tells me she hadn't long to live.'

'Pathologist who's doing the post mortem's just been on the phone. He's talked to her own doctor, too. All four heart valves affected by rheumatic fever when she was seven.' He studied the cigarette he had just removed from the packet, then lit it. 'Always seems to get them in their late thirties. Not so many cases these days, thank God. She knew, of course.'

'Kept it dark, though. I'm surprised Amanda didn't know.'

'So am I.'

'And the cause of death?'

'Up to the coroner. Looked like suicide, but he may give the benefit of the doubt. Call it accident. Which it might have been, of course.'

'Or cardiac arrest caused by an overdose?'

'Of sodium amytal, prescribed when she complained of not sleeping after her mother died. That was more than a year ago, apparently. Small dosage in capsule form. And she was given less than a week's supply. Seems she didn't use them then.'

'You mean she took the lot last night?'

'Could be, from what I've been told so far. But if she knew they were under strength, was fuddled with drink, and didn't realise the danger – for her – of taking too much –' Ewenny-Preece narrowed his eyes to slits against the smoke wreathing from the cigarette clamped between his lips '– then it might have been an accident,' he ended, but without conviction.

'The post mortem would show how many capsules she took?

Or do they dissolve completely?'

'She emptied them into her tea. They found traces of the drug in the cup they took away. Not the capsule shells themselves. Could have disposed of them elsewhere. Bathroom perhaps. I didn't come across them.' There was a touch of belligerence in the last statement as though the speaker expected to be challenged on it. 'The pathologist wanted to know.' So he had been questioned on the subject already.

'Did you say you'd prescribed the same drug for Fleur?'

'One capsule only. Higher strength. To calm her and get her to sleep last night. She was very upset about her father.'

'You carry emergency supplies of that kind of thing?'

'Most physicians do. Which reminds me. Must have used the last capsule last night and chucked away the bottle,' he added uncertainly, and almost to himself. 'Care to join me in a whisky?'

'Thanks.' Treasure accepted the offer chiefly because suddenly he had found the conversation worth prolonging. 'You sure about that?'

The doctor looked up quizzically, his hand already inside the desk pedestal where the bottle and glasses were kept. 'I've no more patients this morning. I usually have a drink about now.'

'Sorry, I didn't mean, should you be drinking? I wouldn't be so presumptuous.' The banker paused, smiling. 'Actually, I meant were you sure about finishing your supply of sodium amytal?'

'Matter of fact I'm not. Not completely.' Ewenny-Preece contemplated his admission. 'Could have sworn there were one or two capsules left in the bottle.'

'But you remember throwing it away?'

'No, I don't. Except there's no other explanation. Not really.' He passed Treasure one of the generous measures of Scotch he had just poured. 'Oh, help yourself to water. Thank you.' He indicated the Thermos jug.

'Jack told me you joined him with the others for a nightcap after you'd seen Fleur. Did you have your medical bag with

175

you in the drawing room?'

The doctor thought again for a moment. 'No. Left it on the hall table.'

'Where Mrs Millant might have dipped into it?'

'She could have done. That's if she left the room. I can't remember.'

'We could ask the others.'

'I'd rather we didn't.' The dissent had come swiftly. 'What you say she might have done is possible, but not very probable. It'd only complicate things with the coroner. Sounds irresponsible, too, when it wasn't really. Doctors don't expect to have their cases plundered in people's houses.'

'It could happen though.'

'It could happen that patients steal things in consulting rooms. It's never happened here though. Never missed anything.' He surveyed the mountain of assorted impedimenta on the desk and then the several other horizontal surfaces similarly encumbered. The expression that went along with this inspection implied its owner would have known in an instant if Treasure had just pocketed so much as an aspirin tablet. 'May look a bit haphazard,' he added, as though to admit as much altered nothing.

'You couldn't have left that bottle in Fleur's room? Or thrown it away there, if it was empty?'

'Thought of that.' The incaution was back in the tone and the confession. 'Had a look when I was leaving the manor this morning. It wasn't in Fleur's room. I asked her if she remembered seeing it. If I'd left it. She didn't.' He gave a prolonged wheeze, then dosed it with a draught of whisky. 'It's only a question of how much sodium amytal Mrs Millant ingested, d'you see?'

'You mean, if it was more than the contents of the capsules she had?'

'That's the point.' He looked uncomfortable. 'I'll know later.'

'It assumes, too, she hadn't used any of the capsules before, I suppose?'

176

'Ah, that's different. They can't prove that. One way or the other.' He had evidently considered all possibilities before the present conversation. 'Don't see how they could. Do you?'

'Not unless someone watched her taking some.'

There was a pause. 'Better when I have all the facts. No point worrying unnecessarily. Nasty if anything comes up to suggest. . .well, professional negligence.'

'Hardly that.'

'Quite. If people steal things from bags.' He shrugged. 'Ready for the other half?'

'I'm all right, thanks.'

'Thank you.' The doctor coughed loudly, then poured himself another whisky.

'Have you heard anything official on the Jarvas post mortem?' asked Treasure.

'Same pathologist. The authorities are a bloody sight more conscientious with dead bodies than they are with live ones, I can tell you. More practice, I suppose. They found a medical sample of some tranquillisers in his coat pocket. Two pills. Machine wrapped in plastic. Unopened. So they were checking if he got them from me. Which he did. If they could have anything to do with his death. Which obviously they couldn't. And if those were all I'd given him. Which they were.'

'He was killed by a blow from a golf ball?'

'Pretty plain, you'd have thought.' Ewenny-Preece shook his head. 'But that's ignoring Clay socked him one earlier on. Could the effects have contributed? That's what they're looking into. I ask you? He bust his middle meningeal artery. You should have seen him.'

'I did.'

'I'd forgotten. Well then. Could you credit a tap on the jaw hours earlier contributed?'

'That's a technical question I'm hardly qualified to answer. On the other hand, I'd certainly have said the cause of death was fairly obvious.'

The doctor had nearly drowned the last comment with a

177

prolonged bout of coughing. 'And I'd say,' he croaked, then had to take a long breath: it sounded like a strong east wind looking for window cracks. He began again. 'And I'd say you were right. Thank you. And I examined him at five-thirty yesterday. Fit as a flea, all things considered.' He searched the desk for his cigarettes, found them, then looked up sharply. 'D'you know something barmy they told me? Strictly between us?'

'They still can't identify the golf ball?'

'Can't they?' Ewenny-Preece lit the cigarette, then ploughed on, effectively ignoring Treasure's contribution. 'Jarvas's blood group. They say he was Group O Rhesus Negative. He told me the same himself. Got it on one of those gold dog-tag things people wear round their necks. Nothing sacrosanct there, of course. Whoever engraved it got it wrong. So has the pathologist. Never checked it. Got it off the tag, obviously. I didn't enlighten them.' He seemed to take an especial satisfaction in this piece of perversity.

'It's important? His blood group?'

'Amanda Figgle is Group B Rhesus Positive. I had to look on my file here, to make sure. Very meticulous filing system.' He waved vaguely in the direction of a sagging wooden filing cabinet in a corner. He bent forward, blowing smoke and looking confidential. 'Needed to get Fleur's blood group done last month. Something to do with going to Hong Kong. Stuck in my mind. Group AB Rhesus Positive.' He sat back nodding, and looking pleased with himself.

'You've lost me. That means something?'

'It means careless pathology. If Kitson Jarvas really had been Group O Rhesus Negative, it'd mean he couldn't possibly have been Fleur's father, that's all.' There was more nodding. 'Thank you.'

# CHAPTER SEVENTEEN

'Ewenny-Preece is a failed and very frustrated haematologist,' said Treasure, then, in answer to his wife's questioning expression explained: 'Blood specialist. Failed to qualify as a consultant umpteen years ago. Reason he has such a down on consultants and hospitals.'

'Poor man. Probably accounts for his drinking too.'

'Accounts for the fact he scarcely knows half his patients by sight but can tell you their blood groups from memory. And the groups their parents could or couldn't have had. Fascinating. He's really very interesting on blood.'

'On blood,' repeated Molly dully. 'D'you think it's stopping?'

The couple were sitting beneath an oak tree, with their golf bags and trolleys, on the fifth fairway – and as far as they could be, on the nine-hole course, from the Orchard and proper shelter. The rain had begun as a slight drizzle shortly after they had started their game. It had turned into a torrent only minutes earlier.

The lunch for disappointed wedding guests had been a dismal affair and only sparsely attended. Even Noah Plimpton had been absent. Just as surprisingly, Jonas had been there, seated at a side table with his great-uncle.

The Treasures had invited the Wares to join them at the meal. This had done little to improve on the air of non-fulfilment pervading the event.

Harriet Ware had spent a good deal of the time deploring the indetermination of young people in general and the inadequate way they dressed in particular. This last barb had been fairly evidently – and audibly – directed at the Bedwell sisters seated, with some others, at the next table. It would have been charitable to assume from their appearances that they had come over more for the swimming than for the eating: Mrs Ware had not been moved to charitable conclusions.

Byron Ware had seemed preoccupied and morose. Even quite frequent views of Alexi Bedwell's bared midriff, as she reached for things, had done nothing to assuage his gloom – they had merely irritated his wife.

Two deaths and an abandoned wedding made unpromising topics for lively conversation, but few other subjects seemed at all appropriate. Treasure was glad he had explained before lunch that he and Molly had a golf game reserved for two-thirty: the problem was they had thus felt obliged to play, risking the threatened rain. Byron had shown no inclination to join them.

'Let's give it another five minutes,' said the banker who was losing by two holes, and anxious to retrieve them. 'Those people behind have given up.'

'All right.' Molly was equally confident of holding her lead if they carried on with the game. She shifted to a more comfortable position. 'Isn't the doctor being a big naïve?' she questioned, reverting to the earlier topic. 'About Kitson Jarvas?'

'Assuming he must have been Fleur's father? I thought so.'

'I know so. If you listen to Mildred Clay, twenty years ago rural Sussex was one big sex orgy. Wife-swapping seems to have been the main county sport.'

Treasure pouted at the raindrops. 'After cricket, perhaps,' he offered soberly.

'I don't think they waited till after anything. Not according to Mildred.'

'So if Jarvas wasn't the father?'

'My money's on the late Basil Millant, even though I don't have his blood group handy. I assume Jack wasn't on the scene in those days?'

'No, they met much later.'

'Well, it was almost certainly Millant. He was dark. Tall, dark and very handsome. Bunty vouchsafed as much at dinner. Several times.'

'I must say, seeing Amanda and Jarvas together made one wonder. I mean how did two such naturally fair people produce a child as dark as Fleur? It happens, of course.'

'And Mr Millant was tense and sensitive. Artistic. Actually he had a breakdown a year before he died. Another extra morsel offered by poor Bunty during the entrée. Our Mildred says keeping up the pace with his female conquests probably made him a nervous wreck. She claims she was one of his few failures. Though only through a technicality. She was one of Kitson's cuddles.'

'She told you that? Good Lord.'

'In total confidence. You don't count.'

'Thank you. So who was likely to have known if Millant sired Fleur?'

'What a nasty carnal expression.' Molly unwrinkled her nose before continuing. 'Amanda.'

'Obviously.'

'Not so obviously. Mildred's still laying bets on who was Rose's father.'

Treasure showed only mild surprise. 'Amanda Figgle is a good deal more switched on than Mildred. Even so,' he went on more thoughtfully, 'Mildred says Dick Clay may not have been Rose's father?'

'Not if he was lorry driving at the time. She really doesn't know.'

'She should get Ewenny-Preece on to it.'

'And have him post the result in the church porch, you mean?'

He frowned. 'I wonder if he's worked that one out already. On his own account.'

'Why?'

'Professional interest. I think he's the Clay family doctor and he seems to take blood groups before temperatures.'

181

'Untapped area there for blackmailing, when you think about it.'

He did – momentarily. 'But not by Ewenny-Preece. This tree's leaking.' They both shuffled closer toward the trunk. 'Look, let's assume Millant was Fleur's father, because there's a good circumstantial case. OK?' She nodded agreement as he went on. 'So who would have known besides Amanda and, presumably, Millant himself?'

'Almost certainly Jarvas. He and Amanda didn't go in for bed very much. If at all. And he didn't care for children.'

'So why didn't he divorce Amanda for adultery?'

'Because Bunty paid him not to? She couldn't have children. That was one of the less choice dinner table disclosures. It's only a theory.'

'But a good one. I see what you're getting at. It would all have been around the time Jarvas was running out of money. You were saying earlier about the yachts and the villas on the Riviera. D'you suppose Bunty was paymaster for the whole quartet?'

'Because it bought her an interest in the child she couldn't have, but her husband could.'

'With her best friend.' He paused. 'Would she have preferred that to adopting a child of her own?'

'I think so. Her medical history might have precluded that anyway. The adoption societies are very particular. In a way she seems to have shared Fleur, for the early part of the child's life at least.'

'Before her husband was killed?'

'And Jarvas left Amanda.' Molly nodded thoughtfully. 'After which, it might not have been so important. D'you understand?'

'I think so. Just. And would you suppose they all four of them openly admitted to the situation?'

'Certainly not. Actual promiscuity would have been covert. I'm sure they'd have played by the conventional rules. That may not be Mildred Clay's opinion, but it's certainly mine. And can you see Amanda admitting to Bunty, or anyone else, that her child was by Basil Millant?'

'Possibly not,' he replied slowly. 'Jarvas and Bunty. . .'

'Would've had to come to some . . . some understanding, probably.'

'Because of the money? It may still have been an unspoken arrangement, of course. Something Amanda never had to acknowledge, even if she knew about it.'

'Would that apply to the terms of Bunty's will, d'you think?'

He pondered for a moment. 'The last involvement with her husband's child. And the final generous gesture – to cut Amanda in for half the income. If I hadn't been there, in that study, I might not have believed it was news to Amanda.'

'But since you were there?'

'And heard her agonised disclaimer.' He shrugged. 'Genuine? She didn't know. Or she's a very good actress.'

'Melodrama's even easier than tragedy,' said Molly dismissively. She invariably played comedy.

'What if Bunty had intended making a new will after Fleur was married? The first might have included Amanda as a beneficiary for cautionary reasons. Not uncommon when endowing the young. Good reason for not telling Amanda.'

'Why?'

'To avoid disappointment, assuming a second will would have cut her out.'

'All rather hypothetical.'

'I don't believe it is. It seems to me Bunty made quite an effort to get to the wedding. She was obviously ill – obvious now, not yesterday when everyone thought she was weird, then drunk.'

'You think she came to inspect Jonas?'

'Her lawyer told Jack she'd been advised not to travel. To avoid all forms of excitement. Yes, I think she was here against that advice, and for reasons she believed more important.' He reflected for a moment. 'Mildred Clay didn't say anything to suggest Millant was Fleur's father?'

'She might have been going to. But no, she didn't. Not even by implication. Come to think of it, implication's a bit abstract

183

for Mildred. She doesn't beat around the bush. She did say Amanda and he were very close, by which she certainly meant they'd been lovers. If she'd known he was Fleur's father I think she'd have said so. D'you really think the Clays could know?'

'They evidently knew a great deal about the private lives of the Jarvases and the Millants. You mentioned blackmail.'

'It was a joke.'

'I know. About Ewenny-Preece's speciality.' He frowned and leaned back on his elbows. 'Clay got the job here, at the Orchard, through Amanda's recommendation. But he and his wife feature from a period in her life you'd guess she'd want to forget.'

'You mean she hadn't really kept up with Bunty?'

'So why resurrect the Clays?'

'Unless she owed them.'

'Unless they had something on her.'

'Or unless they'd been especially loyal to her.' Molly grimaced, wiping a raindrop from her chin. 'My ideas being more charitable than yours. Mildred. . .'

'Mildred may not come into it,' he interrupted, looking up into the leaves. 'It's much more likely it's something between Clay and Amanda.'

'That *they* were lovers? That Clay is Fleur's father?' Molly sat up very straight.

'Neither. Not necessarily, anyway. But it was a very odd ménage they were all mixed up in twenty years ago. Mildred certainly didn't volunteer anything to Clay about her relationship with Jarvas. She says he guessed at it. Could he have had one with Amanda? Or even Bunty?'

'By their standards, yes. I mean Dick Clay is a handsome brute if you like them rugged. More so, I expect, in those days. Of the two women, he'd have been more Amanda's style.'

'For an occasional roll in the hay? So if he'd fathered a child by her, or somehow known that Millant had, would that account for his still being around?' Treasure pushed himself upright. 'Or could he have demanded to be kept around? And if something happened to upset Amanda's plans, would it have been in his interests to thwart whoever was doing the upsetting? Kit Jarvas, for instance.'

'I don't understand.'

'Well, I'll tell you. It's probable Jarvas was engaged yesterday on a pretty sophisticated confidence trick. He'd succeeded in getting Jack to sign that contract letter without giving anything legal in exchange. He gave his word on something, that was all. And I'm beginning to think he wasn't going to keep it.'

'You think he wouldn't have given Fleur away?'

'I think he might not have. We'll never know. What we're certain of is he wouldn't commit himself in writing. And, of course, he had a very good reason. He'd been to gaol once. He didn't fancy risking having to go again.'

'I don't follow.'

'By not approving the marriage – his original plan – he stood to gain a substantial income for ten years. But it involved a fraudulent claim. He wasn't Fleur's father, something any country doctor could prove. One just did.'

'But. . .'

'No buts. It was a risk he'd been prepared to take at one point – until a better idea came up. You see, if he traded his rights to Jarvas Trust income for a contract with Figgle & Sons, he'd have traded himself out of an illegal situation into a legal one.'

Molly frowned. 'Because anyone who could prove Fleur wasn't his daughter. . .'

'Would also be proving she wasn't entitled to Jarvas Trust money.'

'Ever?'

'I'm afraid so. The Trustees could hardly accuse Fleur of making a fraudulent claim since she's never known the facts. And since she's been the only beneficiary to date, if the truth came out, I doubt they'd take retrospective action against her. Nor Amanda. Nor even Jarvas if he'd lived. If Jarvas had become the beneficiary though. . .'

'Which he would if he'd opposed the marriage?'

185

'Right, then he could have risked being accused, at some point, of knowingly taking money under false pretences. Incidentally, Jack told me the Jarvas Trustees had it in for Jarvas. Black sheep of the family, and all that. If they could ever have done him down, they wouldn't have hesitated. He knew it, too.'

'They'd have had to prove he knew he wasn't Fleur's father. That he hadn't been cuckolded.'

'Wouldn't have been difficult. It's pretty obvious he did know.' He lay back against the tree trunk.

Molly's visual interest was now caught up by a figure in the distance: she peered hard through the rain. 'What was it you asked Silvano Grimandi to do?'

'To find out what Jonas was up to on that path last night. And a few other things. I also advised him to get some proper sleep this afternoon. He's meeting us for drinks at six. I'd hoped by then we might have some firmer information on the post mortems. Courtesy of Handel Ewenny-Preece who's also joining us.'

'So why d'you suppose Silvano's running from the hotel to the village under a huge golf umbrella? Can you see him?'

Her husband narrowed his eyes to follow her gaze. 'Because without the umbrella he'd get soaking wet.'

'Very droll. I mean why is he out at all? And running. And don't say because it's quicker than walking.'

'It's hard to tell if he's wearing two suits, but since he hasn't got his case, I'd say he's not doing another bolt. Probably had his rest, and going for tea with the Wares at the manor. They became quite close yesterday.'

'So why isn't he using his car?'

'Perhaps it won't start. Or perhaps he doesn't think it worth it for such a short drive. You know how older people are about economising.'

'You could be right.' But she sounded unconvinced. They watched Silvano, recognisable even at half a mile, as he scampered into the trees in front of the churchyard. 'Was there any significance in what Mrs Ware said at lunch?' Molly

186

asked, returning indirectly to the main subject. 'The bit about Bunty suggesting she and Fleur had become confidantes?'

'Mmm. She made it sound like a sinister aside. Made when Bunty was in her cups, as she put it. It was after someone had announced the wedding was off, too. I noticed Byron Ware didn't approve Harriet bringing it up.'

'Because she said Amanda resented Bunty's involvement.'

'That Amanda thought Fleur quite complicated enough without help from outsiders.' He got up as he spoke. 'Interesting we both noticed. Come on. Let's go in. This rain's with us for another hour at least.' He glanced again in the direction Silvano had taken.

They both opened their umbrellas and set off for the hotel, pulling their trolleys. The course seemed utterly deserted except for them, with water now beginning to lie on the surface in quite large pools.

'Ugh,' complained Molly, jumping aside from where one shoe had sunk into the turf, lace high. 'Bad drainage down here. Can we make for higher up?'

'I think the lower path's a better bet,' said Treasure. 'There's a drainage ditch between.' He led the way down.

The first four of the nine holes were strung out in a more or less straight line to the east along the ridge from the hotel. The fifth, which they'd been playing, dropped southwards quite sharply. The remaining four meandered westwards on sloping or lower ground. The path they joined was the one that led eventually to the Clays' cottage.

Conversation lapsed for some minutes as the two concentrated, heads down, on covering as much distance as possible as quickly as possible. It was raining harder than ever. Then, quite suddenly, Treasure cried 'Eureka!' and delved into the brush below the path.

'Found the other tee marker,' he beamed, drawing abreast again and waving the object in front of him. 'Must be the one Mildred told you was missing. Complete with ball painted with a 9. Hmm, ball's not a very good fit. Must have got loose. Clean though,' he added as an afterthought. 'I'm not going back with it. We'll stick it somewhere prominent. Funny, it just caught my eye.' He winced slightly as he knocked his hand against his umbrella shaft.

'Your finger all right?' asked Molly, a bit breathless. They had come very nearly up to the line of trees where they'd be turning right for the Orchard. They were walking parallel with the ninth fairway.

'Almost forgotten it was jammed in the ecclesiastical step-ladder.' He was still studying the marker he was holding.

'The Vicar didn't mention Bunty's sinister aside?'

'No. He probably heard it though. He was there. So was the doctor.'

'If she hadn't been about to take her life, could it have been meant as a threat?'

'Yes. And if you take the view she wasn't about. . .'

Whatever Treasure intended to say he didn't complete. With loud snortings, much slapping of overshoes on wet gravel and joggling up and down of his massive, borrowed umbrella as though he was coaxing it to take off with him, Silvano had appeared on the crossing path from the Treasures' left.

'Mr Treasure. Mrs Treasure . . . Molly. Is thank God I am finding you. I look everywhere.' He fell in beside them. 'Not that way. Is policeman.' He steered them sharply right on to the uphill path to the hotel which they were intending to take in any case.

'There are police through there again? On the ninth green?' enquired Treasure.

'He says Coroner's Officer. But he's a cop. Policeman's uniform.' Silvano had them all moving at a cracking pace up the incline.

'The Coroner's Officer is usually a seconded policeman, Silvano.'

The older man seemed not to hear. 'We follow Jonas. In your car. Is OK? He's not far. The car, it's out of gas. He should talk with you. For his own good. He shouldn't have gone. I shouldn't have let him. It was all too quick.'

'Whose car's he got? The Bedwells'? Is he with them?'

'No. Is my car. Jonas takes it. Nine, ten minutes back. When he sees cop. After we talk. After he hears what cop says. To Mr Shannon. But he had to get bags. Pack maybe. Then stop for gas.'

'But where's he going?' Treasure demanded.

'He thinks he'll be suspect. Then he's off.'

'Silvano, where's he off to?' This was Molly, quite gently.

'Hong Kong maybe. From there they extradite British citizen. No?'

'They extradite them, yes,' said Treasure. 'Come on then.' He increased his stride.

# CHAPTER EIGHTEEN

'Which road d'you think he took?' asked Treasure. With rain pounding on the roof, he swung the Rolls out of the hotel drive.

Molly had elected to stay behind. Silvano, sitting beside Treasure, was steaming like an over-worked horse and wrestling with the buckle of his seat belt. 'He didn't say. There was no time. No time for persuading him. I guess it was wrong to give him the keys.' He frowned. 'Like they say, he'd lost his cool.'

'So you indulged him like a kind uncle. Sorry, great-uncle.'

'I guess.' The other shrugged.

'Let's assume he's heading for London. Means he'll probably cut across to the Monmouth road,' said the banker, thinking aloud. 'So tell me what led up to this. What did you talk about at lunch?'

'We talk about the deal he did with Mr Jarvas. Private deal that no one else knows about.' Silvano's short neck had sunk entirely below the top of his collar: his usual animation had disappeared too. His face epitomised innocence betrayed, as he contemplated the unfairness of his having been included in that 'no one else' category.

'Jonas did nothing wrong, you understand?' the old man continued. 'He had no option.' The last comment somehow reduced the credibility of the previous one. 'When we find him I make him explain. Is good of you to come after him like this. Is wrong he should run away. You agree?'

The banker made a non-committal head movement. He had acted entirely in response to Silvano's entreaty, judging that if

190

there was any merit in trying to bring Jonas back he had to move quickly and ask the questions as they went along.

'This private deal. You're sure Fleur didn't know about it?'

'Nobody.'

'Was it a trade, Silvano? Jarvas agreed to approve the wedding, provided Jonas got Figgle to sign that contract?' There was much head-nodding from the passenger. 'Only Jonas didn't have an option in the matter because Jarvas could stop Fleur getting any more Jarvas Trust money? For ever?'

'That's right.' Silvano joined the words and brought out the consonants in the markedly ebullient Italian way – a first sign of returning vigour. 'You know that? Only later, when Jarvas has the contract, he's still holding all the cards. Is complicated.'

'Not really. I think they both held good cards. Jonas didn't play his especially well. But Jarvas got killed, of course.' He leaned forward in his seat. 'This road's in a shocking state.' He had just turned the car on to the now familiar country road that ran across the valley, joining the next main highway five miles to the east. The rain was turning the earth at the base of the hedgerows to mud, which in turn was dribbling out over the metal surfacing on both sides.

'Jonas was mad with Jarvas,' said Silvano. He continued to move his lips, indicating he intended to say more but couldn't or wouldn't bring himself to find the words.

'Because he wouldn't sign the formal approval to the marriage,' Treasure prompted. 'How mad was he?' There was no immediate response. 'You know he left Jack Figgle's study before Jarvas?'

'He wanted to talk with Jarvas in private. To say things he couldn't say with Mr Figgle there.'

'He didn't go to join Fleur? To take her to the party?'

'No. Fleur is gone already in a car. He goes to hotel. Walks. There he waits for Jarvas to show. No Jarvas. So he goes back along the path.'

'You saw him go along there with the tee marker. And back again.'

191

'Then he is thinking. He explains he is thinking what to do.'

'He didn't run into Dick Clay?' Then in response to Silvano's quizzical look Treasure enlarged: 'You saw Clay leave his cottage just before you saw Jonas for the first time. They didn't meet each other?'

'Jonas didn't say so. He looked for Jarvas. Then figured he might have gone to the party – by car. Somebody's car.'

'So Jonas joined the party. I saw him.'

'That's right. Then next thing Jarvas is dead.' Silvano sighed. 'I tell Jonas what you say about the hitting with the golf clubs. Like the ball don't go fast enough for killing?'

'I didn't say. . .' The protest was going to be a mild one but it was never completed. Treasure was too busy for the next few moments manoeuvring the car to a stop so that it and a large farm tractor could safely pass in the continuing deluge.

'Is in the hall after lunch we hear the Coroner's Officer,' Silvano continued with his account. 'He's telling Mr Shannon they can't find the ball. Then he's asking about the competition. Also if anyone was playing regular golf last night. In the dark he means! He wants also a copy of the guest list. Said he was going to the manor. After. Oh, and the . . . er . . . what you call . . . the inquest, it'll be delayed, he says. Held over? Maybe two weeks.'

Treasure watched the mud-caked, massive rear wheel of the tractor squelch along the side of the Rolls, until it was revolving only inches from his nose. He had let down his window. 'Notice a grey hatchback ahead of us?' he called up loudly to the driver, a jovial, leather-faced character in yellow oilskins.

'Japanese was it? Arr,' he shouted back, beaming, and as though he felt expressions in a rustic burr might be expected of him. 'Half a mile on. No more. Water's rising. Mind my paintwork, now. Back in a bit. You better get a move on, for fear I'll want to overtake.' The roar of laughter was audible over the crash of gears as the big car accelerated away.

'You were explaining why Jonas decided to leave in such a hurry.' The banker re-opened the conversation some moments

192

later, while gunning the car along a straight piece of empty road. 'Did he seem frightened?' He glanced at Silvano and missed noting the roadsign before a bend.

'Plenty scared, Mr Treasure. And I don't know why. He's not a crook. I know. . .' Silvano caught his breath as Treasure swung the car on to the verge, braking it hard to a halt and finishing with three large brown cows jostling for a view through the windscreen, while others of the herd looked blankly about the road, masticating in the joyless way of cows.

The animals had been only one surprise as the car had breasted the bend. Treasure had forgotten the ford – what the tractor driver had alluded to as rising water. It was normally quite a shallow ford – he had splashed the Rolls through it twice already that day. It was in a hollow, though, in the lowest part of the valley. The rain had swollen the stream that crossed the road here to several times its usual depth. It was still not an obstacle that could have defeated properly-maintained vehicles. But Silvano's hatchback didn't fit that description. It had not adequately recovered from its last immersion.

Now the little car was standing in the centre of the rippling flow; it had expired – with cows on every quarter, like sentinels at a lying-in-state. Beyond, several cars approaching from the other direction were queued up in the narrow road, while the cow-herd – a buxom girl wearing Wellington boots and an unperturbed expression – was calling at her disoriented charges, trying to get them moving in the right direction.

And standing in front of the leading car on the other side, looking concerned under a shared umbrella, were Fleur, the car's owner, and Noah Plimpton. While paddling away from the hatchback, with trousers rolled up, carrying his shoes and socks in one hand and looking furious, was Jonas Grimandi.

'My Dad'll be back with the tractor in a minute. Pull him out quick enough,' the girl said to Treasure, nodding at the hatchback and giving the nearest cow a friendly tap on the rump with her stick. 'Up along, Myrtle, then,' she coaxed. 'They don't understand. It's too early for their milking, see?

Just putting them on higher ground.' She turned her attention to the approaching Jonas. 'Sorry about that. Better you hadn't stopped really.'

Ten minutes later Treasure was driving with Jonas back in the direction of Much Marton. The hatchback had been extricated and re-possessed by Silvano. It had even been made to re-start, but, at the banker's request, Noah had agreed to drive it with Silvano as passenger.

'What could I have done except stop? There were twenty bloody cows in the middle of that flood? Would have been murder,' complained a still ruffled, as well as dejected Jonas – a quite different character from the debonair young man of earlier encounters.

'The cows might have done you more harm than you them, of course. Your instinct was the right one though. Slaughter avoided.'

'Going too fast when I hit that bend.' The tone was a fraction less desolated.

'May I ask why you were going at all?'

'To avoid being part of a long-drawn-out inquest. This Hong Kong job is important to me. All I've got left. You know that? What if I have to hang around England for God knows how long? The company could drop me. Give the job to someone else.'

'Unlikely, I'd have thought. Having to hang around, I mean. In the circumstances, if the coroner needs your evidence he'll probably be satisfied with a written deposition. Your great-uncle was worred you might be clearing off in case of being er . . . unjustly brought under suspicion.'

'You think there was something fishy about Kit Jarvas's death?' The question did nothing to refute the carefully worded comment.

'By the sound of it, a conscientious Coroner's Officer is looking into things while memories are still clear. After all, there've been two unexpected deaths on the same patch within hours of each other.'

'So a connection . . . ?'

'To consider a connection is natural and not necessarily sinister.'

'You told Silvano the police mightn't accept Jarvas was killed by a ball from the golf range.'

'It'd be for the coroner to decide, actually. But, yes, I see grounds for doubt.'

'Meaning that people seen by the green near the time he died could be under suspicion. I was one of them. It's why I was leaving. But I had nothing to do with Jarvas's death.'

'I'm glad to hear it.'

'Silvano saw me down there. He told you. He's sure other people must have seen me.'

'He saw a number of people. You passed along the path twice. You could be asked why.'

'I found one of those tee markers. I was killing time. I took it along the path to the workshop. Stuck it in the ground for Clay to see in the morning. Then I walked back.'

'The long way round. You didn't see Jarvas?'

'Of course not. I was looking for him. If I'd seen him. . .'

'You know Jarvas was then in Clay's cottage? You might have seen him through the window.'

'I didn't get close enough. Anyway, the curtains were probably drawn. I remember there were lights on. At least, I think so.'

'And you didn't see Clay either? According to Silvano you almost had to pass him when you first came along.'

'Well, I didn't.'

'I gather you were angry with Jarvas for refusing to sign the letter I'd drafted. In a way the letter was a formality. Did you have any reason to think he planned backing down on anything?' Treasure waited some moments for an answer. Getting none, he went on. 'If they start official questioning, I think this is a line the police may follow.'

'And it'll make a difference if I tell you now?'

'That's for you to judge. You've thought better of running away or you wouldn't be in this car. If you can clear up some

195

points for me, it might help later if . . .'

'OK,' the other interrupted abruptly. 'When the engagement was announced, Jarvas arranged to meet me in London. It was after that he claimed he was disapproving the marriage. Fair enough. He stood to benefit unless we waited. I was ready to wait, except Fleur was certain at the time she was pregnant. That made the difference.' But the speaker's tone was dubious. 'I had no money. Worse, I'd got deep in debt. Showing off to Fleur, I suppose. Silvano was my best hope. I took a cheap flight to New York. Told him the whole story.'

'Including the bit about Fleur having a baby?'

'Yes. He lent me enough to clear my debts and go on living up to the image. It was on the understanding we got married.'

'I see. And when you found she wasn't pregnant?'

'She still insisted on going on with the wedding. I was for delaying. For a year.'

'What about Silvano?'

'I reckoned I could talk him round. Over the loan he'd made me. It was only a question of postponing, you see.'

Treasure's expression implied he didn't see at all. 'There was a principle involved. You'd have sorely disappointed the old boy.'

'Well, it didn't come to that. I met Jarvas again.'

'At his request?'

'Yes. He put up the Figgle & Sons proposition. The one you know about. He'd done a lot of fact-finding on the company. It was on account of something I'd said at that first meeting. I shouldn't have said it.'

'That you could get the computer sub-contracts?'

'That's right. I was trying to impress. I believed at the time I was being interviewed for suitability as a son-in-law. I said a lot of things to make it sound I was important. In the company. That I was part of top management. That I could swing orders. Help Jack Figgle. I'd told Jack the same thing. I got carried away. I do sometimes.'

'Could you swing those orders?'

'There's a good chance. Chap in the purchasing office at

headquarters. I . . .' He shook his head. 'I can't be certain. It was a bloody fool promise to make. The more elaborate it got, the more I had to stick to the story. I can't help myself sometimes. I was doing the same thing last night.'

'After Fleur called off the wedding? When you were negotiating new terms with Jack? Which he's now cancelled?'

'That's right. I was crazy. I get out of my depth, but I can't admit it. Not to anyone.' He wiped his hand across his mouth. 'I just get to hope everything'll work out. It does quite often.'

'Look, I think it better we finish this conversation before we reach Much Marton,' said Treasure, swinging the car into the walled courtyard of a pub. He glanced at the time. 'It's too early to get a drink but we can sit here and talk. Rain's stopping. Please go on.' Now the car was stationary he had a better chance to examine Jonas's demeanour – the face drained of colour, the quivering jaw, the arms tightly crossed while the hands clenched and unclenched the sleeves of the jacket.

'If I persuaded Jack to sign the contract, Jarvas promised he'd approve the marriage. Give Fleur away. I did my bit.' Jonas glanced fleetingly at Treasure. 'Your letter, the fact he wouldn't sign it, showed he wasn't playing things straight, though. If he wouldn't commit his approval in writing, I figured he'd been counting on using a big loophole from the start.'

'Why did he need one?'

'Because when Fleur came into her money he could still milk us for some of it. And go on doing it for ever.'

'On what grounds?'

'Sort of blackmail.' The young man hesitated. 'I can't elaborate.' There was another pause before he went on. 'Jarvas could prove she wasn't entitled to the money in the first place.'

'But how would that have done him any good?'

'That wasn't the question. It was how much harm it would do Fleur. Having to give the money back – not just what she came into on marriage either. All she'd ever had out of the Jarvas Trust. That's what Jarvas said could happen. I figured

197

he wouldn't sign the letter because it destroyed the hold he had over us.'

'And you believed what he said?'

'Because he was right.'

'And Fleur . . . ?'

'Didn't know anything about it. I didn't tell her. Last night, at the party, I was trying to talk her into postponing the wedding. That was just before you found Jarvas's body. I upset her. You know she's hot-headed? Said if I didn't want to marry right away, I loved her money more than her.'

'What reason did you give for postponing?'

'I said I believed her father was aiming to trick us. That he'd make some excuse for not being at the church. Go sick or something at the last minute. It meant admitting to her how important the money still was. For me. We quarrelled. It was worse later.'

'Because after Jarvas died you wanted the wedding to go ahead?'

'There was no reason why not. All right, I was marrying her partly for her money. Mostly, I suppose. I don't love her – or anyone else for that matter. But I'd have coped with her. Looked after her. She's mixed up. Whoever marries Fleur is in for problems. You don't understand – or approve. Anyway the wedding's off. For good.' The young man had become relaxed: it was clear his unburdening had been a relief.

'I don't approve or disapprove. Not my business. As for the nature of my understanding. Greater than you'd credit, perhaps, and not nearly so warped. I'm still glad the wedding's off. Seems you've learned some kind of lesson. I hope Fleur has too.' He considered for a moment before going on. 'So Jarvas told you he wasn't Fleur's father.'

The other turned sharply to face Treasure. 'You know that? I thought . . .'

'It was a reasonable guess. He was lying, so you'd be very unwise to tell anyone else. But it seems you've decided that already. I suppose to protect Fleur. Does you very great credit. And I mean that. It'll also keep you from being sued for

198

slander. I repeat, he was lying.' There was no purpose in allowing the shadow of his own doubt to blur things – and every point in being adamant. 'Tell me, do you play golf? Or ride? Or fence?'

'I don't understand.'

'Never mind. Just be so good as to answer.'

'No.'

'What sports have you played?'

'Football. A long time ago. Why? I've told you I had nothing to do with Jarvas's death. If you believe. . .'

'I believe he was killed by a golf ball in full flight. No ordinary golfer could have managed the shot on purpose. Certainly not you.' Treasure started the car engine. 'I suggest you let me drive you to Hereford station. Take a train to London, or wherever you were going. Less embarrassing than hanging around this part of the world.'

Treasure was quite certain now that Jarvas had been murdered – but by someone a good deal more brutal and resourceful than Jonas Grimandi.

# CHAPTER NINETEEN

'You can take the call from the box over there. It's Handel Ewenny-Preece,' Tim Shannon announced to Treasure whom he had just summoned from the main hotel drawing room. The banker had been sitting there with Molly and a much relieved Silvano Grimandi.

It was nearly six o'clock. Since leaving Jonas at the station, Treasure had briefly telephoned the vicarage for some information. Then he had changed ready for dinner – specifically a cold collation which the Treasures had been invited to share with the Figgles and the Wares at the manor.

'Mr Treasure, I'm ever so sorry.' This was followed by a long wheeze from the other end. 'Can't make it for that drink after all. Tricky confinement on a farm five miles away. Patient won't go to hospital. Don't blame her. Have to go to her now myself. Thank you. Perhaps later in the evening.'

'We should be back by ten. Drop in then for a nightcap if you can,' Treasure replied, then, pulling shut the door of the tiny phone booth, he continued in a lowered voice, 'Anything about the two post mortems on the medical grapevine?'

'Plenty,' answered the doctor promptly. 'Mrs Millant died of a coronary. Heart attack. For certain. The drink and the sleeping pills played a part, but she was in a very bad way.'

'She'd not over-dosed?'

'Any quantity of what she took would have been bad for her at that stage. She'd ingested five hundred milligrams. That's nearly twice the highest recommended dose for a normal person. Doesn't necessarily point to lethal intent though. And

200

the stuff was prescribed for her in the first place. A week's supply. In hundred milligram capsules.'

'So she obviously took all she had left.'

'By mistake. Or because she was determined to get a good night's rest. If she'd intended to kill herself she would have guessed five capsules might not be enough. Coroner will very likely give the benefit of the doubt.'

'Natural causes, not suicide?'

'That's right.'

'And what about the note she left?'

'Incomplete as a testimony, I'd say. From experience. Easily explained as the start of a formal little apology to Amanda Figgle. About something quite trivial probably. That'd be in character, so I'm told.' There was a distinct sound of lip slapping down the line: Ewenny-Preece was perhaps fortifying himself against the rigours of the confinement. 'Coroner could set the note aside with no trouble if he chooses. He's a sensible chap. By the way, I found that bottle of capsules. Right at the bottom of my case all the time. Empty.'

'You're certain you gave Fleur the last capsule?'

'Absolutely,' replied the doctor confidently, his memory on the point apparently much sharpened since lunchtime. 'And I was right about Mr Jarvas's blood group. I knew he couldn't have been what was on that dog-tag. Being Fleur's father. When they checked properly, they found he was AB Rhesus Positive. What I could have told them. Dangerous mistake to have hanging round his neck. If he'd been in an accident someone could easily have pumped him full of something incompatible.' Then, realising the ineptitude of the comment in the circumstances, he added, by way of recovery, 'Could have happened last night. That's if he hadn't croaked before we got there.' He tutted down the telephone. 'Well, I must go. Hope to see you later. Thank you.'

As he left the booth, Treasure thought he saw Mrs Shannon do one of her disappearing turns – flitting across the hall and down the basement stairs.

'Sorry your golf was washed out this afternoon.' Tim

Shannon had appeared at his side again. 'If you'd care for a game in the morning. . .'

'To get my revenge from the last visit? You still county championship standard?'

'Didn't enter this year, but yes, one makes the effort.' The chin lifted with the emphasis on the last word. 'Don't really get enough practice in the summer, of course, running this place. Try to get in nine holes daily out of season. With Dick Clay, sometimes. He's first-rate. At golf and in every other way. Don't know what we'd do without him. Yeoman stock, you see. Backbone of England since before Agincourt.' The effusion seemed more than a bit extravagant.

Treasure wondered why Shannon's rehabilitation of Clay was continuing so fervently. He looked to see if Rose was behind the desk. She wasn't: another girl was there.

'Didn't realise Clay was a golfer.'

'Could have turned professional, in my opinion. Did a bit of an exhibition this afternoon. For the Coroner's Officer. After the rain. Pity you hadn't been here.'

'What kind of an exhibition?'

The two men had fetched up at the open door to the terrace. 'If you've got the time, I'll show you.' The banker followed the other who continued speaking as they headed outside for the practice range. 'Chap wasn't a golfer. Good policeman though. Asked the right questions. Understood why a lofted shot wouldn't do much damage if it hit someone.'

'And wanted to know, I suppose, what sort of shot from here to there would kill?' They were standing where the competitors had stood the night before.

'Which would either be a mis-hit ball travelling very low and fast . . .'

'Or somebody over-clubbed whose ball ricocheted off a tree behind the green, maybe. That'd be the most deadly, of course.'

'Exactly what we demonstrated. From a bit further away. Over here.' Shannon took several paces to the right. 'Otherwise we'd have peppered the vicarage garden. Chap got the point anyway. Dick kept aiming for that oak.' The tree indicated was near the crossing of the two paths, well beyond the temporary green which was visible in its entirety from where the two were now standing. 'He used a long club. Two iron. Pretty accurate with it, all things considered. About every fourth ball hit the tree and came back like a bullet.'

'And was the Coroner's Officer convinced?'

'Difficult to say. Made a lot of notes.'

'He didn't hint at negligence?'

Shannon's chin shot up fast – almost as though he'd been punched under it. 'Ahead of him there, I can tell you. Pointed out we have warning notices about the range all over the place. No liability.'

'Have they identified the ball that did the damage?'

'Didn't sound like it. Gathered they think it has to have been one of those with blood on.'

'Did he say who hit them?'

'Don't believe he knew.'

'One would still have thought the guilty ball would have more evidence on it than others. Much more.'

Shannon nodded. 'You'd have thought so. Or else it was a ball that was spirited away. But your photograph militates against that. Incredible bit of fast thinking on your part. Coroner's Officer had a blow-up of it. Black and white. But it was all there. Poor Jarvas dropped like a stone with only his own footmarks and the balls to tell the tale.' Suddenly the speaker spun round. 'Oh, good evening, Mr Ware. Didn't see you behind us.'

'Sorry to break in like that,' said Amanda's father, a minute later, as he and Treasure set off for the manor on foot. 'Wanted a chat, though. Urgently. It's why I dropped by. On the off chance.'

Molly had yet to change for dinner. The banker had left her to follow in the car when she was ready. 'You heard what Shannon and I were talking about?' he asked, becoming aware that his companion was in a state of some tension.

'Overheard, and on purpose, I'm afraid. You believe the ricochet story will be accepted?'

'Possibly.'

They were going down the tree-bordered gravel path. The sky was now blue and unclouded, with the sinking sun making the still wet foliage shimmer and throwing long shadows on the fairway to their left.

'You think Clay has a special reason for promoting that idea?'

'Because he wasn't involved in the competition? It went through my mind.'

'No more than that? He loathed Jarvas almost as heartily as I did. Silvano Grimandi told me he saw him last night with some kind of rod . . .'

'A fruit-picker. Clay left it at the back door of the vicarage, which accounts for his not running into Jonas on that path. Silvano saw him too, a few seconds later. Did he tell you?'

'No.'

The banker didn't find the reply surprising. 'Clay would have gone into the vicarage through the wall gate down there. Mrs Sinn just told me she saw the fruit-picker in the porch when they got home. That had to be before Jarvas was killed.' He let out a long breath. 'The thing's adaptable as a sort of golf ball whacker. I tried it. Wasn't long enough to reach where Jarvas was felled though. Not unless whoever was wielding it was standing on the green.'

'But you believe the blow could have been a deliberate act? Made with a device of some kind? Not a golf club?'

'Meaning you don't?'

It was the dapper American's turn to hesitate before replying. 'Let's say I kind of hoped the obvious solution would be acceptable. Most everybody else seems to think it is.'

'Silvano . . .'

'Silvano takes his lead from you.' This came with unusual promptness. 'The police don't seem to be interested. Not yet. Not till some high-up maybe gets . . . alerted in some way to what . . . what could have happened.'

'Are you telling me politely to let things alone? You know if it was an accident, whoever hit the numbered ball that's held responsible – he's going to feel pretty sick about it.'

'But it'll still only have been an accident. My daughter and granddaughter are more precious to me than life itself. Sounds trite, Mark, but it's true. If any . . . any scandal develops, it's going to rub off most on them. No sir, I'm not telling you to let things alone. I'm trying to figure the best way to protect them and the rest of the family.'

'From the effects of a possible criminal enquiry? Difficult.'

Both men involuntarily regarded the temporary green. It was exposed through the gap in the tree line they were just passing. Neither attempted to stop.

'By difficult, I guess you mean impossible,' said Ware. 'Desperate measures aren't always that.'

'You're not contemplating anything heroic?'

'Don't really know what I'm contemplating.' The older man nervously brushed each side of his moustache, something he seemed impelled to do with increasing frequency. 'I've let her down, you see?' He shook his head. 'Not so long ago, when I retired, I was a wealthy man. Could easily have bailed Jack out of the corporate trouble he's into. Except a trusted partner in my brokerage business turned out to be a crook. Put simply, he absconded with a lot of client funds. I felt a moral obligation to help make good, along with the remaining partners.'

'Expensive gesture, I assume?'

'You could say that. It didn't break me, not entirely. We have enough to live on – to live reasonably well. We don't have the kind of money Jack needs.'

'Needed,' Treasure interrupted pointedly. 'I gather the Millant inheritance is substantial.'

Ware shrugged. 'And happened along too late perhaps. I mean . . .'

'I understand. You're assuming Jarvas's death could be linked with the family's financial problems.'

'If it involved foul play, I'm scared an enquiry might begin with that assumption.' He paused. 'Amanda's always had expensive tastes. That's well known. Too well. What has to be gotten through is she wouldn't harm a fly. Wouldn't hurt anyone. Not anyone.'

It was that repeated insistence which recurred to Treasure now as he regarded the glass he was holding. He was alone in Jack Figgle's study. He had been deposited there with a drink while Byron Ware had gone to change.

The banker debated whether the American had been more probing for intelligence than offering it. Had the worthy, fatherly concern for Amanda's reputation been overdone? Certainly it had nurtured a suspicion.

Later in their conversation, Ware had come back to pressing Treasure – without result – for other ideas on how Jarvas's death might have been contrived. But his favoured theory had narrowed the field so tightly as to make sharing it highly imprudent.

Treasure had judged Ware to have been dangerously on edge. The nature of any heroics the man might actually have in mind could only be guessed at. Precipitate action to protect Amanda could involve a confession of Ware's own guilt and then the possible difficulty of proving that guilt, unless. . .

'Sorry you've been left by yourself.' Amanda had entered quietly and was close behind him before he realised she was in the room. Her Nordic kind of beauty was augmented by the blue silk dress that matched her eyes and clung becomingly to her svelte outline. 'Jack won't be long. Went into Hereford to make our apologies to some people. I really couldn't rise to it. Our house guests have left, except Noah. He's taken Fleur to supper at the Broad Oak in Garway. There'll be just the six of us this evening. Cosy.' She smiled and took his arm. 'Daddy told me you were in here.'

'I walked over with him. I'm very early. Have you things to do or can I get you a drink?'

'Drink, please. Same as you have. D'you find Jack's little armoury interesting? I don't much.' When she had come up to him he'd been looking at the exhibits in one of the free-standing cabinets. She leaned back against it as he left her to get the drink. 'Still, it gives Jack and Greville Sinn things to take apart and polish up on long winter evenings. Jack's the one who's crazy about firearms. All rather juvenile, if you ask me.'

Was this more than a bravura suggestion – even a pointed one – that while her husband was playing with his toys, Amanda occupied herself with more adult games? Treasure thought probably so, dismissing the obvious and not unengaging after-thought.

'Is your father interested in the collection?'

The answering laugh seemed genuinely spontaneous. 'Daddy's scared stiff of anything mechanical. More especially anything mechanical that's old and actually meant to be dangerous.'

'Very wise.' He looked around the room as he came back with her drink. 'For my part, I'd prefer to own the pictures in your drawing room.'

'Which, thank God, we can now afford to keep.' She sighed. 'Did that sound heartless? Because of Bunty? It wasn't meant to.'

'Only frankly realistic.'

'Thank you.' She took the glass he offered, touching his hand with both hers. 'I like frankness.'

'If you mean that, will you indulge my curiosity by answering a very personal question?' He had spoken on impulse, but with no following regret. 'It's not idle curiosity, nor even the self-interested sort.'

'Then I can't wait to . . . indulge you.' She fixed him with a wide-eyed and engaging look – more challenging than quizzical.

'Can you tell me why Kit Jarvas sometimes claimed Fleur's father was Basil Millant?'

'You do take a girl at her word, don't you?' The tip of her tongue darted across her lips before she went on. 'The answer is I've no idea. And will you believe he was lying if he said it?'

'Unquestionably.' But he noted the ending question had been put with a good deal more force than the answer preceding it.

'Thank you.'

'He said it all the same. If there'd been the remotest chance of it being true, of course, he wouldn't have dared.'

'I don't understand?'

'If it had been true he couldn't have risked the Jarvas Trustees hearing of it. They'd have cancelled Fleur's entitlements, which always promised residual benefits for him, however remote. As it was, he could risk pretending to confide in a few carefully selected people for ... let's say special purposes at appropriate times.'

'Examples, please?'

'Bunty Millant and Mrs Clay, a long time ago. Jonas Grimandi, quite recently. None had anything to gain in leaking what they'd been told.'

'Do go on.' She turned her head very slowly from side to side, several times.

'With a hypothesis?'

'More exciting perhaps?'

'Bunty was deeply if silently grateful to accept you'd had a child by her husband. So grateful she made Kit Jarvas an allowance that kept both of you in funds for some years.'

'That's preposterous.' She paused. Her eyebrows lifted. 'Almost. I mean, am I supposed to have known? To have told Bunty?'

'Nothing so indelicate. I imagine Kit told the lie to Bunty, knowing she valued her husband too much to admit, either to him or you, that she knew. After the husband's death, Kit possibly argued it could only harm Fleur if the truth came out. It all fits his style. And for good measure I believe he used Mildred Clay to confirm the tale to Bunty, as if she were breaking a confidence.'

'Instead of conspiring over a lie?'

'I'd bet she's never thought to tell anyone else. On strict instructions from Kit. She didn't even hint at it to Molly, for

208

instance, this morning, when she was pouring out her heart. While she was concussed. Made no bones about being deeply involved with Kit. I expect you knew.'

'I knew he bedded our Mildred from time to time. During and after our marriage. What a swine he was.' Yet what Amanda said in an unheated tone made the sentiment sound remarkably bland and dispassionate. 'She'd probably have done anything he said – up to yesterday. I'm sure she used to adore him. And of course he could trust her, too. Knew too much about her. Dick Clay's a very jealous husband.' She looked down into her drink. 'And you think Kit used her?'

'For embellishment. Something he believed in. Seems he had a neck tag he wore on appropriate occasions with the wrong blood group on it. Also for embellishment.'

'You mean to prove non-paternity? All rather elaborate?'

'Convincing though. He may have used it to help convince Bunty years ago. His real blood group was the same as her husband's. Ewenny-Preece asked her doctor this morning. Kit had that tag with him here.'

'Handel's marvellous on blood. You mean he saw the tag and worked out it had to be wrong? Bully for him, and a credit to my virtue. And Kit was wearing the tag here because of Jonas? You haven't explained about Jonas.'

'You're very collected about this.' He smiled an approval which was becoming less guarded. 'Kit told Jonas he wasn't Fleur's father, so she wasn't actually entitled to Jarvas Trust money. Jonas being easily convinced. . .'

'And entirely hung up on the money?'

'Afraid so. And yes, he had the big lie spelled out.'

'You mean Kit had something to prove this nonsense?'

Treasure nodded. 'A run-down on the blood groups of all those involved, purported to have been supplied by a top haematologist. He was pretty thorough. His intention in this case. . .'

'Being obvious, and it worked. He got his contract. Jonas has left believing I . . .'

'Believing nothing he'd dare repeat to anyone. I gave him a

long lecture on the law of slander, and the duplicity of Kitson Jarvas. Actually, he's behaving better as a loser than he did when he thought he was winning.'

'Thank you. I never thought he was right for Fleur.' She looked up at him. 'I can deal with Mildred's. . . misconceptions. Isn't it strange, I can't find any hate for Kit anymore? You know Daddy thinks he might have been murdered? You obviously think the same. I didn't do it. I'm quite hopeless at golf,' she finished with a disarming smile.

'It's what the authorities may think that matters. The coincidence of two sudden deaths . . .'

'But Handel told me they'll decide Bunty died of a heart attack.' It seemed the doctor took a liberal attitude on who could share official conjecture and privileged information. 'And I didn't drop sleeping pills in her tea. I only poured it.'

'She had her own capsules, of course. Didn't someone carry her tea to bed for her?'

'Jack did. She was pretty unsteady. You don't think because Fleur and I benefit . . . ? I mean none of us had any idea about the will. God, how awful. It's as though we're inheriting under false pretences. But Bunty loved Fleur so much. She was such a friend. None of us could have done anything to harm her.'

'Well, as the doctor says, one presumes the coroner will decide it was either natural causes or suicide. There was the note, you see?'

'I've thought about that. It was probably the start of an apology for getting pie-eyed. She was given to doing formal notes over that kind of thing. Guess she intended pushing it under my door.'

'It couldn't have been over anything she'd said to Fleur?'

'Not possibly. Fleur would have told me.'

Treasure shrugged, but not to show the doubt he felt about the last comment. 'If Bunty hadn't died when she did of course, there'd be no reason for everyone to be extra sensitive about Kit's death.'

'You mean suspicious? The police didn't seem to be when it happened.'

'Exactly. Golfing accidents are not uncommon. Trouble is he upset so many people while he was here. If criminal enquiries start, that's bound to come out.'

'And you think they will start?'

'Yes. I also think Jack may be . . . a focus of attention.'

'But he couldn't . . . I mean why Jack especially?'

'Because Kit's on-off attitude over the wedding evidently maddened him. Too many people knew that might involve the future of Jack's company. There are other reasons. I really ought to talk to Jack himself.'

Amanda didn't demur. 'You'll help us if . . . ?'

'It's why I'm being boorish now. And will have to risk being more so. Did you send Kit to see Mildred Clay last night?'

'Yes. She looked so upset during dinner. She was worried about Kit suing her husband for assault. I told him to go and tell her he wouldn't. Right away. Without fail. Jack and Greville backed me up. It was Greville's idea actually.'

Treasure turned again to look at the display case. 'You didn't do the burglary in this room last night?'

'Are you serious?'

'Afraid so. I don't believe there was a real burglar. I think it was staged. Probably from inside the house.' He ignored her attempt to cut in. 'Almost anyone from inside could have done it. Anyone wearing trousers. Dinner had broken up. People were all over the place. That coat of Jack's with the hood. From what Molly says, it could have been worn by a man or a woman.'

'But what reason could . . . ?'

'Any number. The revolver's still missing, assumed stolen. Remember you're indulging me. It's important. You swear it wasn't you?'

'Certainly. If it matters I can prove it. I was . . .'

'Good,' he interrupted, looking at the time. 'D'you think we could have a word with Robin? And don't look so protective. If they brought a case, he wouldn't be made to testify against Jack.'

# CHAPTER TWENTY

'Not in my best, as you can see,' gravelled Penelope Sinn heartily, smoothing the front of the pleated crimson skirt as she ushered Treasure through the vicarage hall. 'Not like last night. Greville's in his study preparing his sermon. Very tedious. He'll be glad of the interruption. Come for instruction, have you? He's good at that.' She threw open the door and leaned into the room, head first, trunk balanced over the forward foot. 'Visitor, dear. Excuse me, both of you. Busy in the kitchen.' She pulled the door shut behind Treasure with another movement of basic balletic origin, even if it lacked basic balletic quality.

The Vicar looked up from his desk. The welcoming expression changed to one of perplexity when he saw what the banker was carrying. Then the smile came back. 'Good to see you. Sherry?' he enquired hospitably, pushing back the chair and rising.

'Thank you, no. I won't keep you. I'm due back at the manor shortly.' It was an irrational opening in view of what he'd come for, and he knew it. 'Your wife's right, I need your advice.'

'Well, do sit down.' Sinn indicated an aged leather tub chair. 'Amanda still entertaining disappointed guests, I expect. Saw a car going up when I was coming from the church a few minutes ago.' One hand went to the buckle of the narrow belt around the cassock he was wearing.

'Afraid that was the police. CID. They're talking to Amanda and her father. Waiting to see Jack. He's expected back shortly. Seems they've started the investigation proper into what killed Kit Jarvas.'

'I see.' The clergyman sat down again, somewhat abruptly. 'Golf ball?' he added uncertainly, his gaze fixed on the implement now lying on Treasure's lap.

'Golf ball undoubtedly. Question is, what propelled it. My money's on this thing.' Treasure lifted the crossbow on to the desk.

'Wondered why you brought it. Not going fishing?'

'It went in the burglary last night. I've never seen a fishing crossbow before.'

'Quite common from earliest times. This one's fairly modern. Engraved 1818. On the silver inlay.'

'Works the same as an ordinary crossbow? You cock the bowstring with this lever on top. And the attachment beneath . . . ?'

'Is a fishing reel. The line comes up through the front of the stock into the slit barrel . . .'

'And you tie it to the arrow.'

'The bolt.'

'I'm sorry?'

'The missile is called a bolt – or sometimes a quarrel. It doesn't matter.'

'One of these?' Treasure removed the stout, eight-inch, feathered shaft from a pocket.

'That's it. There's a small ring at the rear end.'

'And a point at the business end which fits the hole Clay makes in a tee marker ball. I've brought one of those as well. It's a tight fit. But then it would need to be.' He produced the ball and fitted it onto the bolt.

'Bless my soul,' said the Vicar – in his case, an interesting invocation.

'How accurate would that be when fired?' Treasure put the encumbered bolt on the desk. 'I gather you're an expert.'

'Hardly that. I know a little about the art. Accuracy? Severely reduced at long range. But up to fifty, perhaps seventy yards, quite as good as a rifle. In the right hands.'

213

'So that with Jarvas in the centre of the green, someone in the trees – or even your garden – that sort of distance away, could have dropped him with this?'

'I should think so.'

'The bolt and the ball could then have been reeled in. There'd only be Jarvas's footmarks on the green. The decoy ball would still have been there, of course.'

'Decoy ball?'

'To account for his being on the green. He was a golfer. Keen one. So am I. Never passed an abandoned ball yet without pocketing it. Quite sure Jarvas was the same. Whoever killed him was counting on it. Left a perfectly good ball for him to find as he passed. Police have it now. The one PRO-TRUST on the green without a sticky label. Nobody's figured how it got there. Not yet. No blood on it. Jarvas evidently didn't quite reach it.'

'Ingenious theory.'

'Plausible, d'you think? Set up by someone who knew Jarvas would be at the Clays'. Waited for him to come back. Timing wasn't all that critical, but it happened to work out perfectly. The marksman just needed Jarvas to be there before the competition started. The disco music would have drowned his cries, if he made any. Yes, it'd take someone pretty bright to put together an extemporary plan like that in the time available. Cool military tactician, perhaps? Only one mistake. Thought everyone would accept Jarvas was killed by accident. Otherwise brilliant.'

'You think so?'

'Beginning with the fake burglary. Holding on to the revolver while using the crossbow. Mudding the waters, as it were. Poor Jack.'

'I'm sorry?'

'He'll almost certainly be arrested. Eventually. When the police come to the same conclusion I have. He's the one with the motive, opportunity and skill.' Treasure shook his head gravely. 'The motive won't be as simple as money either. Jarvas pushed him too far.'

Sinn shifted in his chair. 'You're surely assuming too much?'

'No more than the police will.'

'I meant rejecting the possibility of an accident?'

'They have already, I'm afraid. They've got the speed the ball was travelling, but not what it was hit by. Except they're certain it wasn't a golf club.' The reply was especially firm. 'Now they're working on motive. They'll get back to opportunity and means. They're sure the ball that did the damage was removed. They don't know how. Not yet. They're bound to come to it.'

'Why?'

'Deduction. They grind slowly but thoroughly. In the process, of course, we'll all find ourselves involved in a good deal of enquiry and publicity. There'll be some muck-raking, I'm afraid. Jack may not be the first under the spotlight. Young Jonas Grimandi, Byron Ware – they qualify for investigation and will probably get it.'

'But. . .'

'They don't know how to handle crossbows? Difficult thing to prove. And it may be some time before the weapon comes into it anyway. Dick Clay, on the other hand, is apparently quite proficient with a bow.'

'Yes, he is.' Was the comment troubled or merely thoughtful? It was difficult to decide.

'Loathed Jarvas, of course. Happily for him it seems he may be able to prove he was at the manor at the critical time.'

'The time Jarvas was hit?'

'Eleven-twenty. He expired at eleven-thirty-two. Clay went to see Jack earlier. He dropped that fruit-picker here on the way. Wanted Jack to intervene for him with Jarvas. To stop Jarvas suing him for assault. Clay didn't find Jack, but he hung around outside the house for some time before leaving. He spoke to Amanda when he arrived, and Ware believes Jack saw him leaving – from a distance. Remembers Jack saying he saw someone. When he was coming back from a stroll. In the grounds. That's what Jack said at the time.'

'So Clay won't be suspected?'

215

Treasure shrugged. 'Initially? Difficult to say. Unless Jack comes forward and admits he's guilty. Save a heap of trouble.'

Sinn was silent for a moment. Only his eyes kept moving – seeking from side to side. 'There was great provocation,' he uttered sternly and unexpectedly. 'Jarvas was taking advantage of the fix Jack was in. Jarvas was a swine. Jail bird. You know that?' He leaned forward in his chair, torso very erect. 'Jack Figgle is a good man. Not wishy-washy good. Man of principle. Stands by the old values. Looks after his family. His employees. His friends. Me.' The veins at the side of his head had begun to pulse. 'Why should Jack have been humbled by a cad like Jarvas?'

'Going to be again, when he's arrested,' the banker offered quietly. 'I was hoping you might be prepared to have a word. The two of us could, of course. I don't believe he'll capitulate otherwise. Not early on.'

'Not even if he's innocent?' The words were stabbed out. 'Such a thing as British justice, you know? You know? You know?' The steep crescendo and the repetition pointed to more than simple conviction: the voice of concern was somehow uncomfortably chilling.

'But British justice is going to prove he's guilty. Your loyalty is admirable. But I think it misjudged. Taking Jack's finer instincts into account, d'you suppose he'd hold out if he knew it was purposeless? If we convinced him he was only prolonging the agony? Heightening the ultimate disgrace? I've always assumed he was a man of honour. So many people are going to be hurt over this. Out of decency, he should get it over quickly. Unselfishly. For the sake of others. There's no escape for Jack, I'm afraid. His. . .'

'All right! All right!' roared Sinn, his whole frame suddenly shaken by some massive convulsion. He lurched to his feet, thrusting back his chair so hard it crashed into the wall behind. He had in the same movement savagely wrenched out the centre drawer of the desk so that it tipped to the floor, spewing out most of the contents. 'Jack didn't kill that vermin. I did. I killed him. So let's . . . let's get it over with . . . Let's get it over with, shall we? That's what you want, isn't it,' he shrieked, waving his arms in the air. 'No. Stand back. Stand back.' The missing Colt revolver was in his right hand.

'And he pulled the trigger. There in front of me.'

'Except the gun didn't go off?'

'Thank heaven. Massive anti-climax in the end. But he kept trying. Till I got the thing away from him. That was after a struggle. I knew there was only one bullet, and it or the gun had to be defective. It was still a trifle too close to Russian roulette.'

It was just after midnight. Some minutes earlier Treasure had joined his wife in their room at the Orchard. He went to the fridge for a second can of lager.

'What happened next?' demanded Molly, propped in bed against the pillows.

'He fell on his knees and started reciting the Lord's Prayer.' Treasure went back to the armchair and took a long draught of his drink. 'Curious, that.'

'For a clergyman to pray?'

'For this one to. According to his wife, he's not the prayerful kind. Not in private. Then he started weeping and at one point I thought he was going to collapse. Anyway he's now in custody for the night. Asleep. Jack's solicitor was with us at the police station. Reckons he can get him committed to a secure hospital tomorrow.'

'When he's admitted to murder?'

'That's changed. Thanks to the solicitor's intervention. They'll go for manslaughter with mitigation. The killing was unintentional. Not that Sinn seems to care, but he was aiming for a leg. Hit the head because Jarvas bent to pick up a ball just as he fired.'

'Still wilful.'

'Don't be difficult. The story is he meant to injure Jarvas so he couldn't attend the wedding. That way, Jarvas couldn't ever say he hadn't attended on principle. Especially since he'd travelled all the way to Much Marton in the first place.'

'And that's the truth?'

'Could be. Complicated but credible, if Sinn can be made to support it. Obviously he's a deeply disturbed personality. Kept insisting he'd been living a lie, but God had suddenly given him faith and directed him in a sound purpose.'

'You think he's really potty?'

'Mmm. Excellent mitigation. Chap's so evidently not a killer. He's a clergyman who's suddenly got religion. Any jury's going to find that pretty bizarre.' He drank some more of his beer. 'I'm the one who should feel guilty, of course. It was very close to the perfect crime till I stirred things. All hunch, too. Otherwise Sinn would very probably have got away with it. Whatever he intended.'

'But you were only concerned Jack shouldn't be accused.'

'That's true. And for a while I thought he would be. Couldn't really be sure he was safe without coming to the truth. But if the coroner decided it was an accident, that would have been the end of it. I mean the police didn't seem much interested – despite the tale I concocted for Sinn. About their knowing the speed of the ball, and so on.'

'What about the CID men. The ones at the manor before dinner?'

'They were there. Sinn actually saw them. They'd called to check up on the stolen property. They certainly helped convince him. My only solid pointer came from what young Robin said. About seeing his father climb out of the study window, put the bag in the Vicar's car, then dash round the side of the house out of sight. It obviously wasn't his father he'd seen. It was Sinn in Jack's coat. Poor Robin, he hated admitting to his mother he'd been up on that parapet.'

Molly's legs shifted under the covers. 'So how did you know he'd seen the burglar in the first place?'

'I didn't. Except, don't you remember he told us today his mother had brought back the bag. I thought it an odd way of describing what she'd done, unless he knew she'd taken it in the first place.'

'And you thought she had?'

'For a bit, yes.'

'Then she persuaded you she was all innocence. During your cosy chat in the study.' She smiled archly.

'Something of the sort. And if it wasn't his mother Robin had seen, I figured it had to be someone else from the immediate family. "Bringing back" fits with "taking away".'

'Not stealing.' Molly thought for a moment. 'Yes, I'll buy that. A prize for your pedantry.'

'It seemed wildly unlikely Jack had burgled his own house and put the proceeds in the Vicar's car.'

'So by elimination it had to be Sinn?'

'Pretty well. And when one looked at the timings and his known movements, it all fell in place. He knew Jarvas was going to see Mildred. All he had to do really was watch for him to go past the vicarage on his way. Half the windows there overlook the manor drive. The rest must have been easy.'

'He laid in wait for Jarvas. Assumed he'd come back along the path, the same way he'd gone.'

'That was reasonable. Most people would use that path. Especially strangers. Incidentally, it was Amanda who told me Sinn was the expert on bows and swords, not muskets and pistols. They're Jack's province.'

'Sinn preferring the silent kill.'

'He hates explosives apparently. Jack says his active service was with infantry commando. Still a popular visiting preacher with the SAS. Their headquarters are in Hereford, of course.' He drained his glass, frowning. 'So it was loyalty that made him do what he did. Then loyalty again that obliged him to confess it. Tough.' He stayed silent for several seconds. 'So. Everything calmed down here?'

'Silvano and the Wares have become inseparables since he tuned up Harriet's vertebrae before dinner. Amanda's asked him to stay over as a house guest at the manor next week.'

'Give him longer to contemplate Mildred Clay.'

'Well, I'm sure that's harmless enough.'

'So am I. But he's devoted to her. I'm not sure it wasn't as much to protect her as Jonas that he flitted last night.

Touching really. . .'

'Oh, I forgot the big news,' Molly interrupted. 'Fleur and Noah came back after dinner to announce they're engaged.'

'Bit swift.' He stood up and began emptying his pockets on to the writing table.

'Not really. It seems he'd been on the point of asking her before. Before he introduced her to Jonas that is. She's accepted. Sensible girl. Nice boy. Apart from his dancing, he's er. . .' She stopped, contenting herself with an approving smile, after deciding it was unnecessary actually to categorise Noah's virtues – as well as mildly challenging. 'Anyway, they plan to marry soon. Want you to do the toast at the reception. So your speech won't be wasted after all.'

'I see.' He began undressing. 'Didn't want to mention it when we were with Silvano, but Jonas hasn't rushed off to Hong Kong. Gone to the Bedwell country seat in Berkshire. Going to present himself unannounced on the excuse he's taking up a standing invitation to stay. By the time I got him to the station he'd become quite his arrogant self again. D'you think he's got it in mind to marry one of those girls?'

'Something less formal, I'd have thought. So they can share him. They both deserve him, after all,' she added with simulated sweetness.

'Not his style. I'd guess it's marriage for money or nothing for Jonas. Practically said as much. Insisted the twin called Alexi started the rot in his relations with Fleur. She invited him to her room. Someone saw them there together and told Fleur.'

'So Alexi now owes him a lifetime of luxury? I really can't understand why that young man hasn't succeeded in vulgar commerce.'

'I can. Thank heaven Jack doesn't have to rely on him.'

'Apart from looking after the Vicar's defence, Jack's problems seem to have disappeared.'

'Because of the Millant money?'

'And Fleur's if he needs any of it, I imagine.' She smoothed a strap of her negligee. 'So Amanda comes out as white as driven snow. Is that right?' she added, without making it clear whether she was checking Amanda or the quotation.

'Intelligent woman,' Treasure observed loudly, from the bathroom.

'And sexy with it. I was sure you'd been noticing.'

'She was singularly unperturbed about Mildred believing Basil Millant was Fleur's father. I'd expected a shocked reaction. But not a bit. She simply told me she'd cope with Mildred's misconception.'

'Too calm by far?'

'I got a strong feeling she'd dealt with that one years ago when she got the Clays employment here.'

Molly watched her husband come back into the bedroom before replying. 'Which made nonsense of pretending she didn't know Mildred had the story.'

'Quite possibly.' He put his watch on the bedside table, before getting into bed.

'Meaning Amanda lied to you. Also . . .' Her eyebrows knitted, then she made the clicking noise in her throat that sometimes followed serious cogitation. 'Didn't the doctor tell you Basil Millant and Kit Jarvas actually had the same blood group?'

'Yes.'

'So Millant could have been the father?'

'I should think it highly probable he was.'

'And Amanda and Bunty could have confided in each other over it? I mean if Jarvas was broke, then suddenly they came into a regular income, Amanda might have guessed who provided it.'

'If she wasn't aware from the start.'

'I see. So, d'you think Amanda knew about the other things? Bunty's health? The will?'

'Also that Bunty was getting too close to Fleur. That business of her confiding in Fleur. I think that worried Amanda.'

'Because the confidence could have involved revealing who Fleur's real father was.'

Treasure nodded. 'It was one thing for Mildred to lie, as Amanda would call it. Anything Mildred let slip could be denied. Even by Mildred. Entirely different matter if Bunty started spilling the beans to Fleur. I'd think that was a potential leak that needed stopping at source.'

'How?'

'How about filching capsules from the doctor's bag? It seems she left the drawing room to get water for Handel's whisky.'

'You're serious? You're suggesting she *could* have laced Bunty's tea?'

'Highly probable. And planted Bunty's own pill bottle by her bed in the night. Impossible to prove, of course. Good thing, too.'

'I don't follow? If you know. . . ?'

'But I don't.' He lay back on the pillows, arms behind his head. 'And would you really want the mother of that nice little boy arrested? Want her tried on suspicion of helping her ailing and oldest friend into a painless demise? It'd serve no purpose, except to blight Robin's life.'

Molly moved down into the bed beside him. 'Either you're fooling or you know Amanda's guilty and she's bewitched you.' She searched his face, pouting.

'You haven't answered my question.'

'Would I want her arrested? For Robin's sake, no.'

'Good. One arrest's quite enough for a long weekend.' He put his arm around her. 'More than one and people could stop inviting us.'